***

Cyber Warfare and the New World Order

Book Four of the World War III Series

By James Rosone and Miranda Watson

****

Published in conjunction with Front Line Publishing, Inc.

Copyright Information

ISBN: 978-1-957634-23-4
Sun City Center, Florida, USA
Library of Congress Control Number: 2022904112

Table of Contents

Chapter 1
USS *Utah*

24 December 2041
700 Miles West of California

Captain Hughes was feeling irritated; as a military man who had had years of punctuality violently punched into his brain, it really sent a bristling feeling up his spine to be running late for anything. Of course, it wasn't his fault that his submarine, the *USS Utah* was the last vessel to make it to Hawaii. The sub had sustained some damage to its targeting system while battling Chinese destroyers off the coast of South Africa, and they had to stop while it was repaired for two days before making their way to San Diego to re-arm. They had made up a lot of time on their long journey from the South Atlantic Ocean to the Californian West Coast, but that didn't stop Hughes from feeling like he wanted to punch a wall.

"Chief of the Boat (COB), can we make any further increase in speed?" asked Hughes.

"No, Sir. We are maxing out our capacity. Anything more and we will begin to cause damage," replied the COB.

Captain Hughes popped all his knuckles, and then took a deep breath. He was eager for action. They were still several hundred miles away from the fleet of U.S. cruisers, SUDs, destroyers and frigates that were ready to engage the Chinese People's Liberation Army Navy (PLAN) off the coast of Hawaii.

To try and calm himself down, he reviewed the battle plans again. The Japanese ships would attack the PLAN from the northwest of the Hawaiian Islands, and then the Americans would surround the fleet from the southeast. Like a shark catching the scent of blood in the water, he was eager for the hunt.

Patience was not Captain Hughes' strongpoint. Even though they were still too far away to participate in the action, when the appointed time of attack arrived, he rushed over to the monitoring stations to get the most updated information about the situation on the frontlines.

What he heard was nothing short of chaos. The Japanese fleet began to send a flurry of messages.

"May Day, May Day! There were unknown Chinese submarines in the water! Please assist!" called one JDF Captain over the radio.

"We are taking fire from Chinese aircraft! Significant damage to our ship!" shouted another.

A third voice cried, "Attention! Cruise missiles have just been launched at us! Our hull is beginning to take on water. Performing evasive maneuvers to make it to the coastline."

Captain Hughes could not imagine a scenario in which the Japanese forces would be so horribly beaten down so quickly. *"Was our intel on the Chinese capabilities that far off?"* he wondered.

He turned to the screen where they had the visual link established with the SUDs, but just as he directed his eyes that way, several torpedoes streaked towards the submarines. Then the video feeds cut out.

Hughes turned to Petty Officer Jack Davis, who manned a different readout. "Davis, can you tell whether the SUDs made it through the attack?"

Jack furiously typed for a moment as he tried to clarify the data he was looking at. "Sir, two of the SUDs were definitely destroyed. A third was badly damaged, but still holding together as far as I can tell. The fourth SUD seems to have disappeared from the face of the Earth."

"Well, get to work Petty Officer! I want to find out what happened as soon as possible," barked Hughes.

"Yes, Sir," responded Davis. His fingers moved so quickly on the keyboard that it practically created smoke.

Suddenly, they received a radio transmission from the operator of the missing SUD. "Captain Hughes, if you can hear me, our readouts show that we've been attacked by three Chinese submarines. Wait…now also detecting several torpedoes that were dropped via helicopter…"

"What just happened, operator?" demanded the Captain.

"Sir, we've lost all transmissions from the SUD. It's been destroyed," he stammered.

Time stood still for just a moment as that information sunk in; Captain Hughes was lost in a quagmire of thoughts. 1ˢᵗ Petty Officer Nguyen jolted him out of that nebulous swirl of contemplation. "--Sir, we cannot detect any torpedoes headed towards the location where the

Japanese fleet was supposed to be. We are still pretty far away, but our advanced sensors should have been able to pick up something."

"Let's send up a surveillance drone immediately," ordered the Captain. "We need to have as much visual and electronic intelligence of what is going on as possible."

The *Utah* rose to a depth of 40 ft. and launched their surveillance drone. This small solar-powered device could stay aloft indefinitely (if needed) and follow the Utah to provide continual surveillance and relay communications to other surface ships. As the drone gained altitude, it activated its long-range radar, capturing a picture of what was going on with the Japanese fleet and US naval ships in the area.

To their surprise, they did not see a swarm of Chinese aircraft or cruise missiles heading towards the Japanese fleet; it looked like the Chinese were only closing in on the small contingent of eight American ships. They could tell that those American ships were desperately trying to fight off the attack, but the numbers were clearly against them. They were going to be sunk. Something was still not adding up…

Suddenly, the communications link they had just established with the American ships was cut off before they could connect with them.

"Captain, we just lost contact with our drone and with the SUDs as well. We were receiving a message from them, but the transmission just cut off," reported Commander Mitcham. He tried to maintain composure, but some of the color had gone out of his cheeks, making him appear ghostly as he spoke.

Captain Hughes was not one hundred percent sure what it all meant, but he had a bad feeling in his gut, so he ordered the ship to dive. "Chief of the Boat, take us down to depth 500 feet and get us under the thermal plain."

The Chief of the Boat (COB), barked some orders to the sailors driving the boat. Over the PA system, a voice suddenly barked, "Dive! Dive! Dive!" Everyone braced themselves for the sudden jolt, and then the ship lurched downward.

Captain Hughes pulled his Commanding Officer (XO) over to the side and leaned in closer to his ear so only he could hear him speak. "Mitcham, go down to the Coms room and see what's going on. We need to figure out what in the world is happening, understood?" directed the Captain.

The XO quickly asked, "You think the Chinese just knocked our communications out?"

"I'm not sure; it could just be a system glitch and those guys back in San Diego didn't correctly fix it, but I want to make sure we know what's going on before the rumor mill starts and people start to get nervous," replied the Captain, running his fingers nervously through his hair.

"Ok, I'll head over now," the XO whispered as he headed off on his mission.

Out of nowhere, the Emergency Action Message (EAM) turned on and began to spit out a message. Lieutenant Commander Grady, the intelligence officer was nearby and grabbed the note as soon as it was done printing and walked it over to the Captain. "Captain, this isn't good," Commander Grady said as he showed the captain the EAM:

****FLASH****COMSUBPAC****FLASH****

SSN-801, DEFENSE COMMUNICATIONS UNDER CYBER ATTACK. REVERT TO UHF FOR COMMUNICATIONS. PEOPLE'S LIBERATION ARMY AIR FORCE AIRBORNE TROOPS HEADING TOWARDS POINT LOMA AND SAN DIEGO. JAPANESE NAVAL TASK FORCE HEAVILY DAMAGED, RETREATING TO LOS ANGELES. TAKE UP STATION 25 MILES OFF OCEANSIDE, SOUTHERN CALIFORNIA AND STANDBY FOR FURTHER ORDERS. END.

****FLASH****COMSUBPAC****FLASH****

The Captain looked over the EAM, digesting what it all meant. From what they saw with the limited drone data, the Japanese task force had not been attacked and it was the American task force that was being wiped out. None of this made any sense.

Looking at Commander Grady, the Captain said, "This just doesn't jive. The message says the Japanese were attacked and are retreating to L.A.--but before our drone was taken offline, we couldn't see any signs that they had been damaged at all. We picked up the same messages from the JDF COMSUBPAC, but the drone's radar and other sensors couldn't find any sign of this supposed battle. What are your thoughts?" asked the Captain.

Commander Grady paused briefly before he responded, "Sir, I agree, none of this makes sense. Before the drone feed cut out, we were analyzing what was going on with the Japanese fleet. What *we* saw was the JDF fleet turning away from Hawaii and heading towards L.A. at what appeared to be flank speed. The JDF continued to emit distress calls saying they were under attack, but we could not detect what confrontation they were talking about. Another strange thing my analyst reported was that he saw several JDF anti-submarine helicopters heading back towards the carriers. Back-tracing their flight tracks, it places them right on top of our SUDs just as they were reporting being under attack by Chinese torpedoes and being destroyed."

Commander Grady cleared his throat before he continued, "My other analyst was looking at the PLAN fleet, and she saw the ships had changed direction from heading towards the JDF to a track that would take them to San Diego...they were also heading at flank speed. Sir, my guys need a bit more time to make a full case, but I believe we may have just been sucker-punched by the JDF and the PLAN." His fists clenched tighter as he spoke, an unconscious expression of his anger.

Despite the mounting evidence, Captain Hughes looked surprised by Commander Grady's implication. He responded in a very calculated manner. "I think you are right... you need more time to analyze the information before making a call like that. We need to be one hundred percent certain before we make that assumption. In the meantime, we will move towards Oceanside at best speed and get on station. I want to have an officer's meeting in the wardroom in one hour. You have until then to determine what in the blazes just happened, Commander."

Nodding in agreement, Grady answered, "Yes, Sir. We'll get this figured out sir. Sorry if I was jumping to a conclusion before I had all the facts."

Not wanting to discourage his newly promoted Commander, the Captain countered, "No, it's not your fault. I just want to make sure everyone has all the full details of this cluster mess before we make a decision that could cost us all our careers. Attacking an ally is no small step."
****

Almost an hour had gone by, and still no one really knew what had happened until Commander Mitcham called from the Coms room.

"Captain Hughes, we've been able to regain control of the surveillance drone by using the Ultra-High Frequency (UHF) system. Once we re-established connection, we moved the drone closer in the direction of the JDF fleet to see what was going on. We've been able to determine with certainty that the Japanese fleet did not sustain any damage or losses; they are still moving at flank speed towards Los Angeles."

"Sir," he continued, "We also saw wreckage and life boats in the vicinity of where the America frigates and destroyers had been when they were attacked. A couple of PLAN ships were nearly to them already, and will probably pick them up, interning the crews as POWs for the remainder of the war."

The Captain turned to Commander Grady, "After we relay this information to the COMSUBPAC, it's time to call the meeting of the senior officers to discuss what our next steps are."

The pow-wow lasted for twenty minutes as they pieced all the information together. Finally, the Captain spoke up, "So, I think we all collectively agree that the JDF must have sunk the SUDs using Chinese torpedoes to make it look like the Chinese were really the attackers. The question remains--was this the action of a rogue JDF Admiral, or did Japan just officially join the war on the side of the Axis?"

"That about sums it up, Sir," replied the COB. "I'm not sure we will be able to come to a 100% conclusion on that one. Should we go ahead and use our drone to send our assessment off to the COMSUBPAC?"

"Yes, go ahead. I want you to also request permission to engage the JDF Fleet. We are closer to them than the PLAN fleet."

"Roger that, Captain."

Chapter 2
Angels in Flight

24 December 2041
Groom Lake, Nevada

Major Theodore Cruse's flight of F41 Archangels had relocated to the Groom Lake Region (commonly referred to as Area 51) two days ago, after a reporter from the Boston Globe wrote a piece that mentioned that the F41s were flying out of Minot, North Dakota. Their team had changed Air Force bases a couple of times to try and keep the Russian and Chinese intelligence guessing at their location. America did not have many F41s, so the few they did have needed to be protected at all costs.

Colonel Leed walked into the flight operations room and found Major Cruse talking with one of the intelligence operations officers. He approached him quickly and signaled to get his attention before he interjected, "Major Cruse, we just received an emergency message via the UHF system, scrambling your flight to head towards Hawaii to assist the JDF fleet that is currently engaging the PLAN. Apparently, the Chinese got the jump on them and they are in trouble. The message also said we lost four of our underwater drone subs, so we have lost all real-time information and intelligence of what is going on right now." The colonel was visibly sweating as he spoke.

The other officers near Cruse who had overheard the conversation were dumbfounded by the announcement. The Air Force had worked up an ironclad plan to support the JDF fleet's amphibious assault of the Hawaiian Islands. Now it appeared that fleet was in shambles.

Major Cruse digested the announcement and then turned around to alert the rest of his officers and get them to their aircraft. It took them twenty minutes to get their flight suits on and get the F41s ready airborne. Once in the air, they immediately began heading towards Hawaii at maximum pace. Even at top speed, it was still going to take the flight of six F41s close to two hours before they would be on station and able to assess the situation.

Major Cruse immediately began to try and get in touch with the JDF fleet via the UHF system until their digital links could be re-established. After several attempts, they were finally able to let them know they were about two hours away from their position and would be on station shortly to assist them. After about five minutes, the JDF responded back, asking if Major Cruse could share their flight information and tracking signal so they could monitor their progress and share information with them as it came available. Not knowing that the JDF had just turned on the Americans, Major Cruse agreed and established a real-time tracking link of their location to help better coordinate the fleet defenses.

****

400 miles east of Hawaii

Thus far, Admiral Tomohisa Kawano's fleet had pulled off the greatest surprise attack in history. The PLA hackers had been able to use their access to the American Defense Communication System to take it down and massively disrupt communications on the West Coast of America. The PLAN had launched a massive missile attack against the ten American ships that were heading towards the JDF fleet to assist them. The U.S. Task Force consisted of four guided missile frigates, three destroyers and one guided missile cruiser--a formidable group, but no match for the PLAN fleet on their own. All but one of the ships was sunk in the attack; however, one of the guided missile cruisers managed to escape, taking only minor damage, and headed at full speed back towards San Diego.

Kawano's fleet had briefly detected a small American navy surveillance drone, probably from a submarine operating in the area. However, before they could identify the location, the drone had gone offline. While they were still trying to figure out what was going on, one of Admiral Kawano's intelligence officers walked over to him. "Sir, we just received a transmission from a flight of American F41 fighters. They say they are on the way to assist us."

Admiral Kawano was briefly startled by the news. He knew it was going to be nearly impossible for their missiles to hit them. In a flash of brilliance, it occurred to him that if he could get the F41s to share their flight data, then his battleships could engage them with their railguns and anti-aircraft missiles. He could also send word to the Americans that he was sending his F35s into the air to help coordinate their efforts against the PLAN. Once the Americans arrived, they could attack the F41s with full force. He issued the orders right away.

Chapter 3
Trojan Horse Update

24 December 2041
Downtown Los Angeles

Near the end of World War II, the Japanese had drafted a plan to combat the inevitable invasion of American forces into their country--codename Operation Ketsugo. The name meant "concluding remarks," and signaled their tenacity to fight to the death, if needed. To General Hidehisa Shinzo, the Commander of the 5th Brigade, it seemed a fitting name for this new offensive against the West Coast of the United States. As his ship pulled into the Port of Los Angeles, he gritted his teeth, eager for battle.

Since the Americans had not deciphered the true intentions of the Japanese forces before they landed, the Port of Los Angeles was relatively easy to secure. Only a few shots were fired by either side; most of the guards surrendered without incident when they saw how hopelessly out-gunned they were. The 5th Brigade was what the Americans called a "heavy" brigade, which meant that along with the typical company elements of reconnaissance, anti-aircraft artillery, engineers, signals and aviation, the group encompassed a tank battalion, three infantry regiments and an artillery battalion. There were 6,500 soldiers in all, each one well-trained, disciplined and full of the zeal and adrenaline that comes from seeing battle for the first time.

At the nearby Port of Long Beach, the Japanese also managed a speedy takeover. There were a few casualties at this facility; a couple of American guards decided to try to be heroes and went completely Rambo. Sadly, this desperate attempt resulted in their swift demise, and did not do very much to inhibit the progress of the Japanese. They did manage to kill four soldiers and wound eight more. As the men pulled the bodies out of the pool of blood to prepare them for a proper burial, the harsh reality of war set in.

The soldiers consolidated their positions, organizing into well-formed groups and preparing to receive the additional reinforcements from the Japanese Defense Force (JDF) and the Chinese Navy (PLAN). So far, everything was proceeding as expected. The JDF and PLAN were headed towards LA and San Diego at flank speed, trying to capitalize on the confusion taking place among their former allies. Because of the cyber-attacks on the cell networks and the internet, the greater public was still unaware of the Japanese attack.

Once the ports were fully secured, General Shinzo prepared to meet with two of his key senior officers. He surveyed the scene as he walked towards a small building that must have been one of the port administrative offices. During this short stroll, he tried to organize his thundering chorus of thoughts. He still had a lot to accomplish within a short window of time; his objective was to secure City Hall and the rest of downtown LA, and then move into the surrounding urban sprawl. He knew that his forces would have to act quickly; it would not take long for the Americans to realize what was happening and dispatch forces to attack his men. His main concern was the Marines Third Division, which he knew to be stationed at Twenty-Nine Palms. They were the most combat-hardened Marine division that the U.S. had, and they were fully-equipped with the new Raptor combat suits. Shinzo knew that they would be a formidable force when the time came.

As General Shinzo entered the building, the smell of cordite and diesel fuel was heavy in the air; all his armored vehicles were lining up near the port exit to begin their task of securing City Hall. He walked over to his commanders. Despite their best efforts to conceal their emotions, he could clearly see their apprehension by their furrowed brows. He knew that both of these men had trained with the Americans in the past, and were now being tasked with attacking some of those very same officers. However, there was no time for emotion, only time for action. He jumped right into the task of the moment.

"Colonel Tenaka, as you know, you are to lead your forces to capture City Hall immediately following this meeting. I want you to convey to your soldiers that they are to put down any resistance that they encounter and secure their target *quickly*. Then I want you to activate the city's emergency broadcast system and have it play the following message," General Shinzo handed Colonel Tenaka a sheet of paper that read, "People of Los Angeles, a Japanese and Chinese invasion force has secured your city. Stay indoors and do not venture into the streets. Do not interfere with our operations, or you will be shot on sight. This is not a test."

Colonel Tenaka nodded and made a mental note to have one of his most fluent English speakers read the announcement for the recording.

General Shinzo continued. "Colonel Watabe, you are to lead your armored division and an infantry regiment to Riverside and San Bernardino. As you travel, destroy as many bridges and overpasses as you can along your route. You will need to establish a defensive perimeter; the Marines will be bearing down on you very quickly, and you are going to have to find a way to hold out until additional reinforcements arrive. Move some of your tanks onto the third or fourth levels of parking garages to give them a better vantage point and increase their range. Position some of the other tanks in alley ways and behind buildings so that you can surprise the enemy as they approach. Fight house-to-house if you need to, but at all costs you must hold the line until the additional forces reach you."

Colonel Watabe nodded his acknowledgement. "Sir, exactly how long should we expect to be on our own before the reinforcements approach?"

Some of the Japanese generals would have found this question to be impertinent, but General Shinzo had a good working relationship with Colonel Watabe. Besides, he would have wanted to know the same thing if the roles were reversed. Without missing a beat, he replied, "Colonel, I have spoken with the Chinese Army (PLA) Commander; he has two brigades of heavy tanks, one brigade of light drone tanks and two infantry brigades that will be reinforce you in about eight hours. It will take some time to unload that amount of equipment. As each battalion is offloaded, I'm going to direct them to head to your location."

Pulling up some information from his tablet, General Shinzo scrolled through some data, then explained, "We also have six attack helicopters that can assist both of your operations. I will hold them back from other actions so they are available to you when you need them. But use them wisely; it will be close to a day before we have more available when the rest of the Air Force finishes ferrying over their aircraft from Hawaii."

Suddenly, there was the loud rush of several jets roaring over their heads—the colonels nervously looked at the ceiling. Having trained with American military throughout their career, they knew exactly what kind of enemy they would be facing. Not only would the U.S. soldiers be tenacious fighters, but they'd be boiling over with desires for revenge. An awkward moment of silence passed in anticipation.

General Shinzo cleared his throat. Knowing this might be the last time he saw either of these men in person, he looked each of them in the eye and said, "Gentlemen, the future of Japan rides on our success over the next several days. I know we have traditionally been an ally of America, but those days are behind us. We need to do our duty to Japan to preserve our way of life and that of our families. Everyone is depending on us. I expect you to do your jobs and win. Dismissed."

All three stood up, and bowed to each other before walking out. Shinzo followed his men out of the building as they each headed off towards their respective commands. He wished them luck…he knew the odds of this invasion being successful were long, but he was determined to succeed.

Twenty minutes later, Lieutenant Colonel Ota (one of Colonel Tenaka's battalion commanders) was leading his column of twelve Type 29 Main Battle Tanks (MBTs) and thirty-four Type 31 infantry fighting vehicles as they passed the exit for Hwy 91 and east Compton. They continued down I-710, towards City Hall and downtown LA. As they drove past an exit, two of his T-31 infantry fighting vehicles made their exit and set up a road block. Once I-710 was secured and cleared of traffic, it would give the JDF and PLA an easy route to move troops throughout the valley quickly.

So far, they had not encountered any resistance. Then again-- what could a car or truck really do to stop a sixty-ton main battle tank? Traffic on the highway was light as it was still early in the morning on Christmas Eve; most Americans were either off work for the holiday or traveling out of the city to see family. His column was making good time as they moved along the interstate; however, when they reached I-105 and Morton, the traffic became a bit more of a problem. Ultimately though, this turned into a minor inconvenience; those cars that failed to move out of the way of the armored column were either pushed aside or run over by the tanks.

Once they reached the correct junction, Colonel Ota had to leave one of his tanks and four infantry fighting vehicles behind to make sure they had the key node secured. Stopping the traffic was not very difficult; the hard part was going to be clearing all of the cars that were already on the road off of it.

As Colonel Ota stood in the commander's hatch of his tank, he could see the expanse of the city as it unfolded before him. It was a beautiful and sprawling city. Tall sky scrapers covered in glass reaching for the clouds in the downtown area gave way to block after block of homes and smaller buildings. He couldn't help but think to himself, "This is going to be an absolute nightmare for our JDF and the Chinese to try and secure. All of these people…and each one potentially has a firearm. Too bad we aren't landing in Great Britain instead, where the worst I'd have to fear is a nightstick."

As his tank raced down the road, he suddenly heard an announcement over the radio. "Colonel Ota, we have a couple of police cruisers approaching our roadblock. Do you want us to engage?"

"Yes, suppress any resistance quickly," he ordered.

He heard a series of loud booms, and there was an eerie silence for a moment before someone came back on. "Sir, our T-31s made short work of the vehicles and the approaching officers. We did not sustain any casualties or significant damage to our equipment."

"Excellent. Please continue to use force as needed," Colonel Ota replied. He was elated that their first encounter had ended so well.

The T-31s were built by Mitsubishi to be a lightweight infantry support vehicle to the T-29 main battle tanks. They were armed with a 30-mm autocannon, four anti-tank missiles, a .50 caliber machine gun above the commander's hatch, and had the capacity to hold twelve infantry soldiers inside. In contrast, the T-29 main battle tank had a 135-mm cannon able to penetrate the American M1A4 and M1A5's armor (as well as the new formidable Pershing tanks), but only carried a crew of three: the driver, gunner and tank commander. The T-29 made use of an auto-loader system, similar to the ones that the Chinese and Russian tanks used. This would be their first operational fielding of the new tank round. If it worked well, then it would go into full production and be disseminated to the European front, which was much more of a tank war than Alaska.

As the column of tanks and infantry fighting vehicles (IFVs) continued to race down the roads heading towards City Hall, word must have gotten around; as they crossed the Los Angeles River on East 1st street, they saw half a dozen police cars and several SWAT vehicles blocking the road. Speaking quickly into his headset, Colonel Ota ordered, "Lead vehicle, engage the SWAT trucks with your main gun and continue through the roadblock on your way to south Spring street and City Hall."

He also radioed his infantry commander. "Have your fighting vehicles engage the road block. I want your last three vehicles in the column to stop, dismount their infantry and clear the rest of the intersection. We need to keep the road clear for additional reinforcements."

The fighting at the intersection was brief and fierce; the column slowed down to 10 mph as they changed formations from a single file line to an arrowhead with three tanks, followed by three infantry fighting vehicles and then the rest of the group staying in a single file column. The tanks and IFVs used their heavy machine guns to fire on the police and SWAT vehicles and quickly decimated all that was before them, shredding the police officers instantly. None of the lead vehicles had to open up the hatches for the infantry to emerge, and they took no casualties in the brief engagement before plowing through the burning vehicles, continuing their way to City Hall.

Colonel Ota climbed back up through the commander's hatch again so he could have a better field of view. He looked back briefly at the armored vehicles behind him and saw the black smoke of the vehicles they had just destroyed start to rise into the sky, marking their brief engagement. For nearly a mile, his armored column stretched across the city as they moved quickly through the highway and streets of LA.

Chapter 4
Bring Me to Your Leader

24 December 2041
Los Angeles, California
City Hall, Mayor's Office

Mayor Jose Perez had been the mayor of LA for nearly twenty years. He was not a fan of President Stein; however, he did have to agree that the President had really turned the country's economy around and that newfound prosperity had greatly benefited his city. In addition, despite the fact that Perez was a lifelong Democrat, the President had been nothing but professional and courteous when dealing with him. He had made many critical infrastructures projects in L.A. a key priority, and had agreed to include several high-speed rail projects in Southern California, with several of them running through LA.

Where he and the President diverged was their opinions concerning the direction of the war and the choice to annex Mexico. L.A. had been the victim of several large terrorist attacks: there was the one that destroyed the police headquarters, the attack against the Universal Studios complex, and several wildfires in and around L.A. county that were most likely arson. Mayor Perez agreed something needed to be done, but was utterly appalled by the President's nuclear response to the destruction of New York and Baltimore. He was concerned the President's aggressive actions would bring more countries into the war (and not on America's side). As the casualty reports began to roll in, the invasion in Alaska began to really frighten him. Tens of thousands of young men and women were being killed each month and it appeared America was losing. He feared the Freedom Party was going to be the death of America.

On this particular day, Jose was frantically trying to finish up some urgent business at the office before he could leave and go home to be with his family for the rest of the holiday. He was doing his best to speed things up so that he could get home to his wife and his German Shepherd, but then his computer started acting up. While he waited for it to restart, he sighed, grabbed his cup of coffee, and flipped on the local news channel. "We are receiving reports of a massive cyber-attack underway against the Pentagon--"

Suddenly, the TV program cut off. It was nothing but static. *"Huh, that's* strange," he thought. *"Let me check another channel."*

Before he could hit the menu button on the remote, someone knocked on his door. "Come in," he said, and placed his coffee back on his desk.

In walked one of his security guards, his police liaison officer and a Homeland Security rep. that he barely knew, Agent Quick. They wasted no time on chit-chat; Agent Quick blurted out, "Mr. Mayor, I have just received a warning from Washington that the Department of Defense communication system has been temporarily disabled. Just before our communications were cut off, I was told a Chinese airborne force was heading towards San Diego." He fidgeted while he spoke, like someone who has had one too many cups of coffee.

Police Liaison Officer Jayko didn't wait for a response to Agent Quick's information; he knew that the mayor would be very concerned with his intel as well, so he just jumped right in, "Mr. Mayor, we have received confirmation from local officers of gunfire taking place at the ports and at LAX International.

Mayor Perez felt his brainwaves overloading as he tried to process everything he had just been told. For a moment, he looked from one man to the other, then he held up his hand. "Obviously, this all needs prompt attention, but right now, I'd really like to hear more from Officer Jayko about what is going on at the ports."

"Yes, Sir. One of our officers reported seeing dozens of military vehicles and soldiers being offloaded from numerous cargo container ships at the Port of L.A. and the Port of Long Beach. Another officer reported seeing dozens of what appeared to be tanks being driven off a large vehicle transport ship."

"Do we have any intel on what they appear to be doing now? Can we tell whose troops they are?" asked the mayor, wringing his hands.

Officer Jayko was distracted; he had cocked his head to one side and appeared to be listening in his earbuds to one of his police units talking on the radio. All the color suddenly left Officer Jayko's face. "Sir, the group of armored vehicles just left the port and attacked several police officers in the area. They opened fire with machine guns and tank cannons--it is unknown if any of them survived."

The room was deadly silent as the reality of the situation sunk in. The mayor was the first to speak. "We need to find out where those vehicles are going. We also need to get the police assembled to respond to this threat. Agent Quick, are there any government troops or forces in the area that can assist us?"

The DHS Agent instinctively grabbed his phone to try to place a call and quickly realized that the phone systems were still down. "Sir, it would appear the phone system is not in operation. I'm not sure we can let anyone know what is going on right now."

Mayor Perez felt that the agent had not adequately answered his question so he asked again. "Agent, are there any government forces in the area that can help us right now?" His voice grew louder and more agitated as he spoke.

Agent Quick looked up at the mayor as if this was the first time he had heard the question. "Um, yes sir, there are troops in the area," he replied. Turning to Officer Jayko, Quick continued, "If one of your officers can get a message to the base commander at the LA Barracks, he can alert the Air Force base there. They can send an emergency message via the UHF radios to other military bases in the area. We also have some Marines and Navy Seabees at Port Hueneme and Point Magu, near Ventura," Quick explained, regaining his composure.

Mayor Perez seized on this glimpse of hope. "Officer Jayko, get a message to the Police Command Center to send a messenger over to the base and request assistance. Also, ask if they can send any forces to the mayor's office while we try to coordinate some sort of defense," he directed.

"Yes, Sir," he replied. "Excuse me for a moment," he said as he began talking to his counterparts in the police through his radio earpiece, turning his body to the side to concentrate on the conversation.

While Officer Jayko was talking, Jose paused for just a few seconds, wading through the sea of thousands of conflicting thoughts. Suddenly, an idea came to him, and he signaled to get Jayko's attention. "We also need to send an emergency message throughout the city, telling people to stay indoors," he ordered.

"Copy that," Officer Jayko responded, then continued talking on the radio.

When he had completed his exchange, he turned back towards the mayor. "Sir, I was able to speak with the police chief; he said they are calling in every available officer they have and are sending them to City Hall and try to organize some sort of defense."

As the mayor and the various law enforcement officials in the city scrambled to organize some sort of defense of the city, the Japanese and Chinese soldiers and their armored convoy continued to head towards City Hall, shooting and killing anyone that got in their way.

Chapter 5
Bird or Plane?

24 December 2041
Catalina Island, California

After the destruction of the Seventh Fleet at Pearl Harbor and Japan, the U.S. Navy was concerned that the PLAN might be able to move ships close to the West Coast and attack the naval facilities and critical infrastructure along the shoreline. They identified thirty positions where anti-ship railguns systems could be built to deter any coastal approach by the PLAN; they could also be used to shoot down any incoming cruise missiles. Battery Twenty-Six on Catalina Island was part of this series of railguns emplaced around the various approaches to Los Angeles.

The sailors at Battery Twenty-Six were busily manning their positions, like any other day. Seaman Paul Rodgers was coming on his shift, relieving the night guard, when he suddenly heard some loud explosions in the distance.

"What was that?" exclaimed Seaman Arturo Gomez, the night guard.

"I don't know…let's find out," Rodgers replied. The two men scanned the coast around them for signs of any kind of smoke or unusual action.

Gomez finally asserted, "It must be coming from L.A. There is no sign of activity here on Catalina Island."

Rodgers moved his head like a dog listening to a strange noise, then interjected, "Hey, do you hear that? It sounds like helicopters."

The two men put their hands above their eyes to block the sun and see if they could try to catch a glimpse of where the sound was coming from. In the distance, there were indeed a few choppers on the horizon.

"Is that a Japanese flag?" Gomez asked. "That seems a bit odd. Why would they be out here?"

"Hey--they just turned to head towards our facility," Rodgers stammered, confusion in his voice.

"What the--Rodgers, they are coming in for an attack run!" He slapped the warning alarm button on the wall next to him in the guard tower, and they both grabbed their weapons. Seconds later, the tower was completely ripped apart by the nose gun of the incoming helicopter. As the chopper continued on, it launched a few missiles at the railguns.

In less than a minute, the two helicopters moved further down the island to the next gun position. In mere moments, they had succeeded in destroying the two anti-ship railguns at their fortified position. As they moved to attack the next railgun site on the island, the crew was prepared for an incoming attack. One of the sailors reacted quickly, and fired off one of the shoulder-mounted surface-to-air-missiles. The projectile whistled violently into the air, hitting one of the Japanese helicopters just as the gunner onboard fired one of his own missiles. The other JDF helicopter launched three missiles at the Americans and then quickly ducked behind a bend in the terrain, preventing the sailors from counter-attacking. With the cat out of the bag, it was going to be a lot harder taking out the remaining gun positions.

Within an hour of the first attack, five other groups of attack helicopters had destroyed their targets, reducing the number of anti-ship railgun positions along the coast from thirty to just six (only sacrificing seven helicopters for their efforts). Those six railgun sites would be targeted by a small contingent of PLA Special Forces, which had been offloaded at the Port of LA. The JDF needed to destroy all the gun batteries before fleets and transports started their seaborne approach to LA and San Diego. The next twelve hours were going to be critical to the success of the seaborne invasion.

Chapter 6
This Is a Test

24 December 2041
Los Angeles, California
NBC Broadcasting Office

The Los Angeles police department was the first to arrive at the scene. As they were unsure of what they would meet there, they decided to send in a SWAT team in full tactical gear. The receptionist at the desk, a man in his mid-twenties with spiked hair and trendy clothing, had possibly never seen a gun except on TV; he screamed like a four-year-old girl when they entered the building. One of the SWAT guys put his finger to his lips as if to say. "Shhh," and then walked over to him.

"Sir, have any soldiers entered the building before us?" asked the officer.

The man fanned himself for a second, then stammered, "Uh, uh, no. You guys are the only ones with guns here."

"Ok, look, we advise you to evacuate the building as quickly and as orderly as possible. Please put your protocol in effect for a fire or a bomb threat so that everyone will leave with the least amount of panic. Advise everyone to take back streets and not freeways and find a safe spot to shelter in place. They might need to stay indoors for a few days."

The man was now sweating profusely. He grabbed a swig from a bottle of water. "What in the world is going on?" he screeched.

"I'm sorry, sir, but I honestly don't have time to explain. I need to know which floor the Emergency Alert System broadcasts from."

"Uh, uh, the fifth floor."

"Thank you," he replied. The officer waved over a couple of security guards to loop them in on evacuating the building, and then he joined his colleagues, who had already hopped the turnstiles for security badge entrance. They knew that during a fire or bomb threat protocol, everyone would be headed down the stairs, so they all piled into two elevators and headed up to the 5th Floor.

As the elevators continued upwards, they could hear the speaker overhead forcefully announce, "Attention! There has been a bomb threat. Please proceed to the stairs and exit as orderly as possible. You are advised to proceed by back roads to the nearest safe location and shelter in place. This is not a drill!"

One of the guys in the elevator chuckled, "That must have been one of the security guards, because I don't think that dude at the front desk could have managed that."

They all laughed for a second. Then the elevator beeped for the fifth floor, and they all went right back to game face.

The doors were opening slowly for some reason. They could hear two men arguing. "There is no way this is real. It is never real! I'm taking the elevator."

"I'm telling you, I've been here fifteen years and I've never heard them announce it that way--"

At the sight of the SWAT team, both men looked at each other and quickly spoke at the same time, "Let's take the stairs." They were gone before you could blink.

The officers made their way down the hall. One young woman, who had been carrying a very large armful of scripts, panicked when she saw the SWAT team headed towards her and created a paper waterfall all over the floor. She turned and ran.

The SWAT team continued advancing, and finally located the room marked "Emergency Alert System."

Several team members stationed themselves by the door, grabbing desks and other furniture to give them some cover if needed. A few more SWAT members picked strategic places along the hall to defend their position. Only three of them went inside.

"Ok, Rita, where's those instructions?" asked Ben, one of her colleagues.

Pulling papers out of her pocket, Rita replied, "I've got it right here."

The three of them started to get to work changing settings on the various equipment. A knob here, a switch there—a few minutes later, everything was ready. They started to record their message.

"This is not a test. Los Angeles is under attack by foreign armies. Go indoors and stay inside until further notice--"

Gun shots were fired down the hall. They paused the recording and grabbed their guns.

"We've got hostiles!" shouted one of the guys outside. "They keep coming! Get ready for a party!"

Rita and her two colleagues took cover behind a desk. The noises outside got louder and louder. First there was a crescendo of flying bullets. Then someone from the SWAT team must have thrown a grenade, because there was a very loud explosion down the hall. Then there was a very loud hissing sound. Rita got as low as she could to peer underneath the legs of the desk. A large cloud of smoke was crawling along the floor toward her.

"Cover your mouths!" she cried.

As the gas continued to advance into the recording studio, all three of them suddenly started coughing and sneezing. Everything burned. "My eyes!" yelled Ben, wiping frantically at tears streaming down his face.

All the other noises suddenly stopped, and what was left was a chorus of coughing and groans of agony. A team of Japanese soldiers with gas masks walked into the room, completely unaffected by the tear gas in the air. The SWAT team members were too incapacitated to fight back, so they lifted their hands in surrender. The JDF zip-tied their arms behind their back and moved them downstairs--they were prisoners of war now. The soldiers broke the windows open and waited for the smoke to dissipate. They had their own message to record.

Chapter 7
Convergence

24 December 2041
Pacific Ocean, 200 miles East of the Japanese Fleet in Hawaii

The Japanese were anxiously awaiting the arrival of Major Cruse's group, Angels' Flight, made up of F-41 Archangels. They could have a fighting chance against them, but it would all depend on the Americans playing into their little ruse. Most stealth fighter planes do not engage their radar, because doing so would make them visible to other planes in the area; instead, they usually utilize the services of Navy ships with high-powered radar or dedicated planes that fly above to send verbal messages to them when an enemy is spotted (commonly referred to as AWACs). The JDF needed the Americans to believe that they would be functioning as their AWACs in order to get them to share their GPS locations and make them an easy target.

Katoshi Abe, one of the JDF radar officers, established connection with Major Cruse in an effort to finalize this plan. "Angels' Flight, this is Aries Five. We are going to be your airborne radar and controller. Please acknowledge."

"Aries Five, this is Major Cruse, Angels' Flight. We acknowledge; can you please send us a view of the region?" Without their radar on, Major Cruse and his flight really had no idea of what was in the area.

The AWAC operator send them a datalink showing a large group of PLAN aircraft starting to assemble over their fleet, probably preparing to attack the JDF fleet again. It looked like a squadron of F35s from the JDF fleet were assembling to help the Americans engage them as well.

"Angels' Flight, you are directed to link up with the F35s and provide air support and missile defense for the fleet. Please acknowledge," said the Japanese radar operator.

"I acknowledge. Angels' Flight moving to join the fleet defense; please keep us updated with radar images." Major Cruse wanted to ensure they had a steady datalink of what the AWACs were seeing in real-time. As they moved closer to the Japanese fleet, they could see a lot of dark smoke coming from the fleet location. Without having any reason to be suspicious at this point, Major Cruse assumed that the smoke was from battle damage the fleet had suffered (instead, the JDF fleet was busy generating black smoke in order to make it appear that they had been damaged).

Cruse addressed his flight, knowing that his enthusiastic fighter jocks were itching for a fight. "All right, listen up guys, we are going to provide missile defense for the fleet down there; you can see they already took a lot of hits, so let's do our best to make sure they don't take any more. Also, if you can get a shot off at any of the PLAN aircraft that get in range, take it. Let's move Angels, and make these guys pay."

As they moved into position, Major Cruse saw F35s moving forward; he assumed they were there to engage the PLAN aircraft as they maneuvered to their own positions. Unknown to him, as they continued forward, another flight of F35s took off from the carrier below and maneuvered behind them. Suddenly, without warning, the F35s fired multiple missiles at them. Within milliseconds, several of the ships below them launched rockets at them as well.

Major Cruse's missile alarms were jarringly loud, jolting him into a reality that he never imagined. The electronic countermeasures on his F41 turned on automatically and performed minor technological miracles to try and jam the enemy missiles. When Cruse regained his senses, he frantically radioed his flight, "Angel Flight, this was a trap! Try to get away and fly back to the rally point two-hundred miles away!"

As Major Cruse began to engage his EmDrive, his aircraft shook ferociously; he had been hit by one of the F35's machine guns. He turned his aircraft hard and went to maximum speed just as several missiles whistled past his aircraft. He activated his rear-view camera so that he could look at the scene behind him as he flew away; he almost immediately regretted this decision because he witnessed three of his fighter pilots murdered in the blazing flames created by the missile swarms. Another one of the Archangels took several hits and began to smoke badly as it spiraled down to the sea; fortunately, he did see the pilot eject, and the chute opened. However, if he were not killed by the Japanese, he would become a prisoner of war, which was not a fate he wished upon anyone. Only one other F41 was able to escape the fray and join him at the rally point. Stunned, they immediately terminated their links with the JDF fleet and AWACs.

"What the blazes just happened, Cruiser? They just blew our guys right out of the air!" exclaimed Flapjack, the only other pilot to escape.

"I have no idea--I think my aircraft is hit, but I'm not showing any warning signs. Do you see any damage?" asked Major Cruse, concerned that his aircraft might not make it back home.

Scanning Major Cruse's aircraft, Flapjack replied, "I see a couple of bullet holes along the wing, but it does not look like they hit anything critical. I'd suggest that you not go hypersonic right now though, just in case it might rip the wing off."

Cruiser signed in relief.

"Can we go back and engage those guys? We can easily take out a lot of those JDF fighters."

Major Cruse took a second to think through his response. "No, we need to head back to base and quick. Without an AWACs, we have to light up our radars to see them. The last thing I want to do is let the PLAN and JDF know our location again. Our advantage has always been our speed and ability to go unseen."

Major Cruse was still a little stunned and shaken by what had just transpired, and it occurred to him that he could have died. That was the closest he had ever come to being blown up or shot down, and it really rattled him. For a moment, he was lost in his thoughts before he could focus on the task at hand. A world passed by in a moment before he resumed giving out orders. "We need to get a message back to headquarters of what just happened. They need to know that the JDF fleet is hostile, that we lost four F41s, and we are now returning back to the base."

"Major, if they can get an AWAC up over California, I could stay airborne and try to reengage them," replied Flapjack, eager for revenge.

"No Captain," replied Cruse. "I won't allow you to go back on your own...that would be a suicide mission. We've lost enough men today."

Chapter 8
Don't Shoot the Messenger

24 December 2041
Los Angeles, California
L.A. Barracks

The base at L.A. Barracks was quite small; over the last few decades it had been cut down until it became a research station that held only about 350 men and women. Despite its small capacity, this little gated community unknowingly shined as the only real beacon of hope in rallying a military response to the invasion.

The guard at the gate spotted a police squad car driving a little too fast towards their entrance, and became alarmed that someone might have stolen the car to try to ram the front access point. He flashed a light at the car, and it slowed down mere milliseconds before he pushed the button to release the cement anti-ramming barriers. The cop car screeched to a halt, and the police officer inside started yelling frantically at the guard.

"I need to get to a UHF radio NOW! There is a foreign army invading Los Angeles!"

The guard was too stunned to respond for a moment. He started to mumble something about needing to see the officer's ID, and the cop got a little agitated.

"--Look, I know you need to do your job. Here's my badge, but you need to let me in!" He threw his badge at the guard.

The guard was practically in a trance, but hit the button to lift the divider so that the squad car could go through.

"Thank you. Now where can I find a UHF radio in here?" the officer bellowed.

"Umm, if you go to this first building on the right, someone there on the first floor should have one," the guard stammered.

"Great," said the officer, calming down. "You might want to call your boss. Pretty sure you guys are going to need back-up really soon."

He sped off down the road, leaving a cloud of dust behind him. When he arrived at the outdated building in front of him, covered in peeling paint, the officer didn't waste any time. He ran up to the first soldier he found. "Ma'am! Ma'am!" he yelled, waving his arms. "I need a UHF, as fast as you can get me to one! L.A. is under attack!"

She was startled, but ushered him to a room nearby where all the coms were. "What in the world is going on?" she asked as she messed with the buttons to get the UHF radio ready to go.

"I'm sorry, but there's really just no time," the cop shot back.

A loud explosion ripped through the air, coming from the direction of the gate. "Oh, for the love--are they really here already?" the officer quipped. "We don't have much time. You might want to grab a weapon," he directed, pulling his own gun from his holster.

"About that...most of us here on base aren't armed," the soldier responded. "You wouldn't happen to have an extra, would you?" she asked.

The police officer grabbed the piece from his ankle holster and handed it to his newfound comrade-in-arms. The sound of gunfire increased in volume, filling the air like a bad garage drummer.

The conflict did not last long. The Japanese and Chinese forces overwhelmed the small base with several tanks and infantry fighting vehicles. They barely met any resistance. The police officer did manage to get out a short message to Camp Pendleton and Twenty-Nine Palms to let them know that the city and the ports were under attack by a foreign army, but he did not make it through the ensuing shootout.

Chapter 9
Delayed Mobilization

24 December 2041
Twenty-Nine Palms, California
Third Army Headquarters

General Gardner's helicopter was approaching Twenty-Nine Palms Marine base and all they could see was chaos on the ground. Several long lines of armored vehicles and tanks could be seen lining up along the main gate, getting ready to move out. Marines were running everywhere, checking equipment, loading water and other supplies they were going to need as they moved quickly to get their force on the road. As Gardner's helicopter landed, a Marine Colonel walked forward snapping a quick salute, then guided the general towards a waiting vehicle that would take them to see Lieutenant General (LTG) Peeler, the Marine Commander on the West Coast and the Commanding General for the Third Marines.

As the vehicle moved throughout the base towards the command center, General Gardner still did not fully understand what was going on. The intelligence they were getting was spotty at best. One report said that the PLAN had snuck several container ships and roll-on roll-off ships into the Port of LA and Long Beach, while another said the soldiers appeared to be Japanese. A third report he received gave an account that Japanese naval task force that was attacking the PLAN fleet outside of Hawaii was mauled and retreating to LA for coastal protection. A fourth account relayed that PLA airborne troopers were heading to San Diego along with a large contingent of PLAAF fighters. He wasn't sure what was true and what wasn't at this point. All these conflicting reports had led to a delayed response time in going to San Diego--they had already sent the order to leave and then called everyone to stay twice.

"Sir!" a voice rang out. "You need to come to the operations center. I've just received word from the flight of F41s that went to Hawaii. Major Cruse says that they were ambushed by the Japanese. Four of their six aircraft were shot down!"

General Gardner was troubled; they were still only able to use the UHF radios and microwave systems while the tech guys tried to figure out how to bring their digital communications back online. He rushed over to see if he could gain anything more from a firsthand account.

As General Gardner walked into the operations center, the Marine guards snapped a salute and opened the sealed doors. LTG Peeler looked up and waved for General Gardner to come to him urgently. "Sir, I'm talking with Major Cruse from the F41 flight that was tasked with coming to the Japanese aid. You need to hear this. Major Cruse, General Gardner has just arrived. Can you relay what you saw again," requested General Peeler.

General Gardner leaned towards the microphone as one of the communications NCOs switched it over to speakerphone, signaling for the general to speak towards it. "Major Cruse, this is General Gardner. I'm the Third Army Commander and the Commanding General in California. I need a frank assessment of what is going on," Gardner said in his usual gruff tone.

Major Cruse was a bit taken back for a second. He was just talking to a Lieutenant General, and now he was talking directly to "the" General Gardner. Gardner was a living legend in the military--he was on the frontlines of defeating the IR, Chinese and Russians in the Middle East. He shrugged off this star struck moment to respond. "Yes, General. My flight had been coordinating our actions with the JDF task force. They told us that they had sent a squadron of F35s up to attack the PLAN fleet, and the PLAN had also sent aircraft up to meet them, so we thought everything was normal. As we were approaching, another flight of F35s took off from one of the carriers and maneuvered in behind us. Then without warning, they fired on us. Four of my fighters were blown up before they had a chance to respond. Only two of us got away. We would have stayed and attacked them, but we had no AWAC support to guide us to our targets or share their radar screens. If we activated our radars it would give away our positions to both fleets."

"Major, you did the right thing; your aircraft are too valuable to lose in a futile effort like that. I am sorry your men were ambushed like that. From your firsthand account and some of the other reports we are getting, it would appear the Japanese have betrayed us and joined the Chinese. Any additional information you can provide us, Major?" asked General Gardner in a much softer tone.

Thinking for a minute, he responded, "Yes, Sir. Just prior to the attack and throughout the engagement, my aircraft recorded the events. I can't transmit it because the digital communications system is still down, but we have the footage of the fleet and what transpired," Cruse said with some optimism that they may still be able to help.

The intelligence officers (and, in particular, the navy liaison officer with Gardner's staff) indicated that this would be extremely valuable. "Major Cruse, can your aircraft divert and land here at Twenty-Nine Palms? We need that video immediately!"

"Yes, Sir. We are about twenty minutes away."

"Major, before we discontinue this call, I want you to fly over Catalina Island, the Port of LA and the rest of the way to Twenty-Nine Palms. Fly low and slow enough so we can get some good images, but do not let your aircraft get targeted or destroyed. Understand?" inquired Gardner. He was hoping to obtain as much visual intelligence as possible.

"Yes, Sir. We'll be at the base in less than twenty minutes with your images," Cruse said, signing off.

He angled his aircraft to get a better vantage point for their cameras. The F41s' cameras had been set up to record engagements for future training purposes and to help with identifying their kills; Major Cruse was very grateful in this moment that they existed. He broadened the camera view; they could see a wide view of the ground below as they flew a little lower and slower over the areas of interest to record what they were seeing. The images could be played back in slow motion or frame-by-frame. Once they were cleaned up, they would provide invaluable intelligence of what was going on.

Back on the ground, LTG Peeler was in the middle of stating the obvious. "General Gardner, if the Japanese have joined the Chinese, then we are in a lot of trouble on the West Coast."

General Gardner was lost in thought for a moment. *The Japanese let the PLA hackers use their link with our defense communications to launch a cyber-attack on our systems. Then the Japanese docked dozens of freighters, carrying troops, tanks and other armored vehicles. The PLA is landing an airborne force near San Diego, and right now, we have no navy ships to stop any of it.*

Snapping out of this depressing moment, Gardner sprang into action. "General Peeler--first, what is the status of the Marines at

Pendleton? Are they on the road to San Diego to meet that PLA airborne force? Second, how soon are your Marines here going to be able to move on LA and engage the Japanese and PLA forces?"

LTG Peeler looked at one of his logistics officers, who quickly brought up the blue force tracker showing the progress of the Pendleton Marines. "They are nearly ready to leave to their base. They will engage the paratroopers shortly, probably after they have landed; it's taken some time for them to get everyone assembled and get their equipment ready. As to the Marines here, they are rolling out of here in twenty minutes. I already have eight scout platoons on their way to LA and the surrounding area to start gathering information. I'm not sure of enemy air defense capabilities yet, so I'm holding my Razorbacks in reserve to support my Marines when they need them," Peeler said as other Marines brought in even more information reports from the scouts.

After a couple of quick minutes, LTG Peeler handed the reports over to General Gardner, saying, "The scouts identified a number of air defense vehicles and missile systems around the port area and moving to a couple of other strategic positions. An armored convoy was also spotted heading towards City Hall in the downtown area. We got a short message from the LA Barracks that they were under attack as well before the message cut out. The radio operator said they could hear a lot of shooting in the background. Another report spotted nearly a dozen attack helicopters moving to various positions along the coast and to Catalina Island. One of the scout platoons reported one of the helicopters attacking one of our anti-ship gun batteries."

"This is not good, Peeler. We need to do what we can to protect those gun positions. If they all go down, it will leave the entire coast open to a seaborne invasion," Gardner said as he waved a hand across the map of Southern California.

"Does anyone know when we are going to get our communications back again?" blurted out a frustrated colonel nearby to no one in particular.

A young-looking Marine sergeant sitting near a bank of computers overheard the remark and responded, "Colonel, I believe we may have the communications system up shortly. I am in contact with a hacker team at the NSA right now on my computer, and we are working on isolating the malware and rerouting some of the data links and ports. After we finish rerouting one more port, NSA is going to restart the system. It will take about twenty minutes to reboot, and maybe another thirty or so minutes to verify that the malware has been isolated and we should be back up and running."

The atmosphere in the room suddenly became a bit more optimistic about things. With communications back up and running, they would be able to coordinate the ground and air operations a lot more effectively. The older radio systems were still working, but they were a lot less effective. There was no way to send videos or other large packets of information, and they were more susceptible to jamming. Also, the newer military vehicles and aircraft did not come equipped with them. Still, right now, they were the only thing keeping the DOD up and running while the NSA and US Cyber Command worked to remove the malware that had taken down the digital system.

Chapter 10
Reckoning

24 December 2041
Los Angeles, California
City Hall, Mayor's Office

Jose was nervous. Cell phones were still down; he had no way to contact his wife. He peeked out the blinds; a group of squad cars was now parked outside his building, creating a blockade.

The mayor turned to Officer Jayko. "So, are our defenses here all set up then?" he asked.

"As best as they can be under the circumstances, yes Sir," he replied.

Mayor Perez paced back and forth nervously. Minutes that seemed like hours melted along. Jose was lost in thought. "*Is there anything else that I can do right now? What am I forgetting?*" he wondered.

A loud pop broke the silence. To Jose it sounded like a car backfiring. He rushed to the window to see what it was. He was greeted by the unpleasant sight of Japanese and Chinese infantry fighting vehicles and tanks, rushing towards his position. That initial pop was followed by several more as each side began to open fire.

"Sir, get down!" yelled Officer Jayko, grabbing the mayor and pulling him to the floor.

Just as he was hitting the deck, the mayor saw a rocket being launched towards the police officers below. The building shook as the projectile exploded. Jose shuddered; the police were clearly outgunned.

The mayor was not a particularly religious person; he hadn't been to church except for Christmas and Easter in a very long time. However, in that moment, he realized that it was very likely that his death was imminent, and he began to pray fervently for forgiveness. Then he grabbed a pen and wrote a quick note to his wife. "*Querida, I know that I have not been the man that you deserve, but I do love you with my whole heart. I want for you to be happy in this life.*" There was so much more to say, but he just couldn't think of the words. This would have to do. He put the note in his pocket.

There was a long, raucous pause. The curiosity in Jose wanted to know what was going on, but at the same time, he was just trying to block everything out.

The noises got closer. It sounded like there might be gunfire down the hall. The mayor checked his surroundings; he was already situated behind a desk. He reached up and grabbed a lamp to use as a weapon. He closed his eyes and focused on his breathing. Everything else faded away for a moment.

The JDF had been outside the office door, unable to enter because of the barricade of furniture that Officer Jayko and his colleagues had put in front of the door. Finally, someone came up the stairs with a battering ram, and they were inside within mere seconds.

Officer Jayko managed to take out two of the Japanese soldiers immediately as they entered the door. He ducked lower behind the desk as they returned fire. One of the other police officers popped up from behind the mayor's armchair long enough to get off a couple of shots; he managed to severely injure two Japanese soldiers, but he paid for it with his life. His limp body slumped down next to the mayor.

Adrenaline flooded through Mayor Perez's veins, but he was strangely very focused. As the JDF soldiers suddenly surrounded him, guns pointed at him, he knew one thing--he wasn't going down without a fight.

Jose grabbed the gun from the fallen police officer next to him and shot at the closest Japanese soldier. Somehow, even though he had never fired a gun in his life, he managed to hit the soldier in the head. It was his last and final act. The JDF opened fire, and he was gone.

Chapter 11
Feel the Heat

24 December 2041
Pacific Ocean, approaching the West Coast

Admiral Kawano was about to rip someone a new one. He had made the order to launch those cruise missiles at the Marines in Camp Pendleton hours ago, but clearly, they hadn't been fired yet. He hated it when he had to repeat instructions. He stormed over to the room where the coordinates were inputted, and opened the door abruptly. Before he could yell at any of his men, one of his officers stepped forward, bowed hurriedly and then held out his hand in front of him as if to say, "Wait."

"Sir, I know, the missiles have not been launched. However, your orders specifically stated that we were to wait until the Marines mobilized so that we could catch them out in the open, and all of our intelligence shows that they haven't moved out yet. We don't know why they are delayed. Do you want us to change the order?"

The admiral let out a deep breath. His rage had simmered down slightly, but he was still aggravated. Now that he was a little less irate, he pulled the officer aside and spoke to him quietly so that he could save face with his men.

"Why didn't you come to give me an update on the status of the launch?"

"Sir, I am deeply sorry, and I humbly apologize. There was an error in the targeting system as well, and I was very focused on fixing that issue so that when our intelligence changed, we could launch the cruise missiles immediately. We had only gotten that system online recently. I admit that I lost track of time," he said, hanging his head low.

The Admiral did not want to kick a wounded puppy. "Apology received. Next time, just keep me more up-to-date if there are delays."

"Yes sir," replied the officer, clearly relieved to have been spared humiliation in front of his men.

"Carry on," responded the Admiral, more loudly so this time his fellow soldiers would hear. Then he walked out of the room and got back to other tasks at hand.

Chapter 12
Planes, Trains, and Taxicabs

O'Hare International Airport
Flight 7975, Tokyo, Japan to Chicago, IL

As Flight 7975 was following their taxi-way directions to the airport terminal, the men of the second battalion of the Japanese Special Forces Group (SFGp) prepared their body armor and weapons for what was certain to be a quick and ferocious engagement once they docked at the terminal. The Company Commander, Katsu Saito, gathered the four platoon leaders together at the front of the plane, and then waved to get everyone's attention. The men immediately went silent.

"Ok everyone, let's review the plan one last time. Platoon One, you will head to the cargo deck of the aircraft and begin offloading all the weapons, equipment and munitions. Several vans will be waiting for us, so just load everything directly into the vans. Then you are to proceed directly to our designated safe houses and secure everything there."

"Yes Sir," replied Platoon One in unison.

"The rest of the company will break into several assault groups. Squad Two, you are going to head down the tarmac and begin throwing grenades into the engines of every plane that is currently docked at one of the terminals. Cause as much havoc and chaos as you can, then make a break for the Arrivals Deck and jump into the vans that will be waiting to take you to our safe houses."

"Yes Sir," came the refrain.

"Squad Three--I want you to move swiftly through the airport terminals and then find your way towards the parking garages. Shoot any security personnel that get in your way; however, your goal is not to kill as many people as possible. Your goal is to get out of the airport as quickly as is feasible. You are going to split into four-man teams and head towards a new set of drop cars several miles away from the airport. Change your uniforms right away so that you can blend into the population, and then prepare for your sabotage operations against the American infrastructure. When you are finished, you will hopefully have destroyed or disrupted all of the major bridges, overpasses, railroads and distribution centers within a several hundred-mile radius of Chicago."

"Yes, Sir," came the reply.

"By distracting the American response on the tarmac with the grenades, and also in the terminal, we should ensure that those offloading our supplies are able to move all of our equipment with relatively little interference. If we have enough weaponry and fighters that make it through unharmed, our success today will mean triumph for many months to come."

By the time the aircraft finally docked, the room was filled with adrenaline and anticipation. As the door was being unlocked, the men inside the aircraft began to line up, ready to rush through the open doorway. Timing was going to be everything; they needed to bust out of the airport quickly and not get bogged down by security. The Americans had beefed up their defenses at the major airports when the war started, and there were more than enough police and security personnel at O'Hare to stop his group if they did not move quickly.

The first several men pushed their way through the exit, throwing the stunned ticketing agent to the ground. She screamed at the sight of men carrying guns, until one of the men punched her in the face to silence her.

As Sergeant Hiro quickly moved off the gangway, he emerged to find a waiting area full of stunned and surprised Americans waiting for the plane to de-board. He did as he was instructed and spoke loudly and clearly in English, saying, "This is a terrorism drill. Everyone remain calm, and get down on the floor." At first, the people were stunned, but as additional members of the group emerged from the gangway, people began to comply. The DHS patches on their body armor seemed to be giving them the authority that they needed in that moment to avoid a massive shootout.

Other people who had not heard his instructions saw men with guns and began to scream. Most people instinctively dropped to the ground with their hands up or over their heads just hoping they were not going to die. The team moved quickly through the international section of the airport without encountering any resistance. Then, as they walked around the corner, two Chicago police officers loaded with full body armor and assault rifles saw them. The officers must have heard some of the screams.

Upon seeing the officers, two JDF soldiers immediately opened fire, hitting one of them several times in the chest and knocking him to the ground. They missed the second one entirely, and he quickly took cover. The police officer who had been hit was lucky that he was wearing body armor; the rounds didn't pierce through, and he was able to quickly recover enough from the force of impact to raise his own rifle and take aim at the JDF soldiers. His bullet found its way to one of the Japanese fighter's shoulders, wounding him enough that he would not be able to fire a gun. However, one of his compatriots quickly took aim at the officer's head, taking him out of the battle.

The second police officer started shooting at the JDF team. Several Japanese soldiers began to lay down suppressive fire against the police officer's position, allowing several other soldiers to advance closer to him. Then they switched roles, and the group that was closer to the officer began to blanket his position with bullets while the other men moved forward. Finally, they were practically on top of the police officer, and they succeeded in killing him.

During this short and violent engagement with the two police officers, nearly a dozen more TSA and Chicago police officers had converged on the position. Suddenly, they opened fire on the JDF men. Sergeant Hiro knew they needed to move so he yelled at his men, "Blanket the field with bullets!"

Then he lobbed several hand grenades in the direction of the TSA guards and police officers. Once the grenades exploded, he immediately ordered his squad, "Advance forward!"

They quickly overwhelmed the stunned guards and officers, killing them before moving forward to the security checkpoint.

At this point, bystanders were running every which way screaming in terror and just trying not to get hit. One of the TSA screeners had hit the security alarm near their station, sending out a loud emergency alert telling everyone in the airport to immediately get down on the floor; it also announced to security the last known location of the assailants. Soon, additional TSA guards and police officers were running towards the scene.

Captain Inada yelled at his men, "You need to continue to move quickly! Follow sergeant Hiro's squad forward. We need to secure the checkpoint as fast as possible and then move to the parking garage!"

As the rest of his company moved through the checkpoint, TSA guards and police officers began to arrive from all areas of the airport; they quickly opened fire. Several of his soldiers were hit; some were killed outright while others were wounded but still able to continue fighting. They were starting to get bogged down…they needed to keep moving.

"Sergeant Hiro, have your men start throwing more grenades and lay some smoke grenades down as well!" Captain Inada yelled as he ducked behind a counter. Several rounds slammed into the wall where his head had been just moments before.

The entire squad began throwing grenades in every direction, along with several smoke grenades and a few flash bangs. Within seconds, his squad sprinted through the checkpoint with Captain Inada and the rest of the company moving quickly behind them. A few minutes later, they were at the edge of the terminal, racing quickly to the parking garage. Once they had arrived, they saw the waiting vans and began to jump into them, speeding off towards their escape.

Chapter 13
Information Overload

24 December 2041
Washington, DC
White House, Situation Room

Mike Rogers, the National Security Advisor, was receiving intelligence reports from across the country of attacks taking place by Chinese or Japanese Special Forces and complete chaos out on the West Coast. He was still trying to determine what the reports he was receiving about the Japanese all meant; they were still getting distress messages from the Japanese fleet, so the reality of the situation on the ground remained murky. The Japanese Ambassador to the United States was supposed to meet with the President shortly; hopefully, he would get some clarity after the meeting. Right now, it looked like there might be a split within the Japanese military, with some supporting the Chinese and others still supporting the Americans.

A Secret Service Agent walked up to Mr. Rogers and said, "Sir, the President would like to speak with you immediately in the Oval Office. Please come with me." Not sure what to make of this, Mike followed the agent out of the Situation Room.

He walked in the Oval Office just as the Japanese Ambassador was being rather forcefully ushered out the door by several agents. As he turned to watch him leave, he almost ran into another group of agents that were ushering out the Indian Ambassador. Mike was confused--it just didn't make sense for both of them to see the President at the same time.

As Mike entered the room, he looked quizzically at President Stein; he saw in his eyes the fire of burning anger and rage. Then a change came over his countenance; he took a couple of deep breaths and then he transformed into a look of intense sadness. He noticed that Henry's hair had noticeably turned more gray, even within the last few weeks. The weight of the presidency was sitting heavily on him now.

"What's going on, Mr. President?" asked Mike, genuinely concerned.

The President sighed deeply and then walking over to the chair behind his desk, plopping down like a man who had expended every last ounce of his energy. He closed his eyes briefly, ignoring Mike's question for just a moment. He thought to himself, *"The enemies are truly at the gate. I am not sure we can overcome them this time. We need to find a way to turn this war around. I will not be the last American President; I don't want to be the man in charge when the country finally collapses."*

Looking up at Mike, the President signaled for him to take a seat at one of the chairs in front of his desk. "No matter how bad things have gotten before, I have still maintained some hope for the future...but I just don't know if there is a way past it all this time," he confided.

"Sir, what just happened?" Mike probed.

The President reached in front of him to grab a couple of documents, and then passed them over to Mike for review. "This just happened," he responded.

As he read both papers in front of him, Mike's eyes grew wide with terror. "Sir, can this really be true? India *and* Japan are making a formal Declaration of War against us?"

"Those are real. It's true," replied President Stein solemnly.

"Sir, we need to assemble everyone right now. The Directors of the FBI, NSA, CIA and Homeland Security, the heads of the armed forces...we need to meet them at the Presidential Emergency Operations Center (PEOC) as quickly as they can arrive." The PEOC had been reinforced heavily at the start of the Stein Administration and now included an underground tram system that linked it to the Pentagon and another undisclosed location in case the President and his advisors needed to leave the city in secret.

The President nodded, exhausted. He signaled to one of his agents to notify the appropriate people. Then he summoned his last remaining strength to stand up and walk out the door, headed for the upcoming meeting.
****

A few minutes later, General Branson walked into the room to see Mike Rogers sipping a cup of coffee and the President milking a 20 ounce half frozen Red Bull, deep in thought. When Stein signaled for him to come and sit down, the general knew this was going to be a long one, so he signaled one of the aides to bring him a coffee with two sugars.

President Stein didn't waste any time while waiting for everyone else to get there. Once the general had sat down, he began to issue orders right away, "General Branson, I do not feel Washington is as safe as it should be in light of the information I have just received. I want you to double the number of soldiers guarding the Capital."

The general sat up even more straightly than he normally did, soaking in each word. The President continued, "I want checkpoints coming and going from the city. I also want you to issue an immediate alert across the country for our military bases to provide military protection to our key critical infrastructure points: railways, bridges, airports, power plants, dams etc. I want this ordered immediately. Please take the time right now to make the calls and make it happen. I will explain more when the others arrive," the President said indicating he wanted these orders issued immediately.

General Branson pushed aside the coffee cup that was being brought to him as he pulled out his smart phone and began to issue the alerts and orders to the Pentagon Operation's Room. As he did, he thought to himself, "*Well, the secure network may still be down, but at least the civilian communication systems are working. I should still be able to get this up and running quickly.*"

The President began to pace as they waited for everyone else to arrive. Then he stopped suddenly, and signaled to the head of his Secret Service detail. "George, how many agents do we have on duty at any given time?" asked the President.

"Sir, we have 105 agents on duty along with 85 Marines. There are also another 60 police officers outside the perimeter. Is there something I should be aware of?" asked his detail chief, with a bit of concern in his voice.

"George, I was just made aware of a new and immediate threat to our nation. I do not have credible information of a direct attack against the White House or the Capital, but I am not taking any chances. I want you to issue Threat Condition Viking and prepare the White House to repel a possible attack--not an immediate attack, but one that could happen at any possible time. Tell the Marines they are to bring in some heavily-armored vehicles; I want their presence tripled, and they should be equipped in full combat gear. Until the situation stabilizes over the next couple of weeks, I want you to be ready to repel a concerted attack." The President was so stoic while he spoke that his face seemed to be made of stone.

A bit alarmed, his detail chief said, "Sir, I will issue the order immediately. If you feel it is this bad, perhaps we should move you to the HIVE and have you work out of there, where we know we can more easily secure your operations as well as the surrounding area."

"If we gain more credible information, we will move. Let's make sure we have some Razorbacks on standby. In the meantime, I do not want to go into hiding unless I absolutely have to." the President replied.

With that, the Secret Service agent nodded, lifted his left arm to his mouth and spoke into the microphone in his sleeve. A flurry of activity began to take place all throughout the White House property.

Twenty minutes later, the Director of the FBI, Janet Smart, walked into the PEOC. Soon afterwards, the Director of Homeland Security, Jorge Perez, and Director Patrick Rubio from the CIA arrived at the same time. They were followed shortly by Attorney General Roberts. The heads of the military branches all came in as a gaggle (there was General Marcy Lynch from the Marines, General Adrian Rice of the Air Force and Admiral Juliano from the Navy--the heads of the Army and the Coast Guard would be joining the group via telecon). The last one to the party was Admiral John Casey, the new Director for the National Security Agency and US Cyber Command.

They all noticed the increased security at the White House; it would have been hard not to observe that the Marine guards were all now wearing full combat armor, and the Wolverines scattered around the grounds were rather conspicuous. Clearly, the President had increased security. The NSA Director was the one with the best inside knowledge of why the precautions were most likely being made; they had picked up some intel about the Japanese and Indian Ambassadors, and he had a reasonable theory regarding the purpose of their visit earlier.

As the group of senior advisors arrived in the PEOC briefing room, they all took their seats at the pyramid-shaped table. The President, already seated at the head, surveyed the group briefly before he began the meeting.

"Thank you everyone for rushing here to the White House. As you all can guess, something major has just happened that, once again, is going to make the war a lot more difficult to win. I have increased security at the White House, within the capital, and at major infrastructural nodes across the country, until we gain a better understanding of the new threat. I want to bring you up to speed on what has transpired these last five hours. An hour ago, I had a meeting with the Ambassadors of Japan and India, who arrived together. They each handed me an official Declaration of War against the United States. Their reasoning for why they declared war at this point is not going to change the fact that they have already taken hostile actions against our forces and our country."

The President saw some people were surprised, others just nodded, knowing this was a possibility. "After consultation with Admiral Casey, and General Gardner out on the West Coast, we have determined that the cyber-attack that temporarily crippled our defense communications system was launched by the Chinese and Japanese cyber warfare groups via our shared communications network with the Japanese Defense Force. The JDF had worked an elaborate rouse to lure our forces into an attack on the Chinese naval forces near Hawaii. This ruse was developed over many months and we fell for it, completely."

President Stein locked eyes with Admiral Juliano, then nodded his head, asking him to continue briefing on this point without saying anything. The admiral nodded in acknowledgement. "It appears the Chinese, with the help of our former allies, sunk four of our five Swordfish underwater drones. Then the Japanese and Chinese fleets sank nine of our ten warships, and managed to shoot down four of our six F41 Archangel fighters."

The room was so silent that the sound of each person breathing suddenly seemed loud.

Turning to Director Perez from DHS, the President asked, "Jorge, would you please bring everyone up to speed on what has transpired at several of our airports?"

Director Perez began to lay out the situation. "Gentlemen, Ladies, just before the communications blackout, several dozen commercial aircraft originating from Japan had either landed or were in the final approaches to their landing at some of our busiest international airports. Our best reports of what happened have come out of Chicago's O'Hare Airport and Hartsford-Jackson Atlanta International Airport. The plane that landed in Chicago was the first one to arrive and dock at a terminal. Once there, a group of heavily armed Asian men wearing DHS uniforms emerged from the aircraft and made their way through the terminal to the parking garages, where vans were waiting for them to rush them off to what we assume are safe houses."

Janet Smart queried, "So, to confirm, these were definitely Japanese Special Forces?"

"Yes, absolutely," replied Jorge, pulling up a picture of a dead body next to a Japanese SFGp unit patch.

He continued, "While making their way out of the terminal, they encountered several of our airport security teams and a massive shootout followed. The police and TSA anti-terrorism groups engaged the enemy soldiers and killed several of their members, but not before taking heavy casualties themselves. Surveillance cameras and eye witness reports lead us to believe that close to 70 of the attackers did manage to escape the airport and make it to vans that were waiting for them in the parking garage. Police forces were able to intercept two of those vans before they left the property of the airport, which resulted in another shootout. They managed to keep those soldiers contained until help was able to arrive and then they finished them off."

Mike Rogers asked, "So how many of them were killed in that shootout? I mean, I just want to know how many armed JDF guys are loose near the city of Chicago."

"There were about a dozen soldiers in the vans that we took down, so I guess that leaves about 58 of these men still out there," Jorge replied. He took a swig of water from the bottle in front of him, and then continued with the briefing, "After the extraordinary events that took place, the TSA agent in charge of O'Hare made a call to alert all U.S. airports and advise them to either deny the landing of all flights from Japan, or delay their arrivals to the terminals so that additional security forces could get in place. Additional quick reaction forces and police units were immediately rushed to the airports as well."

Jorge gestured towards Admiral Rice, "We have the Air Force to thank for a huge win here."

Rice nodded, "Yes indeed. Our fighter jets were able to intercept six commercial aircraft attempting to land in New York, New Jersey, Detroit, Seattle, San Diego and Houston. They shot them down. The planes crashed near the airports, causing some damage resulting in some civilian casualties, but we are certain that those planes held additional Japanese Special Forces."

Director Perez picked the briefing back up, putting a map on the holographic screen. "Nine other commercial aircraft were able to land and dock at other airport terminals. In four of the locations that they landed (Philadelphia, Miami, St. Louis, and Phoenix), a large percentage of the JDF forces were able to make it through the airports after fighting their way through the security forces. We estimate between 40-50 SFGp survivors at each location. The other five groups were thoroughly pinned down at the airports of Boston, Dallas, Denver, Minneapolis and San Francisco and are currently being engaged. We believe that they will shortly be completely wiped out."

Jorge changed the map and then continued, "We were tracking additional aircraft heading to other major metropolitan airports, but it appears that four of the Japanese pilots caught wind of the situation on the ground and rerouted to smaller municipal airports. As you can see on the maps, we had airplanes land at Gary, Indiana, Prescott in Arizona, Richmond, Virginia, and Victoria, Texas. Unfortunately, security at those sites had not been reinforced, and the SFGp was able to unload their troops there, almost without incident. Since these were not planned landing sites, there were no vehicles waiting to help them escape, so they stole maintenance vans to transport themselves away from the airports there. And Admiral Casey, before you ask--yes, we do have BOLOs out on those vans."

The image switched again and Admiral Rice picked back up. "Two other aircraft were identified by our air defense systems and shot down while they were headed to other municipal fields. Those locations were more remote, and the airplane wreckage did not cause any casualties or major property damage based on our most recent assessments."

Janet Smart stepped in, "All of the pertinent FBI offices have been alerted of hostiles in their area, and have begun to dispatch military units to all of the areas with orders to capture or kill these enemy forces."

While most of them had already gained some knowledge of these events, they all had been missing pieces of the puzzle. Everyone just sat there stunned for a moment before people broke out into conversation, slowly raising their volume until they were trying to speak over each other to be heard. The President held a hand up for Monty, his Chief of Staff, to not interrupt their chatter and whispered, "Let them get it out of their systems for a minute, then we'll bring everyone back to the task at hand."

After a few minutes of controlled chaos, the President stood up and smacked his right hand down on the table with a loud crack to get everyone's attention. "Enough. Everyone please be quiet while we sort through the information and formulize our plans on how we are going to respond. Thank goodness, at least the battle lines in Alaska have stabilized and the Russians have halted their operations in Europe after being pushed out of Germany…but any actions that don't require boots on the ground would obviously be highly preferred."

Director Smart from the FBI was the first to speak, "Mr. President, I believe the first thing we need to do is change the parameters of the Trinity program to now include all known Japanese government workers and as much of their defense forces as we have files on."

Attorney General Roberts barely contemplated before he responded, "Agreed. I would recommend that we implement this strategy immediately."

The President nodded, then pronounced, "Let's make it happen."

General Branson piped up, "We can provide all of the biometric dossiers of the Japanese military members that have trained with the American forces over the last forty years."

Admiral Juliano quipped, "That decision to covertly collect biometric data whenever we conduct a training exercise with a foreign national partner is looking better and better."

Admiral John Casey agreed, "The NSA will be very glad to have any additional information to help track these guys. We will add whatever you give us in terms of photographs or other data; it should increase our ability to find them quickly. It shouldn't be too long before their faces show up on one of the CCTVs or security cameras across the country, and now that we are going to flag them as enemy combatants, they won't be able to buy any new supplies here, as they won't have functioning national identity cards. If someone does try to use a card that they previously obtained, we will pick that up right away."

FBI Director Janet Smart spoke in the manner of a fan meeting a celebrity. "This Trinity program really is amazing. It has done such a great job of identifying foreign terrorists operating in America since the outset of the war. I'm really amazed by its ability to predict those who are going to become Russian or Chinese collaborators before they do any real damage."

The President was happy with this course of action, but there was so much more ground to cover. He turned to Admiral Casey and

Director Rubio and asked, "Two questions--1) how soon will we have our government communications systems back in operation, and 2) what can the CIA and NSA do inside of Japan and India immediately, now that they have chosen sides?"

Admiral Casey jumped in first, saying, "Mr. President, the Japanese and Chinese hit us with several types of cyber-attacks. The first was a quick denial of service (DDoS) attack, overwhelming the system with a bunch of useless data until the network came crawling to its knees. This attack was quickly followed up with a nasty malware virus that began to propagate quickly from one directory to the next, erasing everything. Then several key nodes were locked out using a new type of crypto-locker we have not seen before. Couple that with several power transformer nodes being taken offline and it caused a lot of chaos for us. That said, we have already managed to resolve most of the major issues on the East Coast and throughout Midwest."

He took a deep breath, then continued, "Where we are still having some problems is on the West Coast and with our satellites. We have been planning for this type of attack for a while now, so at least we had the UHF radios up and running. We anticipate having the West Coast cell network and our satellites to be operational within the next four or five hours. We need to restart several servers and install a lot of backup information. Nothing that can't be fixed…at least we won't be offline for days like we were at the outset of the war," the Admiral pronounced confidently. He had explained just enough of the technical details to ensure that everyone in the room understood what the NSA was doing and how.

The Director of the CIA spoke up next, "Mr. President, we have several black ops teams operating inside of both countries. In the case of India, I remember we looked for ways to go after their physical infrastructure. They have several key dams and dike systems; if destroyed, these would cause considerable economic and property damage. We can assume they are going to go after our infrastructure, so we should make it clear we can hurt them far worse than they can hurt us."

The President objected. "While I'm OK with disrupting flow of travel and distribution channels that the country may have, I do not want a humanitarian crisis on our hands because millions of people are killed by a faulty dam or suddenly lack clean drinking water. I want you to hit whatever economic nodes that you can while reducing loss of life, understood?"

"Yes, Mr. President," replied Director Rubio. "In the case of Japan, I also recommend we carry out some similar attacks; however, in Japan, I believe there are other opportunities. The population is not going to be fully on board with turning their backs on us and joining with the Chinese. I believe we can work with their opposition groups to help form partisan groups that can carry out attacks against the government."

Admiral Casey smiled. "Those are good starters, but I think the NSA can do better," he said. "We have a contingency plan for almost every nation as far as points of attack…" He briefly rummaged through the files on his tablet until he found what he wanted. "Some of our mission planners thought there was a chance that either India or Japan could turn on America and join the Chinese, so they inserted some nasty malware into several areas of their economy. When you give us the order, we can bring those countries down to their knees," the Admiral said with a wicked grin. Casey clearly liked inflicting apocalyptic scenarios on America's enemies.

"Tell us more about what that would entail" directed the President.

"Sir, India is a softer target, so I will talk about them first. Our first step would be to collapse their banking system. We are going to do that by creating an artificial run at the bank by spreading some stories through social media campaigns about the banks not having enough money to cover everyone's accounts. The story would also explain that the government needed to collect additional funds in order to pay for the war, so they would create a bank tax of 25% to fund India's efforts, and collect the money by seizing people's assets like Cypress did back in the 2010s. This would obviously cause a run on the banks. Of course, all of this will be fake news, made up to generate chaos."

Admiral Casey was smiling at this point and clearly thoroughly enjoying the discussion. He continued, "As the run on the banks begins, our first malware attack will start. The ATMs throughout the country will immediately begin to dispense all their money until they are empty. In addition to the mass chaos this would cause at the scene of each of the machines, with the ATMs across the country suddenly empty, it would be much more difficult for anyone to be able to get any other money. Following that attack, the malware would move through the banking network, hitting each of the banks with a massive denial of service (DDoS) attack. Anything that is hooked up to a network, from printers to building thermostats, computers to fax machines, even some of the administrators' cars, all of the "internet of things" (IoT) items will be DDoS'ed into oblivion, unable to function under the large amounts of data we will use to flood the streams. Finally, within our roster is a worm that will burn through all the personal checking and savings accounts' electronic balances. The only way they will be able to restore people's accounts will be through their off-site backup systems. At that point, it won't really matter if they can restore the accounts or not. The chaos that will ensue will be sheer madness."

Admiral Casey made a swirling motion with his hands that seemed to announce that he was wrapping up this portion of his talk. "Within a week of the financial attacks, we could turn the lights off on several of their manufacturing provinces. Not the entire country (though we could), but as you say we want to shut down their ability to support the war, not destroy the country and kill the population,"

The President raised his hand to interrupt the Admiral and ask a question, "Admiral, thus far, I agree with your plan to cripple their financial system. I authorize you to move forward. However, I do not want you to turn the lights off to the manufacturing districts. Too many people would be killed in a grid collapse like that. What I want your hackers to do is find a way to cripple the Industrial Control Systems (ICS) and Supervisory Control and Data Acquisition (SCADA) systems in those factories—that would disrupt the flow of electricity in a very pinpointed fashion. You may take down the power in those provinces just long enough for your hackers to cause serious physical and electronic damage to the factories." Before the Admiral could launch a protest the President added, "This war is against their government and military, we are not going to go after their population unless they go after ours. Is that understood?" asked the President.

Nodding in agreement, the Admiral continued, "For Japan, we have a different surprise in store for them. As you know, we have made remarkable strides in cyber warfare the last twelve months. We've worked with the tech companies and have developed some nasty surprises. First, I will address the Japanese navy as they pose the most pressing threat to our country and forces. We were able to insert a couple of zero-day malware systems inside the propulsion systems of their carriers. When activated, the malware will cause their turbines to burn out and disable the ships' propulsion and power systems. We also have the same virus in their railgun systems on their battleships. We may have given them the railgun technology (which I am sure they have now given to the Chinese), but not before we laced it with malware that would make it impossible to use once we activate it."

The President interrupted, "So essentially, you can turn most of their fleet off at the flick of a switch?"

"Basically, yes. That is, once we regain our defense communications system. That should happen within the next hour or so. We've isolated the malware they introduced and are currently rebooting the various systems to get our communications up and running again."

The President nodded, then motioned for him to continue along his original train of thought. "Mr. President, moving on to the economic aspect of Japan. Like India, we have gained access to their banking system as well as their communications system and their entire country's electrical grid. The Japanese have made heavy use of the Internet of Things (IoT) over the past three decades, integrating everything from their cars, homes and every aspect of their daily lives into the digital world. We plan on turning it off. Not everything, just parts of the economy that will make life hard on the average citizen, with the promise to turn it back on once their government surrenders." Admiral Casey had a smug look on his face. He sat back, satisfied with the plans he had presented.

Casey had only been the Commander of NSA and US Cyber Command for six months. Prior to that he had worked in various cyber warfare areas within the US Navy and had also worked with several Silicon Valley tech companies for several years, honing his skills in cyber-warfare and writing multiple military manuals and white papers on the subject. He was an obvious choice to become the NSA Commander after the previous commander died from a heart attack. Though he was very young for his position, he was smart, and more importantly, he was cunning and ruthless in defeating America's enemies. He had turned a small cadre of US hackers at the NSA into a powerful group of individuals with access to nearly unlimited resources, totally dedicated to the electronic destruction of America's enemies. The only thing restraining them was President Stein, who wanted to keep the war confined to combatants and the government, and not the civilian populous.

"Admiral Casey, I want you to move forward with the financial attack in India and Japan. I want you to hold off on attacking the Japanese navy until we can coordinate an attack with the navy. I want our guys to hit them when they are most vulnerable," the President directed.

"Yes, Mr. President," replied Admiral Casey. He would have to be satisfied with what had been approved, at least for now.

The President looked at his military service chiefs and General Branson and asked, "What is the situation on the West Coast? Let's start with the Air Force."

General Adrian Rice, the Air Force Chief of Staff brought up some information on his notepad and paired it to the holographic display in the center of the table. "Mr. President, as you know, we lost four of our six F41s that were sent to aid our former allies near Hawaii. We still have one other flight of F41s that is currently providing fighter support to Alaska. It is imperative that we keep them on that mission; our situation in the Northwest is precarious, to say the least. Right now, the two F41s we have left on the West Coast are going to be used in a reconnaissance role, providing us with real-time visual intelligence once the satellites are back up and running."

General Rice brought up another slide on the presentation. "We are short of aircraft everywhere. We just completed refurbishing 70 F15s and 68 F16s from the boneyard. We had planned on moving them to support our forces in Alaska, but I am now having them rerouted to our air bases in California to bolster our forces there. If the NSA can cripple the Japanese carriers, then our air assets in California should be able to eliminate any air defenses that the JDF and Chinese manage to establish and hammer the invasion force." General Rice spoke confidently as he showed several quickly drawn-up scenarios.

"Thank you, General Rice. I look forward to reading your full weekly update in a couple of days. Let's move to the Marines next," the President said as he turned towards the Commandant of the Marine Corps.

General Marcy Lynch was the first woman to make four-star general in the Marines and now was the first female commandant of the Marine Corps. She had been a protégé of General Tyler Black (the previous commandant) before he was asked to take command of the First

Army just prior to the Chinese/Russian invasion of Alaska. General Lynch was a dynamic leader with a warrior's heart and intellect to match. Thus far, she had been doing a remarkable job increasing the training capacity of the Marines and integrating that force with the latest in military technology.

Looking at the President, General Lynch brought up several disturbing images on the screen and began to explain what they were looking at. "Mr. President, I just received these images and a SPOT report of what happened to my Marines while Admiral Casey was providing us his brief. The reports of the Chinese airborne force that were heading to San Diego have now been proven to be false. As you know, we had ordered the base commander at Camp Pendleton to dispatch as many Marines as he could to the landing zones. He sent a force of nine thousand Marines with a second force of eight thousand more Marines two hours later to San Diego and our naval facilities in the area. Within thirty minutes of arriving at the various locations and beginning preparations to defend the area, they were hit by hundreds of cruise missiles. The missiles appear to have originated from both the Chinese and Japanese fleets that are currently heading towards the West Coast."

An audible gasp was heard by several people in the room and the sudden realization of what this meant. General Lynch continued, with a slight tremble in her voice, "Our local radar systems identified the Chinese cruise missiles, and the laser and railgun systems immediately began to engage them. They destroyed nearly 96% of the 540 cruise missiles the Chinese launched. What the radar systems did *not* detect was the 560 missiles that the Japanese fired--at least not until it was too late. They did manage to shoot down about 230 of the cruise missiles, but the rest got through--"

Admiral Juliano interrupted to add, "--I've just gotten another update while General Lynch was speaking. They've hit us hard, Mr. President. I have a partial report that says our facilities on Coronado were heavily hit. The Fleet headquarters on Naval Base San Diego has been pretty much wiped out. So was our naval air station on North Island. Fourteen of our ships in port have also been heavily damaged." He sighed then blurted out, "They nearly wiped out our West Coast naval capability, Mr. President."

General Lynch interjected to finish talking. "--Mr. President, before you respond, I do not have casualty figures just yet, but they are going to be high. My Marines were out in the open when the attack happened. They appear to have also hit Camp Pendleton pretty hard, but I have not received a full report of how bad it was."

The President just sat back in his chair for a minute digesting what he heard. The rest of the room began to come alive with chatter as people began to check their tablets for additional updates and any other information being sent to them. Monty, the President's Chief of Staff and personal friend, leaned in to be closer to the President asking him, "Sir, are you all right?"

His thoughts were swirling, *"This is just too much information all at once. Crud, my migraine is starting to come back--I don't have time to deal with a migraine. I need to take a break and lay down for a few minutes."*

The President stood up, which got the attention of everyone in the room. "OK here is what we are going to do. The situation right now is too fluid and changing too fast for us to formulate a strategy and respond to this new situation. Right now, we are just reacting, and we need to start anticipating what they are going to do next and make them react to us. Clearly, we need more information to start making good decisions here."

The President continued, "I don't really see that I will be of use to you until we have some more information about what the situation is on the ground, so I am going to take a break from the meeting to go eat dinner with my wife while you sort some things out. In the meantime, I will have dinner brought down here while you continue to work and consolidate the information coming in."

"I am going to come back down here in two hours, and I would like the following information to be ready. 1) I want confirmation that our cyber-attacks have been initiated and are underway. 2) I want the best possible damage assessment of this recent cruise missile attack. 3) I want to know where and what the Chinese and Japanese fleets are doing and what we can do to counter them. 4) I want a full report of what is going on in Oakland and LA... Please coordinate with whomever you need to and have this information ready when I return." With his instructions issued, the President proceeded to leave the PEOC and let his senior military leaders and cabinet members to do their jobs.

Monty began to follow the President out of the room when the President turned and said, "Monty, I need to spend some time alone with my wife and rest for a short bit. I'm getting another migraine, which I absolutely cannot afford to have right now. I want you to stay down here and manage the information and workflow. Guide them if need be, but we need to right our ship quickly." Henry spoke with confidence, knowing that Monty could fill in for him for the next couple of hours.

Monty was becoming concerned for his lifelong friend as these migraines appeared to be happening more often. "Yes Sir. Perhaps you should call for the doctor. We cannot afford to lose you even for a couple of days if something more serious is going on."

"I appreciate your concern; I will set aside some time to talk with the doctor tomorrow and see what he has to say." With that, the President left the PEOC to return to the residence and have a quiet dinner with his wife.

The information pouring in to the PEOC over the following two hours was nothing short of disastrous. The Marines had suffered some horrific casualties as they were mostly caught out in the open during the attack. Thousands of civilians had been killed by the cruise missiles as well. The Coronado bridge had also been destroyed, along with the police headquarters. The City of San Diego was a mess. Camp Pendleton had been hit extremely hard, killing thousands of Marine recruits and severely damaging the base facilities. In LA, two battalions of the Third Marines had been nearly wiped out by several cruise missiles and several buildings and the airstrip at Twenty-Nine Palms had been hit as well, killing several hundred additional Marines and soldiers and destroying dozens of Razorback attack helicopters and other aircraft.

When the President returned to the PEOC two hours later, he was feeling much better; although he was not one to take medication for a headache normally, his wife had convinced him that the state of the free world was at stake, and he had acquiesced. He was quickly brought up to speed and new orders were issued for the navy to dispatch the newly created Carrier Strike Group 12 (CSG-12 which was a consolidation of CSG-10 and CSG-11) to cross the Panama Canal and destroy the Japanese and Chinese carrier fleets.

This new strike group consisted of three Supercarriers: two of the newly designed *Reagan* class carriers and one of the older *Nimitz* class that had been reactivated from the Ghost Fleet along with a lot of other mothballed ships. The *Reagan* class carriers were enormous. At 1,350 feet in length with a flight deck width of 376 feet and 290 feet in height, the carriers displaced 140,000 tons, making them the largest warship in the world. The strike group also had twenty escort ships, including two of America's newest battleships, the *USS Iowa* and the *USS Wisconsin*, named after the two famous World War II battleships. The President was not playing around.

Chapter 14
Send in the Marines

24 December 2041
Riverside, California

The Japanese had succeeded in taking America by surprise. The Army and Marines were stretched thin in Europe and Alaska; the US Pacific Fleet had been destroyed a year earlier, leaving most of the West Coast exposed. People had been assured the Japanese would eventually come to America's aid, then, just as they appeared to come to America's rescue, they betrayed the U.S. and led the invasion of California. As the first Japanese tanks began to roll off those freighters, the LA police and Orange County sheriff tried to organize a defense; they were not going to lay down to this invading army without a fight, and neither were those civilians who owned personal firearms.

The 3rd Battalion of the 3rd Marines (or 3/3 as they called themselves), moved into Riverside, a suburb of LA. As they moved through the various neighborhoods, they could see some artillery and cruise missiles had already landed in the area. As Captain Thornton led his men through the area, he saw a broken swing set, lying on its side next to a blackened crater and several children's bicycles. That's when it hit him, "*The homeland has been invaded, and nothing is ever going to be the same again.*"

Captain Thornton's company had been ordered to move through Riverside and destroy any enemy forces they encountered. The 3/3 was moving to secure the road junctions just beyond the city of Corona leading in to the LA basin. The Japanese forces in the area had put up stiff resistance as the Marines moved forward, forcing them to fight block-to-block in some areas, and leveling buildings in others. It was dirty close quarter combat that had not been seen on the streets of America before. Fortunately, some neighborhoods had also banned together, using their own personal firearms to attack the Japanese soldiers (who had not anticipated the population being so heavily armed with their own assault rifles). This unfortunately also led to a lot of civilians being killed by enemy soldiers, who were not taking any chances.

The Marines would have moved through the area faster; however, the cruise missile attack had destroyed a large part of the Marines air support elements, forcing them to have to fight with limited air support. The Marines had also lost two battalions of tanks and wolverines just north of Riverside on the San Bernardino freeway. Several other major freeways had been destroyed by Japanese demolition experts, forcing many of the Marine armored units and foot soldiers to have to move through various side streets going through many of the smaller cities leading to LA. To further compound the problem, many civilians who were being caught up in the fighting were now trying to flee eastward, heading away from the battles, further clogging up the road system the Marines were trying to use to bring in additional reinforcements to attack the Chinese and Japanese already in the area.

To their credit, the Japanese forces fighting the Marines were giving ground as needed while doing what they could to slow the Marines progress. They did not want to get caught up in fights they could not win. Their only goal was to buy time for additional forces to arrive and to be offloaded in the ports. As hundreds of thousands of people began to escape the city, it quickly became nearly impossible for the Marines to move enough of their heavy forces to the front lines to begin recapturing LAX and the ports, which were being used to ferry in thousands upon thousands of enemy reinforcements.

Chapter 15
One if by Land, Two if by Sea

25 December 2041
Norfolk Naval Station, Virginia

Rear Admiral Michael Stonebridge was the youngest Admiral in the Navy at just 41 years of age. He had distinguished himself as the Captain of one of two American ships that had survived the nuclear attack against the American Fifth Fleet by the Islamic Republic in the Gulf of Aden at the outset of the war. His guided missile cruiser had sustained heavy damage, but also managed to destroy six IR naval vessels, including two submarines. During the fighting, they shot down 84 missiles and destroyed 31 enemy drones. After being hit by four enemy anti-ship missiles and sustaining heavy casualties, they were forced to limp away along with the lone surviving destroyer (which had also sustained heavy damage). It took nearly fourteen hours to control the fires that threatened to send their ship to the bottom of the ocean. Stonebridge's leadership was definitely one of the key reasons that so many of his sailors had survived that confrontation. Upon returning to the U.S., Captain Stonebridge had been awarded a purple heart (with V device for valor) and the Medal of Honor. He was also promoted to Rear Admiral for his heroic defense of the Fifth Fleet.

Several months later, as a newly minted Admiral, his task force assisted the *HMS Queen Elizabeth* and *HMS Prince of Wales* in the fighting against the Russian Navy in the North Atlantic and the North Sea as they attempted to push forward and disrupt the supply lines to Europe. Admiral Stonebridge's task force of guided missile cruisers and three Zumwalt-guided missile destroyers helped to defeat a Russian surface fleet in the North Atlantic as the Russians tried to push past the NATO fleet between Iceland and the Faroe Islands. The French carrier that had been a part of the task force, the *Charles de Gaulle,* was destroyed during the engagement, and the *HMS Queen Elizabeth* had been severely damaged. Admiral Stonebridge was awarded his second purple heart after this skirmish; his ship had been hit by several cruise missiles during the fray, and he broke his left arm and lost a finger on that left hand. He had also received the Navy Cross for his actions during the Battle of the Faroe Islands; because the NATO forces managed to hold the line, the Russians had not been able to break out into the Atlantic, giving the Allies a huge win.

After recovering from his wounds, Admiral Stonebridge was given his second star and given command of CSG-12, arguably America's most powerful strike group. Admiral Stonebridge was a dynamic leader and not afraid to get his hands dirty. He could often be found in the flight maintenance deck helping the mechanics conduct routine maintenance on the drones or mentoring young seamen and junior non-commissioned officers during weekly professional development training. He was a sailors' sailor and cared about the men and women he was commanding.

Admiral Stonebridge's work had now brought him to be stationed on the USS New York, just off the coast of Virginia. As he sat at his station, reviewing some emails on his tablet, the captain of the ship, Captain Baker, walked briskly up to Admiral Stonebridge to bring him the latest personnel report. "Admiral, we are still missing about 223 people with only an hour left before we pull out of port. What do you want to do about the missing men?" It was a question he asked rather facetiously, having already resolved to leave them behind if they missed the deadline.

"Under normal circumstances, I would leave them behind and write them up for missing the recall. However, we were not scheduled to leave for another six more days and most people have been on leave for the holidays. I still want the fleet to pull out of port and begin to head towards the canal; then we can dispatch several helicopters and aircraft standing by here in Norfolk to fly the missing individuals out to the fleet as they continue to arrive. We are going to need everyone for this mission."

Captain Baker had not expected that response. He found that his mouth had kind of hung open while the Admiral spoke. He quickly checked his facial expression and then nodded in agreement. "Yes sir."

"Are the contractors still coming with us?" asked Stonebridge. The fleet still had several technical systems that needed to be completed before the ships were technically ready for combat, and the navy had enlisted civilians to help speed up the repair process in order to get things rolling.

"Every contractor that was working on the ships has agreed to accompany us to Panama, and directly into combat if we need them. They all want some payback for what the Japanese just did to our forces."

A broad grin spread across the Admiral's face, "Excellent, Captain. When we get underway, I want the defense systems run through their paces, and make sure we are not going to have any further issues with them. We are going to need them soon."

Captain Baker could see that Admiral Stonebridge kept glancing down at his tablet, so he left him alone to finish up his emails while he went back to getting the ship ready to leave.

Once he finished getting his Christmas message written, the Admiral moved down to his quarters, where the media team was waiting for him. He wanted to get a video pre-recorded now rather than giving it live. Once the ship was out to sea, he was going to need to hold a series of meetings with various department commanders within the ship and the fleet as a whole; he was going to have to hit the ground running.

"Admiral, we are ready to begin when you are," said the Lieutenant Commander who was the media department chief for the fleet. The Admiral nodded and began his prepared speech.

"Merry Christmas my fellow sailors and marines, and to the civilians who have volunteered to accompany us on this dangerous mission. As we prepare for combat, I want everyone to take some time to remember those who have been lost this past year and to be thankful that we are still alive and able to fight for our country. I am grateful for those of us whose families are safe, and that we have been given the opportunity to bring vengeance and retribution to our enemies. 2040 and '41 have been rough years for the Navy and our country. We have lost a lot of friends and family members, and our country has been invaded twice. Not since the war of 1812 has America's very survival been at stake. We have been punched, sucker-punched, and kicked while we were down. President Stein said it best in his Christmas Day address to the nation a few hours ago, 'America has been given a bloody nose and a kick to the teeth.' Unfortunately for our enemies, the military giant that is America has been rousted from its slumber, and soon we will be taking the fight to the enemies' own homelands."

Pausing for a second and looking at the sailors in the room with him, he continued, "Carrier Strike Group 12 is the most advanced naval fleet the world has ever seen. Group 12 is anchored by the carriers *New*

York and *Baltimore* in remembrance of our two great cities that were destroyed by the IR, and with the strength of their memory, we are going to destroy the PLAN and JDF fleets."

"I want everyone to enjoy this evening and the camaraderie of your fellow sailors and marines. Those on shift tonight will be replaced by their commanding officers at the end of your shift for four hours while everyone enjoys a few extra hours of sleep in the morning. Starting tomorrow, we are going to be working longer and harder than ever before to get this fleet ready for combat. We will reach the Panama Canal in 67 hours at flank speed, and we will be in range of attacking the PLAN fleet within six days."

"We do not have a lot of time left to get our ships ready for combat. I want everyone to know that your nation and I are counting on you to be ready. I have full confidence in your abilities; we will win this coming fight. The men and women you see around you will be the guiding force in turning the war in our favor. Please take a few minutes to pray and give thanks for everything that we have been given, and trust that your commanders have your best interests at heart. That is all."

The media director had a few small edits and wording changes to the speech, but otherwise it was ready to be broadcast to the crew. The entire fleet would hear the message just before their Christmas dinner.

Chapter 16
Rude Awakening

26 December 2041
London, Great Britain
10 Downing Street

The political and military leadership of Great Britain had been following the latest developments of the war and the invasion of California with rapt attention and shock. They could not believe the Japanese had betrayed the Allies like this and were leading the invasion of California. There were images all over TV and streaming on the Web of millions of residents fleeing San Diego, Los Angeles and the San Francisco Bay Area as refugees; the sight was shocking and horrifying. Nearly ten thousand civilians had already been killed across the three major cities from cruise missile attacks and the fighting currently underway.

The massive flow of refugees fleeing the warzone was hampering the American military from getting forces into the cities to repel the invaders, and had stopped additional reinforcements from arriving. The American President had gone to the airways to assure the American people that the military would soon repulse these invaders and that Japan and India would pay a steep price for their betrayal. Images were being shown of General Gardner's American Third Army moving from their bases across Colorado, Utah and Nevada heading towards California. The President had declared that all 1,300,000 soldiers of the Third Army, as well as their armored vehicles were on their way to California and would retake these iconic cities.

The Prime Minister pulled away from the images on the television and turned to the Director of MI6. "George, you've always been one for candor. How bad is it really in America right now?"

The other members in the briefing room all looked at George to see what he had to say. "Good and bad sir."

Annoyed at the cryptic and unhelpful answer, PM Bedford shot back, "Please, elaborate a bit for us, will you?"

Snickering could be heard by a few of the military men as they saw the director stiffen a bit. He was not very well liked; he had been one of the few senior members of the British government to dismiss the idea that Russia was going to invade the EU, citing the same logic as the EU intelligence services (who were claiming that the Russian economy was too tied to Europe to risk a military conflict). He had been proven utterly wrong, but had still managed to cling on to power.

"Sir, the Americans have restored their military communications systems again, so in that respect things are looking up. They can effectively communicate with their ground and air forces. Unfortunately, in the invaded cities they are having a hard time getting reinforcements to the fight with the refugees clogging the roads. The ground war in Alaska has finally become a stalemate now that winter has moved across the state, making it hard for the Russian and Chinese armies to effectively attack the American defenses there, so at least they can focus solely on these new invasions."

The MI6 director was not telling them anything more than what the media was already providing. Feeling frustrated at the lack of information provided, Admiral Sir Mark West, First Sea Lord, felt he needed to interject. "Prime Minister, the war in the Pacific and on the West Coast is about to change dramatically in the next week. President Stein ordered the secretive American Carrier Strike Group 12 to set sail for the West Coast in order to retake the Pacific. Admiral Juliano just provided us with a brief on their mission and shared the details of the new *Reagan* class carriers and the new *Web* class battleships. They have also agreed to share the designs with us, if we wish to pursue building them ourselves." Sir Mark West was clearly hoping the PM would be interested in building one of these new revolutionary warships; he spoke as a child who is hinting about a new toy they would like for Christmas.

The PM was still feeling rather irritated with his intelligence director, and chided him. "George, you seem distracted; I want to know about what is going on in Japan and India at the end of the meeting. Please collect yourself and be prepared to provide a more detailed response than what you just gave us."

George nodded to acknowledge the PM, and then he began to look through some of his notes, writing down a few specific points to bring up.

Looking back to the First Sea Lord, the Prime Minister inquired, "Sir Mark, I am not familiar with these new ships; would you please bring us up to speed on them now that they have shared the details with you?"

Smiling, Sir Mark happily complied. "Sir, the *Reagan* class carriers are a completely new design. They have the command island in the center of the ship with runways on all sides of it. The ship is 100 meters longer in length than their current carriers, 65 meter wider, and 36 meters taller. The carrier can accommodate 36 F35Cs and 150 fighter bomber drones, along with Razorbacks. The defenses on the ship are incredible. They have 32 20mm anti-aircraft/anti-ship railguns surrounding the edge of the flight deck. Just below the flight deck, the ship has two twin-mounted five-inch anti-ship railguns, one on each side of the ship; these have a range of 143 kilometers at a flat trajectory--"

The PM interrupted, "--How were they able to increase the railgun range that much? I thought the railgun only had a range of--at best--39 kilometers."

"The Americans incorporated the new Angelic reactor, providing the carrier with enough power generation capability to power one quarter of Great Britain. The increased energy, along with a five-foot increase in barrel length, allows them to shoot the projectile significantly farther than previously possible. The real power of the fleet though is going to be the new *Web* class battleships," the Sea Lord explained giddily.

"Let me guess--it also has this new railgun as well?" Bedford asked with a wry grin on his face. He was rather amused by watching the Sea Lord (who was normally a very serious and dry person) become this excited about something.

"Yes, it has two-twin turret railguns, but these guns are ten-inch guns with the same range. The ship also has two pulse beam laser turrets, which are capable of engaging aerial targets as far away as 439 kilometers out and enemy ships up to 132 kilometers away, which is basically the limit due to the curve of the horizon. They shared some data on the pulse beam; it shot an eight-inch hole through a ship they were using for target practice. The ship also carries six hundred cruise missiles and has a myriad of anti-aircraft and missile defense systems. Sir, these four new ships are going to single-handedly destroy the Chinese and Japanese fleets once they get in range. Once they secure the ocean along the West Coast and Alaska, the Axis forces there are going to wither and die."

The group continued to talk for a while about these new ships and what they would mean for the war effort going forward. Finally, PM

Bedford turned to the MI6 Director and asked, "George, are you ready to brief us on what is going on in India and Japan?"

Trying to reassert himself, the Director replied, "Yes Sir, there is a lot of information to share. As you may be aware, the Americans are now waging a cyber-war against India and Japan. One of my top analysts believes that the Indian financial system may collapse within the next few weeks; the Americans have caused all the ATMs in the country to empty, creating havoc throughout the cities as people tried to grab as much 'free' money as possible. Then, rumors spread on the internet about a new bank tax and possible insolvency of several of the major banks. People have been trying to withdraw as much money as possible from their accounts, and I am getting reports that this run on the banks may result in the government closing all of the banks by later today in order to prevent a full run on the banking system. Of course, that would only further fuel the disinformation the American hackers have been spreading everywhere."

The Sea Lord flipped to a different slide on his tablet as he switched topics. "The situation in Japan is still taking shape; the cyber-attacks there appear to be slightly different. The Americans have gone after the financial system there as well, but they have also attacked a lot of the Internet of Things (IoT) integrated items; this has affected the communications system, among other things. The systems that control the digital glasses people often wear was taken offline. They also disabled the automatic vehicle driving systems within the major cities, effectively disabling a large portion of the vehicles in Japan from being used until they patch the system. To further complicate the transportation system, the Americans disabled the rail systems by attacking the electronically controlled engines and forcing them to burn out."

The PM was amazed at the ability of the Americans to effectively disable these two countries' digital capability. "Clearly, the Americans have improved their cyber capabilities since the beginning of the war. This is an impressive display," he remarked.

Turning to one of his generals, the PM asked, "General, what is the status of our forces here in Europe with regards to the new attack against the Americans?"

All eyes turned to the general, hoping he had good news to share as well. "Sir, 300,000 new soldiers from the South American Multi-National Force have just arrived in France and England. The Americans had also sent us an additional 20,000 soldiers to replace the ones they've lost during the last several months of fighting. Right now, we have the Russians contained; they cannot break out of their current lines, nor can we break through. That situation will change in the next couple of months as more of the new German and French tanks come online and the Americans send some of those new F41 Archangel fighters. Our goal right now is to hold our positions and continue to consolidate our gains while we plan for another offensive in February or March," the general explained.

The prime minister thought for a minute before responding, "General, perhaps it is time we reconsider launching a new attack against the Russians, but not along our current battle lines. Let's consider a plan to hit northern Norway, with the goal of driving on Murmansk. That northernmost Russian naval base leads to the White Sea and the heart of the Russian navy."

"We could, PM, but we would need to look at late spring to conduct an attack like that. Most of that area is frozen over during the winter, so moving troops, vehicles and ships would be extremely challenging. I can have our planners put together an invasion plan, but I would like this to be in conjunction to a spring offensive along the western front as well. This way, we can catch them off guard."

"Excellent, then let's move forward with the planning phase. We'll evaluate the strategy in a couple of months once your planners have had time to put things together."

With the needed updates completed, the PM ended the meeting and everyone moved to execute their orders.

Chapter 17
New Directive

26 December 2041
80 Miles Southwest of Los Angeles, California

Admiral Tomohisa Kawano's fleet was now in range of launching their heliborne assault forces to reinforce their troops already fighting in the city of LA. It was critical that they hold the city and its port facilities long enough for the invasion force to arrive and bring the follow-on troops coming from Japan, China and India. As they neared the coast, several of the ships began to take aim at the coast, providing fire support to the JDF soldiers desperately trying to hold their ground against the US Marines.

One of the communications officers walked towards the Admiral, signaling that he needed to talk with him. "Sir, Admiral Xi from the PLAN has sent us new orders." As he spoke, the officer handed the Admiral the newest directive from the PLAN fleet.

The Captain of the Carrier, Nagasaki, saw the exchange and walked over to Admiral Kawano to ask, "What do they want us to do?" He was curious to know what the "new masters" had in store for them. Not all the officers in the fleet were happy about turning on the Americans and attacking them like they had. Captain Nagasaki had honored his orders, but he was not happy about it. He also feared what would happen to his fleet and to Japan once the Americans rebounded from their treachery.

Admiral Kawano forgave the intrusion of his senior captain and explained, "Admiral Xi wants us to offload our ground forces as quickly as possible, and then prepare to join them as they head towards the Panama Canal and attack the American carrier group that is close to traveling through it."

Admiral Kawano could see the concern in his officer's eyes; the PLAN had been able to successfully defeat the American Seventh Fleet at the outset of the war, but the Americans had built a new series of warships and none of them knew what they were going to be like. They only knew that they were going to incorporate a lot of new technology that they had not been privy to, even when they were allies. He didn't judge his captain for those feelings though; he felt the concern too.

Instead, he tried to bring him back into the process, asking, "Captain, how soon until our transports can dock at the ports and we turn our attention to the new threat?"

Nagasaki sighed before responding, "Sir, the transports are already moving ahead of the fleet as we speak; they will be docking in the ports within the next three hours. Once they are in the port, we can turn the fleet to join the PLAN after they have offloaded their invasion forces." As he spoke, the Captain resigned himself to the fact that they were going to have to fight the US navy toe-to-toe and hope for the best.

Suddenly, one of the action officers walked towards their little group and announced, "Sir, one of the destroyers has detected an American submarine in the area and is engaging it. The sub apparently fired off a series of torpedoes at the transports and one of the cruisers...."

Their jaws hit the floor in genuine surprise.

Chapter 18
On my Mark, Engage

26 December 2041
Off the coast of San Clemente, California

Captain Hughes had guided the *USS Utah* as close to the path of the JDF transports as possible without giving away his position. Their goal was to fire a spread of torpedoes at the transports and get a shot off at the Japanese cruiser guarding them. Those transports were bringing troops, tanks and other material to support their ground forces in LA; if the *Utah* could send a few of them to the bottom, then maybe they could give the ground forces a better fighting chance of repulsing the invasion.

Looking at his XO, Captain Hughes said, "Commander Mitcham, do we have a firing solution yet on those ships?"

Receiving a nod from his weapons officer, Commander Mitcham replied, "Sir, we have four torpedoes targeting the freighters, one each. The other two are targeted at the guided missile cruiser escorting them. We are ready to fire when you give the order," he said nervously.

The tension in the air was immense; once they fired their weapons, the Japanese would know where they were. Their sonar technicians had already detected two enemy submarines in the area, in addition to the five destroyers with the Japanese fleet and the rest of their anti-submarine helicopters. The chances of them surviving this attack were slim, and they all knew it. They also knew they had a duty to try and stop the enemy troops from landing in America, if at all possible.

Looking at the men and women manning the Con, the captain could see fear in their eyes, but also anger and determination to avenge their fallen brethren. Captain Hughes steeled his own nerves and ordered, "Fire all tubes!"

"Tubes one through six are firing! One, two, three, four, five, six. All tubes fired. Torpedoes are tracking their targets," one of the sailors said as he read off the times to impact.

Without missing a beat, the Captain yelled, "Chief of the Boat, take us down to five hundred feet! Launch the decoy now and get us out of here!"

As the *Utah* began to dive, they deployed their submarine decoy, which was essentially a large torpedo that was designed to sound just like the *Utah* at a higher rate of speed. This would make it appear to the enemy sonar operators that the *Utah* was trying to flee the area. If all went well, they would go after and attack the decoy and the *Utah* would be able to slip away to fight another day.

Within a minute, several enemy torpedoes were in the water heading towards the decoy. Just as the men of the *Utah* thought they might have escaped, a Chinese submarine who had been monitoring the area spotted the *Utah* as she descended to below 500 feet. The Chinese sub was less than 5,000 meters away from the *Utah* when they fired two torpedoes at nearly point blank range. The *Utah* was still reloading her own torpedo tubes, so they were unable to fire back. Within two minutes, the Chinese torpedoes zeroed in on their mark and struck the *Utah*, imploding her hull and killing everyone on board.

Chapter 19
Another Beach Invasion

26 December 2041
Oceanside, California

Corporal Chang had recovered from his wounds during the beach invasion of Anchor Point and was once again back with his old unit. He had also been promoted to Sergeant and now commanded the entire platoon, along with a lieutenant who had just been assigned to their company. Word had it they were going to be the lead element landing on the beach near the Marine Base, Camp Pendleton. Chang had never fought the American Marines before. He fought the American Army soldiers in Alaska, and they were tough as nails. He had been told the Marines fight like devils. He thought that hard to believe because the Americans he fought in Alaska fought like men possessed, and they were Army soldiers. If the Marines were supposed to be tougher, then he was not sure he wanted to meet them.

As their ships approached the coast of California, they received the order for them to suit up and move to their landing craft. They were going to be hitting the beaches of Camp Pendleton before the end of the day. For some reason, there was a lot of urgency to get the ground troops ashore; the Admirals must have known something they were not willing to share with the rest of the men.

Chang looked over his platoon and saw a lot of green faces. He also saw a lot of hardened combat veterans who had fought in Alaska and lived to tell about it. This would be their third beach assault of the war, and hopefully their last. The platoon loaded up into the landing craft, and soon they were on their way to the beach. From what Chang could see, the beach looked like it was not prepared to repel an invasion; this was good news. They might land unopposed. No sooner had that thought crossed his mind than the whistling of artillery could be heard as artillery shells began to explode all around their landing vehicles. As they got closer to the beach, they could start to see the silhouettes of Marines moving into fighting positions along the top of the rise, about two hundred meters away from the shore.

Using his binoculars, he could see these Marines were also equipped with their exoskeleton suits, though theirs looked to be a fully enclosed suit. As they neared the beach, they could start to hear the familiar sound of machine gun fire intermixed with explosions and yelling. Lots of yelling. Suddenly, the landing craft hit the beach and the rear ramp dropped. The platoon immediately began to run through the back ramp and headed towards the low rise at the end of the beach.

Chang also began to run towards the beach, yelling at the soldiers in his platoon to keep advancing and secure their objectives. The platoon ran as fast as they could, ducking and dodging as best they could through the hailstorm of gunfire being rained down on them. Dozens of soldiers were being hit, some getting back up and firing back at the Marines, others just simply dropping to the ground, dead. Chang raised his rifle as he ran and began to fire at the Marines. Suddenly, dozens of claymore mines were triggered and nearly three platoons of soldiers in front of Chang's group were shredded to pieces.

He dropped to one knee and sighted in on a small group of Marines manning a heavy machinegun. He fired several rounds, hitting one of the Marines in the face, killing him instantly and wounding the other two Marines near him. Without missing a beat, those two other Marines he had hit got right back up and began firing at him and the men around him. He thought to himself, *"Their armor must be stronger than we thought. This is not good."*

One of the Chinese destroyers came closer to the shoreline and began to provide direct fire support, hitting several of the Marine heavy machinegun locations and other strongholds that the PLAN infantry was having a hard time securing. Chang's platoon made it to the edge of the beach and proceeded to fight several of the Marines who stood their ground in hand-to-hand combat. He shot one of the Marines several times in the chest, only to see that Marine pull out his pistol, shooting and killing two of Chang's men. He put several bullets into the Marine's face shield, finally killing him.

That first wave of Marines lost the beach quickly; they did not have nearly enough time to prepare a proper defense that could stand up to the PLAN infantry like the American Army soldiers had done in Alaska. Chang looked back at the beach and saw bodies everywhere. Then he saw the second and third wave of Marines starting to move towards the beach. Just as the PLAN soldiers began to run up the beach to reinforce his men's position, the soldiers started to stumble and fall. At first it was just one or two, then it was everyone he was looking at.

He thought for a second, "*Maybe the Americans just hit us with some sort of chemical weapon*." However, as he looked around, the men weren't dying, they just could not move in their suits. Just as Chang went to stand up and try to help some of them get to cover, his suit suddenly stopped responding. He couldn't stand. In that moment, he knew something bigger was going on.

Chapter 20
Zero Day Arrives

26 December 2041
Ft. Meade, Maryland
NSA Headquarters

Neven Jackson was drinking his second 16 oz. Rip It energy drink and eating some chicken wings when his boss, Colonel Jeff Blount, walked in and interrupted his blissful meal. "Neven, you need to be ready to activate your zero-day virus on the Chinese exoskeleton suits soon. The Chinese are going to be launching a massive beach invasion along several points in California. It's go time."

Colonel Blount escorted him and another hacker to the command center that was monitoring the various landing sites. As Neven walked into the room he couldn't help but be impressed (this was the first time the colonel had brought him into the command center). He quickly showed him and his friend Milo two open seats near some of the airmen who were controlling the various drone feeds that were bringing up real time images of the invasion on the beaches. As Milo and Neven took their seats, they saw explosions taking place across the shore. In between the various blasts, they could see what appeared to be soldiers being thrown into the air like rag dolls. Some of them had legs or arms simply ripped right off.

Milo asked one of the sergeants, "How many people are in each of those landing vehicles?"

The sergeant replied, "The armored vehicles carry ten soldiers and have a crew of three; the landing craft can carry as many as thirty men, and the larger hovercraft can carry close to one hundred people, or several armored vehicles."

As they watched the scenes unfold, Neven couldn't help but realize he was witnessing the death of hundreds of Chinese soldiers. In the past, Neven had never seen the results of his hacking actions, just read about them. Now he was going to witness the entire scene live.

Colonel Blount turned to Neven and Milo and said, "It's time to activate the virus."

Neven's fingers began to tap away on the keypad in front of him; he was opening various windows while Milo began accessing the backdoor they had established so Neven could begin dropping in the various activation codes. Glancing up from his monitor, Neven saw the first wave of Chinese soldiers hit the beach; he was amazed at how fast the enemy soldiers moved across the beach in the exoskeleton suits. He was also appalled to see how fast many of them were being killed by the Marines trying to defend the beach.

"Neven, when the second wave of soldiers hits the beach, we need you to activate the code. Our Marines are going to get wiped out if you guys cannot turn their suits off." Jeff was normally a big tough guy, but as he spoke, there was genuine concern in his voice.

Neven and Milo could tell the situation was very tense. These men and women were scared that the Chinese might succeed--what would that mean for the war? Though Neven had never really been scared before, he was starting to feel a bit nervous.

As Milo opened the backdoor, Neven brought up the files and execution codes that would disable the exo suits. They saw the second wave of landing craft and vehicles hit the beach and thousands upon thousands of new soldiers began to rush up the beach. It was scary to think that so many men with guns were storming an American beach, trying to kill Americans.

Colonel Blount turned to Milo and Neven, directing, "It's time gentlemen. Turn their suits off."

With that, Neven hit the enter key on his computer and saw that the code had been accepted. He looked up at the monitors and waited to see if the suits would turn off. At first nothing happened. Then, sporadically a couple of suits started to fail, then seconds later all the suits began to seize up. At first it was funny to see the soldiers simply fall over as their suits were disabled. Then after a few minutes, it appeared the Chinese figured out the suits were not going to work so they began to climb out of them. They once again resumed their charge up the beach to join the rest of their comrades.

Neven looked at Colonel Blount and said, "Sir, I thought this would stop them. What did I do wrong?"

Colonel Blount responded with uncharacteristic compassion in his voice, saying, "Neven, you did not fail. What you just did is give our guys a fighting chance to win. We knew the Chinese would leave the suits and continue to fight, but without their suits the odds of our guys winning went up significantly. Now the Chinese must fight as regular old-fashioned infantrymen while our Marines and Soldiers attack them using the Raptor suits."

Neven felt better that he and Milo had not failed, but as they sat there together in silence watching the battle unfold on the monitors, he couldn't help but feel sick to his stomach as he watched thousands upon thousands of Chinese and American soldiers battle it out, in some cases engaged in hand-to-hand combat.

As the battle raged on, a new drone feed was being shown. This one was looking at the Port of LA and Long Beach, which showed dozens of large transports and container ships offloading tanks, troops and helicopters. These were clearly Japanese soldiers that were also a part of the invasion. The drone zoomed back out, and they got a glimpse of smoke and fire in a number of different locations. There were two ships near Santa Monica Island that were on fire and not moving and then there were hundreds of smaller little fires throughout LA and the surrounding cities.

Milo leaned in towards Neven and whispered nervously, "It looks pretty bad out there, do you think we are going to lose California?"

"I'm not sure Milo, but it seems like they might. If we do, I think America is in serious trouble."

Chapter 21
Breathe Through the Pain

26 December 2041
Apple Valley, California
Third Army Headquarters

General Gardner's left hand was throbbing; the medic had asked if he wanted some pain medication for it, but he had declined. He needed to keep his wits about him, so he would have to endure the pain for the moment. General Gardner had relocated the headquarters element of his command to a National Guard Armory in Apple Valley after Twenty-Nine Palms had been hit by a dozen cruise missiles. The Command Post he had been working out of along with Lieutenant General Peeler had been hit; the attack killed a number of his staff and General Peeler's staff as well. His Marine Commander had been seriously injured, and was taken to the base hospital while General Gardner tried to have the XO located so he could take over command of the Third Marines.

The missiles that hit Twenty-Nine Palms had devastated the base. Several columns of Marine tanks and infantry fighting vehicles had been destroyed, along with 32 Razorbacks and a lot of the ground support aircraft. The Air Force lost 109 aircraft at March Air Force Base alone. The Japanese cruise missiles had also hit Nellis Air Force Base in Las Vegas.

Gardner had to admit, the Japanese had really blindsided them. As he tried to plan what the next possible actions were, he was distracted by his own pain. "*My hand is really throbbing,*" he thought. "*I may need to take a pain killer just so I can focus…I think I might even lose that finger.*"

Snapping himself out of these thoughts, General Gardner barked at his operations officer. "Colonel Mason, what is the status of the beach invasion at Pendleton and San Diego?" (Colonel Mason had been the J3 executive officer or XO when they arrived at Twenty-Nine Palms. His boss, Major General Pina, had been killed during the cruise missile strike, so for the time being he was General Gardner's J3 or Operations Chief.)

"Sir, the Base Commander reports the Chinese have broken through the beach and are currently fighting all throughout the base. He has been slowly moving most of his troops to Oceanside, where they are going to make the Chinese fight house-to-house. He has also established the blocking force you requested at Pala Mason and I-15."

Showing a new image with data overlaid on it, Colonel Mason moved to San Diego, "Sir, the PLAN infantry have secured most of the naval bases in San Diego and the harbor. There is currently sporadic fighting taking place throughout the downtown area and around the Navy SEAL training facility. The SEAL Commander there said they should be able to hold out for a while, so long as the Chinese do not bring any heavy naval gun support."

"I hope those SEALS are able to hold out; unfortunately, I doubt we are going to be able to get them any reinforcements any time soon. What about downtown LA? How are things going?" asked Gardner.

Colonel Mason grimaced slightly as he pulled up the latest reports. He explained, "Things are not nearly as good as we would like to have seen by now. The problem we are running into is the mass number of residents trying to flee the city. We have over one million people, either in vehicles or on foot, all trying to use the main highways and the side roads leading away from the city. Meanwhile, our armored vehicles and soldiers continue to try and get to the port. To make matters worse, the JDF carriers are now in range of using their aircraft and they have been strafing the civilians who were trying to flee. I'm sure they are doing this in part because they know that our forces will stop to render aid and it further slows our progress."

An idea seemed to pop in Colonel Mason's head, and he changed topics for a moment. "A suggestion that came from that one of my NCOs was for us to temporarily stop the advance into the city and just focus on using our transport trucks and helicopters to evacuate as many people as possible to get them out of our way."

"Hmm, that is a thought. However, we cannot leave our forces already in the city to die on the vine while we work on relocating hundreds of thousands of people," Gardener responded. He turned to his Air Force LNO, "Colonel Drewing, how soon can we gain air superiority?"

Colonel Drewing looked at General Gardner with a disappointed looked, saying, "Sir, I would say maybe another day, two tops. The Navy says the JDF carriers are starting to head south, so if that's true, then the number of enemy aircraft over the city will drop significantly. We lost a lot of aircraft at March, Nellis, and the naval air station in San Diego. We'll get air superiority, but it won't be for at least twenty-four to forty-eight hours."

Gardner took a deep breath, during which time he seemed to process millions of possible scenarios in his mind. "All right. Here is what we are going to do then. Colonel Drewing, what aircraft we do have, I want them to focus on hitting the enemy air defense systems they have established. We need to take them down so our helicopters have a better chance of survival. Colonel Mason, have our soldiers dismount from the trucks and move into the city and reach their objectives on foot. Use the trucks to move as many civilians as possible to San Bernardino. We need to get them out of our way so our tanks can get through. Second, I want to get our Razorbacks to start ferrying in as many soldiers and marines as possible to their objectives (or as close to them as they can). We have to get at those ports or we are going to be up a creek without a paddle."

"Yes, Sir," both colonels replied.

General Gardner looked down at the holographic map again. "Mason, how soon until the Blackjacks arrive?" (The 2nd Armored Brigade from the 1st Armored Division also known as the Blackjacks was the closest heavy armored brigade General Gardner had, and he wanted to get them into the fight soon. The Marines had several battalions of Pershing main battle tanks, but the Blackjacks and the rest of the division had 900 of them--more than enough to steamroll through whatever the JDF and Chinese had on shore.)

"The lead elements are about six hours away; the rest of the division should arrive in San Bernardino in about 16 hours. They will be ready to advance into the city in about 24 hours."

Gardner grunted an acknowledgement. "What's going on with our forces near City Hall and the downtown area? Also, have we been able to get some eyes on the ports yet?"

"Unfortunately, Sir, we lost City Hall and the surrounding area. Our troops put up one hell of a fight in the city, but just as we thought we had the enemy on the run, two battalions of heliborne troops from the JDF Marines arrived and reinforced their troops on the ground. We did shoot down seven troop helicopters and four attack helicopters--"

The Air Force LNO interjected, "--We also lost five F38A fighter drones and two A10 Warthogs in the battle as well."

General Gardner let out a quiet groan.

Colonel Mason continued with his brief. "Sir, what's left of the soldiers we sent in have fallen back several blocks further to the east and are hunkering down and waiting for reinforcements. They took some pretty heavy casualties."

"Why are we not sending more Razorbacks into the city to provide our guys with more support?" asked Gardner huffily.

"We have, Sir. We've lost thirteen Razorbacks in the last three hours alone, bringing more troops into the city and evacuating casualties out," Colonel Mason said, exhaustion dripping from his voice.

Seeing the frustration and exhaustion on the faces of his officers around him, General Gardner said, "Look, I know everyone is tired and frustrated right now. We are going to have to deal with this one problem at a time. You all know what needs to be done, and I know I cannot snap my fingers and make things better. What I need from you is to take a deep breath, calm yourselves down and put your thinking caps on. We need to reason through this problem; come up with ideas on how we are going to get more troops into the city in a coordinated manner and defeat this invading force. Intelligence says there are over forty freighters and transports lining up to unload their troops and tanks at the port. Time is not on our side. Just focus on the task at hand and do not let your anger or frustration get the better of you. I need to go call General Branson and see if we can get some additional help. In the meantime, execute the orders you've been given."

With that, General Gardner picked up his secured smartphone, left the room, and began to call General Branson.

General Branson was not keen on the idea of using the limited supply of X59 scramjet cruise missiles to hit the port facilities on the West Coast. "Gardner, you have to understand," he explained. "The US is still in short supply of these missiles--the manufacturers only produce between ten and fourteen a month. The President has been wanting to build up the inventory of them to launch a massive cruise missile attack against the Chinese ship building industry in order to cripple the PLA's ability to replace the losses in the PLAN fleet. So far, we have managed to build up a supply of about eighty-seven missiles, but President Stein directly expressed that he was reluctant in using them against the ports."

General Gardner shared some not-so-choice words with his compatriot. Branson shrugged it off though. "Look," he said. "The new American Carrier Strike Group is going to be entering the Pacific soon. At that point, CSG12 could secure the ports in a week, two weeks at the most, and then we can use the cruise missiles to cripple the PLAN and starve their forces in Alaska."

Clearly, General Gardner's mood did not improve after that phone call.

Chapter 22
Fall Back

26 December 2041
Corona, California
Near the Junction of Highway 91 and Highway 71

Captain Thornton's company had been fighting all out for the last five hours, and they had finally pushed the Japanese to the canyon entrance leading to Anaheim Hills and Los Angeles. The combat had been brutal; just as they thought they had mopped up the remnants of a Japanese infantry company, dozens of helicopters landed nearly 400 additional Japanese Marines not far from their position. As they moved to engage the new arrivals, seven Japanese main battle tanks also showed up, providing direct fire support. This forced Thornton to have to order his men to disperse and try to find a way around the enemy positions so they could destroy the tanks from the rear. His company was taking heavy casualties, but they continued to press on.

It took them close to two more hours, but they were finally able to force the Japanese to fall back to Anaheim Hills. Despite numerous requests for air support and artillery support, none was available. This lack of assistance meant they were not able to get around the heavy tanks and the two additional companies of Japanese light infantry. Thornton's men were now facing close to 800 troops and seven main battle tanks along with two dozen light armored support vehicles. His men were busy using their anti-tank missiles and rockets, slowly grinding down the number of enemy armored vehicles.

Lieutenant Colonel Lee had called Thornton for about the third time, trying to get a status update. "Hey Thornton--has your company broken through the lines yet?" he asked.

"I'm sorry, Sir, but without air support, we are stuck. The Japanese are not going to bust through our position, but we do not have enough men to overwhelm the enemy force."

Lee attempted to encourage him. "I understand, honestly, but do whatever you can to try. The Army has an armored Cavalry division arriving later in the day. Tomorrow, you will have heavy armor support."

Thornton didn't care about tomorrow; his Marines were dying now, and they needed more support. Unfortunately, none was coming at least until tomorrow. "*What was it they used to tell us in Boot Camp? Ah, yes. 'Semper Gumby' Marines.*"

Chapter 23
A Man, A Plan, A Canal--Panama!

28 December 2041
Panama Canal

As the *USS New York* exited the Panama Canal, the ship moved to join the rest of the battlegroup. The remaining three ships of the group were set to pass through the canal over the next few hours, and would join their fellow sailors as they prepared themselves to meet the joint Chinese and Japanese fleets sailing south from California to meet them. The naval battle that was brewing up along the Pacific coast of Mexico was gearing up to be the largest sea battle between modern naval forces since World War II.

Captain Baker approached Admiral Stonebridge in the Combat Information Center (CIC) to get his attention. "Admiral, we have the latest intelligence on the enemy fleet. The Chinese and JDF are merging their fleets and starting to make their way towards us. With both fleets moving towards each other, we will be in striking range of them with our anti-ship lasers and railguns within three days. Our fighters will be within range of each other in two days."

Placing his coffee cup down on the table as he looked up at Captain Baker. "How long until we are in range of launching our cruise missiles?" asked the Admiral, wanting to be the one to draw first blood.

Baker smiled before responding, "We will be in range in about eight hours; then it'll take the cruise missiles close to three hours' flight time before they hit the fleet."

Thinking about his strategy for a minute, the Admiral had an epiphany that it might be better if they did not attack first. Maybe they should draw the enemy in closer, let them expend their cruise missiles against his superior defenses, and then cut them apart. "Hmm, on second thought," he said, "I want to wait to launch the cruise missiles until tomorrow. I want more time for our subs to get in range before we launch them. Then the submarines can launch their attack once the enemy fleet is fully engaged with their own cruise missiles; hopefully this will give us an opportunity to overwhelm them," Stonebridge said as he pointed at a few sections on the map of where he wanted his ships to be when the attack began.

Captain Baker mulled over this change in strategy for a moment. "Sir, if we launch the cruise missiles tomorrow at 2100 hours, they will arrive around 0100 in the morning. Close to half of their fleet will be asleep; this will also put us in range to use our attack drones. We can also have our aircraft attack at the same time the cruise missiles and submarines are hitting them." As Captain Baker spoke, he moved a few aircraft, submarine and cruise missile icons around on the map to illustrate his idea.

"The one thing I do not like about this scenario is that we are going to get hit first," the Admiral said.

"We will, but we also know what direction the missiles are going to come from. We can move our destroyers and cruisers forward to act as a picket screen and have the battleships move in front of us. When we do spot the missile launches on the satellite readouts, we can scramble our fighters to go missile hunting as well."

Thinking for a minute and taking a long sip of his coffee, the Admiral surveyed the map, trying to calculate how much damage his fleet would possibly sustain. It was hard to determine if it was worth the risk of waiting to let the enemy strike first so that he could launch a three-pronged attack.

"I generally do not like the idea of letting the enemy get the first punch in. That said, our attack against their fleet is going to be a lot more effective if we hit them with all three elements as opposed to using a piecemeal approach. If we are going to do this, then let's have the fleet move to their battle stations and be ready to repel the attack when it comes. I need to send a message to the Pentagon and let them know what we are going to do. Admiral Juliano said we have to keep them fully appraised of any changes from our original strategy." Stonebridge was not happy about the thought that others, several thousand miles away from him, could potentially override his tactical decisions.

Chapter 24
Tung and Shinzo

28 December 2041
Port of Los Angeles
Japanese Command Center

Major General Hidehisa Shinzo was starting to feel overwhelmed in his role as the operational ground commander of the invasion of California. Nearly half of the units he landed with four days ago had either been killed or captured by the American Marines rushing towards the city from the Marine Base at Twenty-Nine Palms, and now they were having to deal with the Army airborne units as well. The port would have been lost a day ago, if they had not unloaded that PLA heavy tank brigade and the aviation unit that came along with them. A battalion of Pershing battle tanks nearly broke through their lines in Anaheim Hills.

In the last ninety-six hours since the start of the invasion, they had offloaded nearly 98,000 soldiers, 1,200 armored vehicles, and 800 main battle tanks. The Japanese Air Force and PLAAF had ferried over 620 fighters and ground attack aircraft from Hawaii to the various airports in and around LA. However, their foothold in the city was still tenuous at best; the Marines were still pouring in like water around every strongpoint they had established around the city. Fighting was fierce and constant in most of the suburbs. So far, they had managed to keep the Marines away from the ports, but it was only a matter of time at this point.

He had watched President Stein address the nation a couple of days ago, saying the entire American Third Army was heading to California and would soon throw the invaders back into the sea. This is what General Shinzo had warned his superiors about; if they did not get enough reinforcement into the city before the American Third Army arrived, then the invasion was doomed to fail. Another 60,000 soldiers were going to be offloaded today at the port while 15,000 more flew in by commercial air. It was a race to see who could get more troops to LA. Tomorrow, the first wave of transports from Indonesia and India would start to arrive. General Shinzo had not fought alongside soldiers from either of these nations before, so he did not know how well they would fair against the Americans. Time would tell.

Seeing General Shinzo deep in thought, General Zi Tung of the People's Liberation Army walked up to him and bowed. "General Shinzo, are you all right?" he inquired.

General Zi Tung had just arrived; he was supposed to take over command from General Shinzo. Tung had fought against General Gardner in the Middle East before being wounded and flown back to China. That was several months before the Chinese were defeated by General Gardner. He was then given command of a PLA Corps in Alaska and had helped lead the PLA in capturing Anchorage. Now he had been transferred to California and was going to be the joint forces commander for the Chinese, Japanese, Indian and Indonesian forces in California. This was a great honor, and not one Tung took lightly. If he failed, chances were that he would be executed or at least placed in exile; if he won though, he might be able to secure a position on the ruling committee as one of the great Chinese generals.

"Ah, General Tung, it is great to finally meet you in person. Yes, I am quite well. I am looking over the maps and the intelligence we are receiving, trying to figure out what General Gardner is going to do next and what we can do to stop him."

Tung nodded before responding, "General Shinzo, you have done a superb job leading the invasion up to this point. I know you feel as if you have betrayed the Americans, but they turned their backs on Japan and the rest of the world when they committed genocide against the Muslims in the Middle East. The collapse of America is for the betterment of mankind, not the end of it. Japan is on the right side of history in this war," Tung said, praising Shinzo.

Then he let the hammer drop. "General Shinzo, I am here to take over as Commander for all Axis forces in California. I would like to know if you would be willing to take over as the ground commander for the joint Chinese/Japanese First Corps once they are fully unloaded and ready to move?" General Tung was trying not to insult his counterpart; he knew that General Shinzo was probably the best ground commander in California, and he wanted to use his skills to his advantage.

The Joint First Corps was going to be a 45,000-person armored and mechanized infantry unit. To counter the American Pershing tanks, the Chinese and JDF had developed a new tank round for use by the

Type-29 JDF main battle tank and the new PLA Type-43 main battle tank. Both tanks used a 135mm main gun, but the new projectile incorporated the same armor component that the Pershing tanks used into a penetrator. Essentially, the new tank round was a glorified lawn dart that was made of the same armor as the Pershing tanks, traveling at speeds of 4,000 feet per second. Once it hit the Pershing, it would punch right through its armor and bounce around inside, killing the crew. Or it would blow a hole right through the Pershing so fast it that would cause a massive vacuum, collapsing the lungs of the crew members inside. The advantages that the Pershing had had up to this point were its range and its armor. However, in a close-in city and urban warfare fight, the Pershing would not have a range advantage, and the new penetrator would remove any advantage from the armor. The leader of the Joint Corps was bound to witness some marvelous victories.

General Shinzo was swelling with pride. "It would be my honor to lead the joint force in attacking the Americans," he said. Then his face changed to a somber expression, "…I do hope you understand, General Tung, that our time to beat the Americans is slowly coming to an end, so we have to act quickly."

Somewhat stunned by General Shinzo's pessimistic attitude but willingness to fight on despite it, General Tung asked, "What did you mean by that statement? I would caution you not to express such defeatist statements in front of the men."

"General Tung, the Japanese do not view talk like that as defeatist; it is a statement of fact to spur us on to the action needed to win before it is too late. What I mean is that the American President announced two days ago on television that the entire American Third Army is heading to California to 'throw the invaders back into the sea.' The American Third Army consist of 1,300,000 soldiers. That is significantly larger than our invasion force. It will still take them several days for most of the units to arrive, but once they do, they will push us into the sea if we are not able to secure enough of the strategic points in the valley leading into Los Angeles County. There are currently 90,000 Marines at Twenty-Nine Palms Marine Base, not more than sixty miles from here."

"One of my lead tank elements reported they encountered a battalion from the 2nd Cavalry Division earlier this morning. That division had been in Colorado three days ago; now they are in California.

I need your help in marshaling the needed forces to re-capture these areas and reinforce them so we can hold the valley while reinforcements continue to arrive. I also need our air forces to attack the columns of enemy tanks and armored vehicles driving to California. No matter how many aircraft we lose, we need to attack them while they are on the road and destroy the streets and rail infrastructure heading into California," General Shinzo explained. He spoke with conviction as he pointed to several different locations on the map.

General Tung thought to himself for a moment before responding, *"They were right about General Shinzo; he is a very smart and astute military commander. Perhaps I should keep him here with me."*

Tung acknowledged, "General Shinzo, you bring up some great points. I can see why the military leadership believes you to be one of the rising stars in the JDF. You are smart, and clearly see the second and third order effects of decisions. It also seems that you anticipate the enemy well. I have also fought against General Gardner in the Middle East, so I know what it is like to go up against him (as well as General Black); both commanders are tough and smart adversaries. The battle for California will not be easy, and it will cost both of our nations a lot of men. But it is just one part of the greater global chess game being played. We need to continue to bleed the Americans dry of forces and material. Especially here in California."

"I want you to take command of the First, and the Second Corps and implement the strategy and plan that you just discussed. I will coordinate with our reinforcements, the PLAAF and PLAN to bring in the support and supplies you need to win. You need to deliver though. The PLA does not accept defeat, and it is imperative that we hold our gains here in California." Tung spoke with a toughness in his voice.

"If you can get the PLAAF to attack the American reinforcements and specifically destroy the rail and highway systems leading into California, we can hold our ground," Shinzo said with determination in his eyes.

Chapter 25
Analyze This

29 December 2041
Ft. Meade, Maryland
US Cyber Command

Admiral John Casey was pouring over the intelligence information reports from the previous night and comparing them to the global picture of the war. Three of his best contractors (who specialized in military operations) and his two most trusted intelligence officers were also sifting through the information and the maps, trying to piece together the bigger picture of what was going on with the worldwide conflict.

One of the contractors blurted out, "This doesn't make sense. Why would the Chinese stop attacking in Alaska? They have the upper hand there."

Another contractor said, "Think about it for a second. Look at the units in Alaska. Over the last month, they have rotated out some of their best frontline units and moved them to support the California invasion. All of the new Chinese units and reserve units are being sent to Alaska, and their combat veterans are being redeployed to California. The forces in Alaska are clearly meant as a distraction at this point to tie down our resources and troops. They control everything of value; now they just need to make sure we continue to think they are going to pose a threat," he explained, pointing to charts and maps as he spoke.

A smart young major from the Marines interjected, "My concern with these unit rotations is not that they are all going to show up in California, but that some of them may be used to invade Washington State."

The room erupted in grumbles and murmurs, as others clearly disagreed with his assessment.

"No, hear me out. The Russians just moved all their amphibious troop ships to this point here in Alaska. My money says they are loading up troops and will ferry them down to Seattle. Think about it…we have very few forces in Seattle, and now with the invasion of California, what forces we have in Seattle are being sent to California to try and retake the ports in Oakland and the San Francisco Bay Area."

Another contractor jumped in, "It's an idea. If we start to see all the troop transports and other support ships move from Oakland and LA up to Alaska to pick up more soldiers, then you might be right. Until that happens, even with the help of the Russians, they do not have enough sealift capability or support ships to make it happen." He was somewhat flippant in his dismissal of the Marine's idea.

The third contractor (who had not said anything up to this point) broke into the conversation to add, "What everyone is missing is what the Indians and Indonesians are doing. Both countries have sent troops to participate in the California invasion, we already know that. But what we have *not* talked about is the massive troop movements showing up on our satellites to the Chinese railheads. These forces are moving by rail to Russia. Thus far, the Indians have not made a move against our forces now occupying the Islamic Republic, but all indications are they are moving hundreds of thousands of soldiers to Russia, then possibly on to Europe. If that is the case, then our forces in Europe are going to be in some serious trouble come spring." He sat back in his chair, waiting for the information to sink in.

Admiral Casey finally chimed in with his own thoughts, "I believe Russia and China are trying to distract us by attacking everywhere, knowing if they hit us in enough different places, they can bleed us dry. What we have to figure out is how we can hit them hard enough to take them out of the war without them going nuclear."

Everyone nodded.

Casey continued, "I have an idea and I want you all to vet it and see if it is possible. As everyone knows, we are systematically destroying Japan and India electronically. The US has a limited supply of X59 scramjet cruise missiles, which the President currently wants to use to destroy several major Chinese port facilities being used to build PLAN naval ships and super carriers. What if we used those cruise missiles to destroy key rail bridges linking China, India and Russia together in Siberia? How would that impact the logistics of the war? Also, if we hit the Three Gorge Dam in China, how bad would that hurt the Chinese?"

Casey didn't wait for a response, instead plowing on to the next tactical point. "I want you guys to look at how we can go after their transportation industry and how we can systematically destroy these countries from within. I do not care how many civilians may be killed in these attacks or because of them; I want you to consider all angles and find a way to defeat them before they tear our country apart. I want your ideas ready by the end of this week."

"Yes sir," the group responded.

Admiral Casey then got up from the table and left to go check on his next think tank group to see what they had come up with. That was the one that was systematically destroying Japan electronically...Casey may have been slightly too happy to learn about how his enemies might be suffering.

Chapter 26
Vampires During the Day

30 December 2041
100 Miles off the Coast of Mexico

"Vampires! Vampires! Vampires!" yelled one of the petty officers in the CIC as the radar screens started to show one, then dozens, then hundreds, then *thousands* of cruise missiles heading towards the American fleet. Immediately, the fleet's automated defense system began to take over, slaving every ship in the fleet to the central command at the heart of the fleet, the *USS New York*, the flagship of the fleet. Admiral Stonebridge would now be able to control all of the ships' defense and targeting systems.

The carriers immediately began to launch their drone fighters to get them heading towards the missiles to engage them. The missiles were still several hundred miles away, but they were closing that distance fast. As the naval attack came into range of the first ships in the strike group's screening force, the frigates, destroyers and cruisers began to engage them with their railguns and anti-missile interceptors. A curtain of projectiles was flying at the thousands of missiles streaking in towards the strike group. Dozens of missiles started to disintegrate as they were shredded by the railgun projectiles, while others were destroyed by the missile interceptors. As the ships desperately fought to destroy the waves of incoming fire, several of them started to find their marks, ripping through the frigates and destroyers. Fireballs appeared as the missiles ripped through the hulls and superstructures of the ships like hot knives through butter. As the enemy swarm overwhelmed the outer screen of the strike group, the heavy cruisers and battleships began to throw up their own wall of projectiles, missile interceptors and point defense lasers, engaging as many missiles as their systems could target.

Several anti-ship missiles plowed into the two heavy battleships, the pride of the American Navy. To everyone's amazement, they sustained little damage. The reactive armor added to the battleships had held, and the ships just shrugged off the hits, only sustaining superficial damage to the exterior structure. As the final wave of missiles flew towards the three carriers of the American fleet, they disintegrated in a hail of railgun projectiles and laser point defense systems.

America had learned a hard lesson early in the war when they had found out that the carrier fleets were vulnerable to a missile swarm attack. It had been a difficult lesson to accept at the time, but now it was paying off through the new design of the carrier fleet's defensive systems. The JDF and PLAN had just thrown over 2,100 anti-ship cruise missiles at the American fleet, and all but 62 missiles had been destroyed. The Americans did sustain damage, losing three destroyers, four frigates and one cruiser to the missile swarm. However, all three carriers survived with no damage, and the battleships (which packed most of the fleet's heavy firepower) had taken little damage. The core of the fleet was still intact despite the losses, and now they were moving into their own strike range; soon the JDF and PLAN would feel the wrath of American ingenuity.

Chapter 27
Don't Forget to Turn out the Lights

30 December 2041
Ft. Meade, Maryland
NSA Headquarters

Neven Jackson and his partner in crime Milo had received a lot of congratulations from the bosses at the NSA for their successful hack of the Chinese exoskeleton suits during the PLAN beach invasion of Oceanside. The Chinese had still captured Camp Pendleton and San Diego, but they had suffered horrific casualties and lost the ability to use their exoskeleton combat suits until their programmers could figure out how to remove Neven's malware and get the suits operational again. Neven and Milo had even been invited for lunch with President Stein as a reward for a job well done.

Meeting the President was not something high on either of their minds. As hackers, their natural inclination was to have little respect for authority figures, let alone the President. However, after their lunch, they both walked away with a better understanding of Stein, and may have even started to see him as a real person. For a politician, the President had a very strong grasp on cyber warfare and cyber security, something neither of them expected from any president. They also felt a renewed purpose to not let the country down after seeing how their direct efforts were affecting the war.

Colonel Jeff Blount may have been a little jealous of Milo and Neven's facetime with the President. He walked into their little hacker fiefdom on a mission, and with barely any gesture to politeness, bluntly asserted, "Ok gentlemen, sorry to disrupt the joyful reverie of your 'lair,' but it's time for you to launch your next malware attack. We need you to move against the Japanese Fleet off the Pacific Coast of Mexico."

As the drone feed was directed to their large screen monitors, they could see that the naval battle between the joint Chinese/Japanese fleet and the Americans was well underway. They saw the missile swarm heading towards the Americans and thought for certain the fleet was finished. To their surprise, they saw hundreds and then thousands of enemy missiles being destroyed, reducing the swarm into a manageable flock.

Several bright flashes could be seen as multiple American ships were hit. Then numerous large explosions occurred.

"What was that?" asked Neven, as he began work on another screen.

Colonel Blount was almost callous as he responded, "That was 291 people being killed. Those ships just blew up."

As the missiles converged on the battleships and carriers, it seemed that they were all but destroyed.

The Colonel walked to the front of the room, standing in front of the monitors. Then he announced, "Now it is our turn. I need you guys to go in through your established backdoors and turn the Japanese ships off. We know you cannot access the Chinese ships; our fleet will handle them. Disable the JDF ships and let's finish this battle, bringing the war one step closer to victory." Then he walked to the side of the room to let the hackers do their work.

Neven pulled another Rip It out of the fridge near his work station, turned on his favorite music and began to type away. Neven was working on three different twenty inch monitors while reclining in a soft leather chair with his headphones on, and Milo was setting up the malware that would jump from the JDF fleet to the PLAN and begin to bog down their communications system with a concerted DDoS attack from every IoT device in the JDF fleet.

As Neven moved from folder to folder, system to system within the carriers and battleships of the JDF fleet, he began to activate a series of viruses and crypto-locker protocols that would shut down the carriers and battleship and then summarily lock them out of their systems when they tried to reboot them. The ships would effectively become dead in the water, unable to move or defend themselves when the American fleet started to carry out their counter attack. It was going to be a bloodbath.

Chapter 28
Battleships

30 December 2041
100 Miles Off the Coast of Mexico

An intelligence officer walked onto the bridge and handed Stonebridge a memo. "Admiral, this message just came in from NSA. They said the JDF fleet has been taken offline and is dead in the water. We should conduct our attack now before they are able to bring their systems back online." The officer waited for the Admiral to finish reading the report and issue his next set of orders.

"*Now it's time for some American justice*," thought the Admiral to himself.

Stonebridge turned to Captain Mason and directed, "Captain, order your attack aircraft to engage the enemy fleet immediately." Then he turned to his operations officer and said, "Captain Lacey, order the battleships to launch their missiles and continue at flank speed until they are in range of the enemy fleets ships with their laser and railgun turrets. Once they are within range, they are to engage the enemy at will."

Admiral Stonebridge looked back at the holographic map and the distances between the two fleets; the gap was closing quickly as the Americans were moving at flank speed towards the enemy. The Chinese and JDF continued to move towards the Americans to get their battleships in range to use their main guns, unaware of what awaited them.

****

Captain Jeremiah Wright had just completed his twenty-first year in the US Navy and his second year as the Captain of the *USS Iowa* Battleship. He had been selected to be the Captain of the *Iowa* after completing his assignment as the executive officer of the *USS George H.W. Bush* just months before it had been destroyed in the Pacific by the Chinese during the opening engagement of World War III. He had felt terrible about the loss of his previous ship; he knew a lot of the officers and enlisted personnel on board that had died, so it's sinking hit home. He had lost over a hundred people he considered to be close friends. His assignment to the *USS Iowa* had been a blessing and a curse. He had needed time to emotionally heal and grieve the loss of so many friends;

he had gotten that in a way because he had been sidelined from participating in the war up to that point while he worked on getting the *USS Iowa* ready for battle for more than 18 months.

Now, as Captain Wright stood in the CIC of America's most powerful warship ever built, he felt almost god-like at the power and sheer destruction he was about to unleash on America's enemies. His orders were to target the Chinese Supercarriers and battleships and leave the Japanese ships for the drones to destroy. With the cyber-attacks crippling the Japanese fleet, his real concern was the Chinese navy.

He turned to his weapons officer, "Commander Lewis, do we have a firing solution on the first Supercarrier?" he asked.

Lewis replied, "Yes, sir, we do. We have both weapon systems locked in right now. Do you want to hit them with the railgun or the laser?" he asked with a grin.

"First, let Admiral Stonebridge know we are ready to fire and make sure everyone can see the drone footage. Let's hit the first carrier with the railguns. Then we'll hit the second carrier with the pulse beam and see which one has the most effect." Captain Wright had been told by Admiral Stonebridge that President Stein himself was going to be watching the battle, so he wanted to impress.

The communications officer replied, "All outstations are reporting ready, and the various feeds from the drones are coming in nice and clear."

Looking at the men and women in the CIC, Captain Wright ordered, "Commander Lewis, FIRE guns one through four!"

There was a slight increase in the mechanical hum of the ship as the reactor increased power and then an ear-piercing *SNAP, SNAP, SNAP, SNAP*, as the four railguns fired one projectile each at the Chinese Supercarrier one hundred and eighteen miles away. It took nearly a minute for the projectiles to fly the distance to the Chinese fleet, and then the rounds hit the carrier. They saw on the drone feed the impact against the side of the carrier, causing it to rock heavily to one side before it righted itself from the impact. Initially, there was a somewhat small entry hole into the hull, and then a massive explosion detonated as the projectile flew through the ship and out the other side. The projectile was traveling so fast when it hit that the shockwave caused a huge section of the hull on the opposite side to blow right open. Critical sections of the ship started to catch fire and explode. The carrier was still floating, but clearly had suffered a critical hit. Flames burst out of the entrance and exit holes where the projectile had been.

Captain Wright looked at his weapons officer and ordered, "Fire a second volley."

The *USS Iowa* shook a second time as the main guns fired a second volley of projectiles at the Chinese warship. When the second round hit the carrier, it shook violently. Several additional explosions erupted, and the carrier began to rip apart. Within minutes, the carrier began to list heavily to one side and started sinking quickly. An audible gasp could be heard in the CIC as the men and women watching saw the ship start to roll over on its side and quickly descend below the waves.

"Commander Lewis," barked the Captain. "Fire the lasers at the second carrier!"

The reactors of the Iowa began to spool up again, and this time the ship's two pulse beam lasers discharged. Upon hitting the ship, each laser burned a three-foot round hole into the hull of the ship, just below the flight deck. Within seconds, the laser had ignited the fuel and weapons used for the drones, causing significant damage and secondary explosions.

"Commander Lewis, have the gun battery aim for the waterline, and let's see if we can sink that ship with the next shot," the Captain ordered.

Commander Lewis nodded, then picked up a phone to talk with the targeting officers for the laser battery, who quickly made the requested adjustment. The second laser shot impacted the carrier, burning a hole several feet below the waterline and causing the water surrounding the new hole in the hull to quickly bubble away until the laser turned off. In seconds, a huge rush of water could be seen swooshing into the vacant hole left by the laser. In less than a minute, the ship began to tilt heavily to one side as the flames from the drone fuel and ammunition continued to rage.

Admiral Stonebridge came on to the fleet PA system, "Impressive show, Captain Wright. It's time for both battleships to fire at will now. We need to begin to systematically destroy the Chinese fleet while the carrier drones fly in to finish off the Japanese."

The battle lasted less than thirty minutes. In that time, the Japanese lost three Supercarriers, their two prized battleships, and their entire support fleet. The Chinese recognized what type of weapons they were being hit with, and the ships that were left immediately began to sail away from the American fleet as fast as possible to try and get out of range of the American super weapons. Three of the four Chinese Supercarriers were destroyed, while the fourth sustained a hit from the *Wisconsin's* railgun, causing significant damage. Only three other Chinese surface ships escaped the battle as they ran quickly towards the waters of Hawaii.

Chapter 29
In the Middle of the Night

30 December 2041
Tokyo, Japan
Prime Minister's Official Residence

Prime Minister Yasuhiro Hata was asleep with his wife when a knock at the door woke him out of his slumber. As he fumbled with the covers and placed his feet on the floor, he reached for a robe and slowly walked to the door just as the knocking started again. "Shhh--you are going to wake my wife. What is so urgent that it could not wait until morning?" PM Hata asked the military officer standing in front of his bedroom door.

"Sir, I was told by Admiral Hito to come and get you. He said to tell you there has been a major naval engagement with the Americans in the Pacific," the officer muttered. He seemed to be completely out of breath.

"Perhaps if the officer hurried that much to see me, the situation is truly serious," thought the Prime Minister.

"Tell the admiral I will be over shortly," Hata responded aloud. "I am going to get dressed," he said, and he closed the door, not waiting for a reply.

Twenty minutes later, PM Hata walked into the operations center in the bowels of the PM's offices and saw several military officers talking animatedly around a holographic map while others were reviewing several different drone feeds. The room looked every bit the military headquarters it had turned into these past few weeks since the start of the war with America.

Up to this point, the invasion had been proceeding better than expected. Their forces in Los Angeles had done a marvelous job fighting the American Marines, though it did appear the war was about to take a turn for the worse as more and more American soldiers continued to pour into California from other areas of America. Their Special Forces raids in the heart of America via the airlines had also been yielding great results. They had already destroyed several critical rail bridges and tunnels in the cities surrounding the airports where a number of operatives had gotten out through security. The attacks against the transportation infrastructure of America were going to have a long-term effect on the Americans' ability to defend themselves. However, the optimism of the situation was about to change.

Admiral Hito looked up and saw the PM had finally arrived. "PM, please, if you will come this way. We need to discuss the recent naval battle," he said urgently.

As the PM walked towards the Admiral, he saw the look of sheer anxiety on the faces of many of the military officers. "What is so important that it could not wait until morning?" demanded Hata, clearly not happy with having been woken up in the middle of the night.

"Prime Minister, there was a major naval battle between our forces and the Americans off the Pacific coast of Mexico. The Americans had moved their new battle group called Carrier Strike Group 12, along with their newest battleships and supercarriers to the Pacific several days ago. Three hours ago, the fleets came into range of each other and the battle started," began the Admiral.

"Near as I can tell Admiral, this battle was a success, we sunk nine American warships," shot back the PM, not sure why his officers were acting like this was some sort of disaster.

"Sir, there is more. Following our initial attack and success against the Americans, they launched their own assault using their newest super weapons. We had no idea they had these types of weapons, and they were incredibly deadly. They destroyed three of our five carriers and both of our battleships, along with nearly our entire support fleet. What is left of the fleet has retreated to Hawaii." As the Admiral spoke, he hung his head low, not making eye contact with the PM.

PM Hata began to fill with rage and anger. He had been assured by the PLAN and his own Admirals that the American navy would be defeated, that their navy no longer posed a serious threat if they were to join the Chinese in this war. Now most of their fleet had been destroyed in just one engagement with the Americans...this was unacceptable.

Barely able to contain his ire, the PM yelled, "What happened?!" Then he softened his voice and hissed, "Start from the beginning, Admiral."

The Admiral stiffened his back and looked the PM in the eyes as he relayed the sequence of the battle and what led to their defeat. "The Americans hacked into our computer systems on the carriers and our battleships. They took the ships' power systems offline; then they began to disable specific combat systems like the point defense weapon systems. In the battleships, they disabled the railgun turrets. By the time our computer specialist could regain control of the power system and some of the defenses, the battle was well underway and the Americans were already attacking them. The best they could do was turn the fleet towards Hawaii and move as fast as they could to get away from the American guns."

He pulled up some drone footage to show the PM. "They hit us with two new weapons we were not prepared for. One was their railgun turrets--we have them on our battleships as well, but the American railguns were shooting projectiles significantly larger than anything we thought possible; they also had a range of more than 120 kilometers, which was way beyond what we thought possible. Next, they hit the Chinese ships (and ours) with a pulse beam laser. Here is a video of the laser hitting a Chinese carrier; you can see how it only hits the ship for about five seconds, but cut a hole more than ten meters deep and two meters in diameter. It devastated the ship."

"As our ships began to turn towards Hawaii, the American fighter drones began to pounce on our ships from the sky. Our support ships luckily did not have their systems hacked, so they were able to shoot down many of the drones, but not before they destroyed a large portion of our support fleet and three of our five carriers."

PM Hata stood there in silence for a couple of minutes watching the drone feeds and thinking to himself, "*If the Americans could do this to our fleet, how much more will they be able to do when the rest of their navy on the East Coast is ready? I fear I have led Japan down the road to ruin.*"

"Admiral, this battle has been clearly lost; I need time to think about what this all means and what our next steps are. I am going to go get some food and talk with the Foreign Minister. We will both return to this room in three hours, and I would like a briefing on what the military heads' recommendations are." The PM was in a state of shock and resignation as he looked at the military officers standing around him. He knew he should say something inspiring at that moment, but he could not think of anything to say, so he turned around and left the room as he dialed the phone number to his foreign ministers.

Admiral Kawano could not believe he had lost 9,600 sailors in the span of thirty-five minutes. What had been the pride of the Japanese navy was now reduced to two supercarriers and a handful of escort ships. The PLAN had suffered a similar loss in capital ships. His officers were also still in a state of shock at what just happened; they continued pouring over the drone images of the attack to try and determine how this all happened. He knew the Americans had been working on pulse beam lasers and heavier railguns, but had no idea they had moved from experimenting with them to full implementation of them on their next generation warships. If they did not find a way to counter this, then they were going to be in some serious trouble.

What troubled him more was that all the transports were still heading to the American ports. With his naval force unable to protect those ships, a lot of men were going to die before they ever set foot on American soil.
****

Hours later, Prime Minister Hata and his Foreign Minister Hirohita walked into the Command Center and made their way over to a corner in the room where the briefing table was. Several officers were setting up equipment near the table, while another aide was filling the glasses on the table with water and getting cups ready for tea.

Admiral Hito directed the officers around him to head to the table so they could begin the briefing. Fortunately, they had found some valuable information intermixed with the drone feeds and they were eager to share it. As everyone sat down, Admiral Hito cleared his throat and began to speak to the group. "PM, Foreign Minister, after careful review of the drone feeds of the battle, we have found some useful intelligence that may help us to defeat the advanced American warships. During the battle, our forces and the PLAN carried out what we in the navy call a missile swarm attack. Our ships and aircraft fired a series of waves of anti-ship cruise missiles at the American fleet. The American support ships and their capital ships did manage to destroy most of them, but a small percentage did still get through. During our attack, we managed to destroy three Zumwalt destroyers, four guided missile frigates and one heavy cruiser. That only leaves the carrier fleet with two of their older missile destroyers, three frigates and two heavy missile cruisers to assist their two battleships and three supercarriers." The Admiral seemed to be boasting about the damage they had inflicted.

The PM seemed puzzled by the Admiral and other officers' excitement and asked, "I commend our forces in destroying these

American warships, but it sounds as if most of their fleet and their capital ships are still intact. What am I missing?"

Seeing that the PM and the Foreign Minister had not grasped the significance of what they had accomplished, the Admiral explained, "Sir, the American capital ships are powerful, but now they are vulnerable to a missile swarm attack. We launched 2,100 anti-ship cruise missiles at them. During that engagement, only 68 of our missiles got through to cause damage, but even those small numbers sank half of their missile screening defense. If we can launch another missile swarm of this magnitude or greater, there is a high likelihood that we can sink their fleet." The Admiral's face glowed with a genuine smile.

PM Hata's face relaxed out of its permanent frown for the first time that day as he finally realized what his officers were saying. Yes, they had just suffered a stinging defeat, but they had also discovered a way to sink this new and powerful fleet. "Admiral, how soon until we can launch another swarm attack like this?"

After calculating in his head for a moment, the Admiral responded, "Sir, we are moving as many anti-ship cruise missiles as we can to Hawaii right now. Our ships that are left can carry and launch 810 missiles; our drones can launch another 340. We believe the Chinese ships can launch a combined 940 missiles. I have a meeting with the PLAN Admiral in two hours to discuss our findings with them. I would like to believe we can coordinate a new attack against the Americans within the next couple of days."

****

Over the next two days, the Japanese and Chinese naval forces would work feverishly to bring as many anti-ship cruise missiles to Hawaii as possible. They also moved any available ships and support aircraft that were still available as well. Despite the tremendous loss, the mood of the commanders was now one of optimism.

Chapter 30
Meet Me in St. Louis

31 December 2041
Washington, D.C.
Presidential Emergency Operations Center (PEOC)

The President and his staff were still celebrating the great naval battle from the night before when Jose Perez walked in on the celebration with a very somber expression. "Mr. President," he began. "I'm sorry to sour the mood, but it's about St. Louis."

"What happened, Jose?" asked Stein, turning serious.

"Sir, last night a Japanese Special Forces group placed explosives on the supports of the South I-235 bridge near the St. Louis airport…it dropped into the Mississippi. Not only is it stopping road travel there, but it's also blocking river traffic."

There was no more happy chatter in the back of the room. Director Perez continued, "It's not just that, either. In addition to dropping the South bridge, they also dropped the North one, the I-64 bridge and I-70 bridge in downtown St. Louis. Twenty-Three National Guard soldiers who had been guarding the bridges were killed, along with seven police officers. As if the attack against the bridges were not bad enough, another attack group blew up the canal locks along the Chicago River, reversing the direction of the water flow and causing all sorts of pollution to be transported to Northern and Central Illinois."

These weren't the first successful attacks by the JDF; recent memories flashed back in everyone's minds. Two days ago, a major shootout had occurred near the White House as a Japanese Special Forces group attacked and then subsequently destroyed the 14th Street bridge joining Northern Virginia and the District of Columbia across the Potomac River. Using several recoilless rifles, the attack force had also destroyed a section of the rail bridge that crosses nearby before they were killed by an Army unit that responded to the attack. The attack had been so close to the White House that it had reinforced the President's assumption that Washington DC was not safe as long as enemy Special Forces were still prowling around.

The advisors turned back to business, discussing the attacks against the transportation grid and their potential military and economic impact. The President asked, "So, Admiral Casey, what is the status of the Trinity Program in tracking these guys down?"

"It's a work in progress, Sir," replied Casey. "We have managed to track down a large number of hostiles in Miami, Philadelphia and around Victoria, Texas, but obviously, there are still quite a number of them at large. It's just a matter of time before they trip up though, Mr. President."

FBI Director Janet Smart added, "We've also picked up smaller groups of the JDF Special Forces Group in Atlanta, Phoenix and outside of Gary, Indiana. We are currently utilizing enhanced interrogation methods to help close in on any of their compatriots that they may be able to locate."

The President nodded.

Mike Rogers, the National Security Advisor, decided to lighten the mood a little. "Sir, I've been going over Admiral Casey's reports from India and Japan. Not only are the cyber-attacks impacting the economies there, but public opinion in those countries has definitely moved against participating in the war in attacking the United States." General Branson saw an opportunity and chimed in, "Speaking of good news, Sir, we have officially deployed the first Bodarks in Alaska. We've set them up behind the Russian and Chinese lines, hoping they will cause as much chaos as possible."

"So, have we had movement in Alaska, then?" asked the President.

"No, Sir. Not yet. The lines have been well established at this point; it seems that all sides are content to wait until spring before they resume killing each other. Although we've definitely lost Alaska, there is a glimmer of hope. After the Russians secured Fairbanks and oil fields of Prudhoe Bay, they withdrew most of their forces, leaving an occupation force to deal with the American militias there. The Chinese also seem to be moving a lot of their troops and heavy equipment to the ports; perhaps they are trying to move them to California."

The President wondered, "So, speaking of California, how soon do you think we will be able to end the invasion there and restore order?"

General Branson brought up the map of Southern California and the various military divisions and their locations. "We have 121,000 soldiers fighting in Los Angeles against about 148,000 enemy soldiers. As of right now, our intel estimates that an additional 12,000 enemy soldiers are arriving in Los Angeles through the ports every hour. Our naval forces are starting to move towards the ports, once in range they will begin to interdict the enemy transports."

Zooming in closer to the map of Los Angeles, he continued, "As you can see, we have moved forces throughout the LA basin and encircled the enemy. We now have them blocked in, so they cannot expand their footprint while we continue to move additional forces into the area. We also have several armored divisions arriving now, so we should begin the new offensive shortly."

Pulling up a different map of the San Francisco Bay area, General Branson explained, "The enemy forces in this area are much smaller in number. They have not moved nearly as many forces into the area, and we have managed to get an airborne brigade to the mouth of the bay and close it off from any additional transports that arrive. Right now, they are holding the area until we can get additional forces to them. We have two armored divisions and three infantry divisions about a day away now."

"Well, that's encouraging at least," said the President. "What about San Diego?"

Branson changed the map again before he began, "Now that we have the enemy contained in LA, we have some of our forces heading down to San Diego. This pocket here is a bit more concerning. The enemy managed to offload six armored divisions and another twelve infantry divisions. They are gearing up to move north and attack our forces currently holding the lines in LA."

General Adrian Rice took over, giving the Air Force perspective. "Mr. President, as you can see, the JDF and PLAN have ferried over roughly seven hundred fighter drones to provide air support. The Japanese moved 110 F35s, the PLAAF brought in 125 J20s and 90 of their new J39s, their newest stealth fighters. Right now, the skies are a cluster mess. Neither side has air superiority yet, and I'm not sure how long it will be until we can regain control of the skies. The two F41s that survived the ambush with the JDF fleet were destroyed on the ground when Twenty-Nine Palms was bombed."

"Mr. President," interjected General Branson, "I would like to pull the other flight of F41s from the air campaign in Alaska and move them back down here. We need the help, Sir."

President Stein knew Branson was right. However, he also wanted to keep the F41s fighting over Alaska. He was hoping to find a way to get the Air Force into a position where they could maintain air superiority in the Klondike without the F41s. Until Operation Pegasus fully got underway, they were going to be months away from building any additional F41s.

"General Branson, before we bring the F41s down, I have a question. What will happen to our operations in Alaska if we do take them away from the forces there?" the President asked, turning to the Air Force Service Commander.

General Rice responded, "Mr. President, the Russians have pulled a lot of their forces out and moved them back to Europe. The Chinese are still giving us a lot of problems though. Our issue is we just do not have enough fighters or drones to fight everywhere. Having the F41s in Alaska has allowed us to beef up our air forces in Europe and now to divert additional forces to California. If we move them, we risk the Chinese being able to break out of our air defenses and launch further attacks in the Pacific northwest. We are moving tremendous amounts of aircraft from across the country to California. We will gain air superiority; we just need to be patient while we get everything in place," he explained.

The President looked at Branson, "General, I agree with the Air Force on this one. You are going to have to make do with what you have."

The General shrugged a little, but he decided not to fight the President on this one.

Stein moved on. "Changing subjects, I want to transition to the Pegasus project. Are we still on track?"

General Branson sat down, knowing that his part of the briefing was over. Dr. Peter Gorka came to life as his holographic image began to display from Henry's tablet. "Yes, Mr. President; Pegasus is still on track. We are going to move forward with the launch in March. We anticipate the mining operations starting within four days of landing on the lunar surface. Our first shipment of Tritium4 will be ready for transport back to Earth beginning in April. We will also have the first delivery of Helium3 available in April as well."

As everyone was listening to Dr. Gorka speak, on another screen they could see video clips of what the lunar operation would look like. Henry Stein thought to himself, "*I don't think I can really get used to this--the future is really here.*"

Chapter 31
The Beatings Will Continue until Morale Improves

01 January 2042
Tetlin Junction, Alaska

Lieutenant Paul Allen and his beat-up company of infantry had been pulled back to the unincorporated township of Tetlin Junction, which sat at the split between Highway 5 and Highway 2. Most of the US Forces left in Alaska had been pulled back either to this point or further down the Peninsula towards Vancouver. Allen's company had fought hard in Fairbanks, but ultimately it was a losing cause. The Russians had too many men and the Chinese had dislodged the American stronghold further south. For the time-being, Alaska was lost. Now their objective was to keep the enemy bottled up in this frozen wasteland in order to keep them from capturing the Canadian states and pushing further down into the Pacific Northwest.

The mood of the soldiers was low. They had lost many of their comrades, and they had suffered defeat in the war in Alaska after enduring nearly six grueling months and hundreds of thousands of casualties. Then, just as Christmas was about to arrive, the media had started to report on a major invasion of California by the Chinese and the brutal betrayal of Japan and India as both nations officially declared war against the US.

The rumor mill was rampant in the 12th Infantry Division; some soldiers were reporting that LA and San Diego had fallen to the enemy, while others bragged that the Marines had pushed the invaders back into the sea. Eventually, a message was sent down from General Black, the First Army Commander, detailing the events of the past several days and explaining the current situation. Once the soldiers knew what was going on, a lot of things settled down as they knew the Third Army was in-route to California and would crush the invaders. Many soldiers had already fought with General Gardner in the Middle East; they felt confident in America's chances with him at the helm on the West Coast.

Now that it was New Year's Day, there was a special lunch for the men and women at the Tetlin Defense. While they ate, they watched videos of what military experts were calling the largest naval battle since World War II. The footage of the two new American battleships in action was awe-inspiring. They were massive futuristic looking ships and the display of their weapons against the joint Chinese/Japanese fleet was incredible. They shredded the enemy fleet, forcing the remaining ships to flee back to Hawaii. Per the Pentagon, the Carrier Strike Group was going to sail up the coast to San Diego and Los Angeles and assist the Army and Marines in crushing the enemy invasion force. Their help would go a long way toward recapturing the territory lost during the Christmas Day invasion.

Following the celebration, Lieutenant Allen was informed that he was being promoted to Captain and taking over command of his company. He was also invited to a high-level briefing being given at brigade headquarters. Unbeknownst to the officers in attendance, the division commander, a one star general, was also with their brigade commander to discuss a new secret weapon. During the briefing, they were shown images and then videos of the newest drone weapon that would be used in Alaska, the Bodark. What they saw terrified and excited them at the same time.

When Allen looked at the Bodark for the first time he was not impressed; then it transformed from a large rock-like form into a Werewolf looking creature with red glowing eyes, razor sharp claws and a howling shriek that caused a shiver to run down his back. The general explained how the Bodark was a mythological creature in Russian folklore. The goal in creating this new weapon was instilling psychological terror. As more and more units were built, the plan was to drop thousands of them behind the lines to wreak as much havoc as possible.

As Allen left the briefing room, he was glad his forces would not have to deal with facing a new weapon like that. They had seen enough horrific things in their lives; they did not need to add fictitious mythical creatures to their repertoire of frightening memories. Some of the new guys in his company were disappointed that their battalion was not being rotated back to the States to go fight in California. He had to remind them that less than a few hundred miles away were hundreds of thousands of Russian and Chinese soldiers spoiling for a good fight. Their chance at combat would come soon enough. As it stood, the 12th ID was going to hold this position until spring and then see what the higher-ups had planned for them.

Chapter 32
A Man Named Bucky

01 January 2042
Pacific Ocean, 200 Miles South of San Diego

After the naval victory off the coast of Baja California, Admiral Stonebridge directed the fleet to move up the coast towards San Diego. While the remaining ships of the enemy fleet retreated to the Hawaiian Islands, Stonebridge wanted to go after the now vulnerable transports and supply ships heading to the Californian coast and disrupt the supply of equipment being offloaded at the ports. Though his objective was to destroy the enemy fleet, the more pressing demand from the Pentagon was to hammer the enemy forces in and around the ports.

Captain Baker was deep in thought when Admiral Stonebridge walked up to him and rudely interrupted his daydreams. Without any sort of small talk, he probed, "Captain, how many aircraft do the *New York* and *Baltimore* have available?"

Captain Baker jarred himself back to reality quickly and responded, "We have 12 drones and seven F35s down for maintenance; it will be the better part of a day, maybe two, before they are operational. The Carrier Air Group Commander (CAG) reports having 19 F35s ready for combat, another 36 F38As and 42 F38Bs. Are you wanting to send them ahead of the fleet to engage the enemy transports?" asked the Captain quizzically.

Stonebridge smiled for a second before responding, "Yes. It's going to be another five more hours before the battleships are in range, and I do not want to waste any cruise missiles on trying to destroy their escorts. We need the cruise missiles for land targets. Have our aircraft take out the escorts, and we'll let the battleships handle the supply ships."

Walking over to the coms position, the captain asked one of his officers to signal the captain of the *Baltimore* that the Admiral needed to talk with him immediately. A few minutes later Captain Bruck, the commander of the *Baltimore*, came on the video link.

Admiral Stonebridge looked at both of his captains, "Gentlemen, we are not out of danger just yet. The Pentagon has ordered us to interdict the enemy troop transports and equipment ships heading to California before we finish off the enemy fleet. To that end, I want you both to order your remaining aircraft to attack the escort ships guarding the transports heading to San Diego and Los Angeles. As we sail closer to LA, we'll send a second or third wave if necessary to hit the transports heading to San Francisco. Is that understood?" Stonebridge asked.

"Yes, Sir," they replied in unison.

Within an hour, the air wing of both carriers was heading towards San Diego and the enemy transports. Commander John Buckley ("Bucky") was leading his squadron of F35s in the direction of the enemy transports. As they neared their targets, they saw dozens of enemy ships queued up, waiting for their turn to dock at the port and offload their cargo. They also saw half a dozen enemy destroyers and frigates, which immediately began to engage the F38B drones as they began to make their combat runs against the ships. Dozens of anti-ship missiles began to streak away from the attack drones heading towards the enemy destroyers and frigates guarding the fleet.

Missile after missile began to leave the various frigates and destroyers as they tried to intercept the incoming anti-ship missiles and counter-attack the American drones. Shortly after the conflict began, a swarm of Chinese J20s began to gather over San Diego and started to head towards the American fighters. Bucky briefly saw the J20s show up on his radar from the AWACs controller before they disappeared. The J20 was China's version of the American F22 stealth fighter and was exceptional in combat. Like the American aircraft, it was also a stealth aircraft, only visible when taking off or landing, making it very difficult (although not impossible) to track once in the air.

Bucky got on his coms to call his squadron. "I want you all to gain altitude and put some distance between yourselves and the fighter drones. I just saw a group of J20s taking off; let's use the fighter drones as bait and get them to give away their position while they are engaged with the fighter drones. Each time you locate one of those J20s, I want you to lock onto that target and attack them with your long-range air-to-air missiles."

"Yes, Sir," the squadron replied.

The enemy fighter drones began to engage the American drones, and within minutes, drone aircraft on both sides began to fall out of the sky. The enemy J20s heavily outnumbered Bucky's squadron, but he needed to at least try and thin them out. The fleet was going to be moving his direction soon, and they needed to do their best to gain some sense of air supremacy.

Had the fleet intelligence officers known the enemy air strength, they never would have recommended the carrier air wings attack. They were heavily outnumbered, and not likely to succeed in their mission. It was unfortunate as most of the carrier fighters and ground attack drones would be destroyed during the battle.

After a while in the air, Bucky concluded that their situation was not very optimistic, and got back on his coms to change up the plan. "OK everyone, here is what we are going to do. We have four missiles each; everyone is going to be assigned a target by our AWACs. Once you have a target for your missiles, launch and then immediately go supersonic back towards the fleet. Don't stick around to see if your missiles were successful or get in closer to engage with the Sidewinders. I want everyone back to the safety of the fleet as quickly as possible."

The fleets air combat controllers in the AWACs had linked their screens to the C3 surveillance drone that was high above the fighting. The C3 had monitored the takeoff of the J20s and had been tracking them ever since. Using specialized heat scanners, the C3 fed the AWACs controllers the enemy coordinates, and they in turn fed the data to the targeting computers on the F35s. Once all 64 missiles had been assigned intended targets, Bucky's squadron of 16 fighters began to send the volley of missiles on their way. Within seconds, the J20s (whose radar had spotted the launch) began to fire their own air-to-air missiles at the F35s. Now it was a race to see if the F35s could get back to the laser and missile defense screen of the fleet or not.

As Bucky's squadron retreated to the safety of the fleet, their 64 missiles scored 19 hits; the remaining missiles were either evaded or ran out of fuel while the J20s performed evasive maneuvers. Bucky's squadron lost only one aircraft from the enemy missiles before they made it back to the safety of the fleet's missile defense system. As his squadron landed, they learned that most of the attacking F38Bs had been destroyed during their attack run, and half of the F38As has been shot down while trying to provide air cover for them. The fleet had effectively lost half of their airpower during the battle.

However, they had managed to destroy the remaining enemy frigates and destroyers and sink seven of the 22 transport ships they had engaged. Unfortunately though, if the fleet was going to interdict the remaining enemy cargo and transport ships, they were going to need to get in range of the battleships' main guns and laser batteries.

Chapter 33
Brazilians in Germany

10 January 2042
Hamburg, Germany

General Eduardo Temer had been the second-in-command of the Brazilian Army when the Americans began to develop the South American Multination Force to fight the Russian and Chinese forces. After being sent to America to participate in several general officer training courses, he was then deployed to Germany to observe and assist General Black and General Gardner's staff for three-month rotations. The experience was designed to give him a sense of the enemy his army would be fighting, and to gain some experience from working with these two dynamic generals.

Now he had finished training up his MNF, and they had finally been deployed to Europe to bolster the NATO lines. It took nearly a month for the Americans to move the bulk of their military equipment and troops from South America to Hamburg, Germany. After nearly three weeks of unpacking and reorganizing their equipment, they began their preparations to move towards the frontlines. Many of his soldiers experienced a rude awakening when a major snowfall blanketed the countryside; a lot of them had never even seen the cold fluffy flakes in their lives, and now they were going to be asked to fight a war in it.

The NATO lines had stabilized along the German/Polish border one week after the New Year. However, the Russians had been moving men and equipment back to the European front now that they had accomplished everything they set out to achieve in Alaska. With the arrival of the MNF force, the NATO forces were now planning on launching a winter offensive to recapture most of Poland before any Indian reinforcements had a chance to arrive from Russia. The latest intel suggested that the Indian Army would arrive in Poland sometime around April, bringing close to 600,000 soldiers with them.

In Europe, it had taken the better part of a year to recruit and train a sufficient army to stop the Russian advance. Now France, Spain, Germany, Italy and the UK had the troops and equipment needed to retake the lands captured by Russia early in the war. Shortly after arriving in Hamburg, General Temer was flown via helicopter to

Brussels to meet with the NATO Commander and other political leaders. The Allies were going to hold a war council to devise the end-game strategy for the war, much like the Allies of World War II had during the meeting between Roosevelt, Churchill and Stalin at the Yalta meeting.

As it turned out, Brussels was not his final destination. Once General Temer arrived at the military base, he was ushered into a blacked-out vehicle that drove him to yet another airport. Then he was scurried onto a plane that flew him to a small French island called Saint Anne, not far from the French coastline. This sleepy little island had been taken over by the military just four hours ago, in preparation for the arrival of the leaders of the Allies, so they could meet face-to-face for the first time in nearly a year. Saint Anne had been chosen because of its remoteness and the fact that it could be easily guarded and secured for the twelve-hour meeting. At the end of the gathering, everyone would be flown back to their respective countries to continue with their activities.

Some had questioned the wisdom of having an in-person meeting. With technology, people could just as easily meet virtually and not have to risk leaving their secured facilities. However, President Stein had insisted on the meeting, arguing that technology could never replace a face-to-face meeting or the interaction between participants in a room.

As General Temer exited the aircraft that brought him to the island, there was a vehicle ready and waiting to take him to meet with the other military commanders. General Wade, the Supreme Allied Commander Europe (SACEUR) had arrived a couple of hours ahead of General Temer and had already met briefly with President Stein, General Branson and the National Security Advisor Mike Williams. President Stein wanted to give General Wade a heads-up on the conversation they were going to have with the rest of the Allied leaders before the rest of the group arrived.

Soon Prime Minister Bedford and Chancellor Lowden both arrived; everyone stood and exchanged pleasantries and handshakes and then quickly took their seats at the table. Some attendants brought in some drinks and snacks, and then quickly left the room; security personnel then ensured the room was secured and locked.

President Stein immediately got down to business, "Gentlemen, thank you for agreeing to meet in person. I know we could have done this via the holograph system, but I felt a face-to-face meeting was needed as we discuss what the future of the world will look like once the war is over."

Everyone in the room nodded and appeared ready to listen to President Stein's suggestions and then offer their own.

Stein brought up an image from his tablet and linked it to the holographic projector at the center of the table. A series of floating maps appeared: one with the current breakdown of nations, one with the current disposition of enemy and allied forces on the global map, and a third map. The third map had a very different looking picture than the first. This map had several countries broken up and others merged. This map, everyone realized, is what President Stein was going to propose be the new world post-World War III.

President Stein began, "For more than one hundred years, the world has been given geographical borders with no regard as to the ethnicities, religions or people who live there. This, I argue, has given rise to numerous wars and tensions across the world and led to many genocides. This is our opportunity to right that wrong and to redraw the borders, taking into consideration the ethnicities, religions and people that will live within them. I do not propose that we impose our form of government or democracy on our vanquished foes, but we will replace the existing countries and borders with ones that will better represent the people living in them."

Stein paused for a moment to take a sip of his water and to let his proposal settle in for a minute. Then he continued, "It is incumbent upon us to ensure that once this great war has been won, that we do not also sow the seeds of another conflict. I am not going to be so naïve as to believe that this will be the war to end all wars, but we need to be cognizant in how we handle our victory so as not to breed permanent enmity and hatred within our current adversaries, like what happened with Germany at the end of World War I."

The leaders seemed intrigued; Chancellor Lowden seemed the most amicable to this philosophy, and Prime Minister Bedford would need the most convincing. They talked at length about the implications of what President Stein was suggesting. After several hours of discussing the post-war future, the conversation turned back to the matters at hand. They needed a plan to defeat Russia, China and the other countries that had just joined the war. Without that, discussions of a world after the conflict were meaningless.

Chapter 34
Plotting Revenge

Pearl Harbor, Hawaii
Joint Chinese / Japanese Naval Headquarters

The remnants of Admiral Tomohisa Kawano's fleet had limped into port alongside their PLAN counterparts two weeks ago. By the time their engineers and computer specialists could get their power and engine systems operational again, the Americans had nearly wiped them out. Admiral Kawano was able to escape with just two of his five carriers and about a quarter of his support ships. The battle had been a bloody disaster; not since the battle of Midway had the Japanese lost so many ships and sailors in a single battle.

After the battle, Admiral Xi had been recalled to China and replaced by Admiral Ye Shengli, a young, energetic naval officer who was eager to prove his mettle against the Americans. When Admiral Kawano explained the missile swarm plan, Admiral Shengli had become extremely excited to move forward with the attack. After nearly a week of preparation, both fleets had been refitted with anti-ship cruise missiles, and their drones and fighters had received anti-ship missiles as well. It was now time to launch the next assault against the American fleet and return control of the Pacific back to China and Japan.

While the two fleets had been regrouping and preparing themselves, the American fleet had moved up the West Coast and caused complete havoc. Many of the transports bringing troops and supplies to the ground forces had to be rerouted back to Hawaii until the sea lanes could be secured. The situation on the ground for their troops was becoming increasingly perilous as they ran through supplies and failed to bring in more troops. The American Third Army had now surrounded the three invasion sites and was slowly tightening the noose. The Japanese and Chinese needed to regain control of the sea or their invasion force would be doomed.

With little time to spare, the combined fleet left Hawaii and embarked on what they hoped would be the final battle for the Pacific.

Chapter 35
Showdown Looming

12 January 2042
6 Miles Off the Coast of Los Angeles

Admiral Stonebridge had been elated when their battle group had finally been able to choke off the enemy supply ships from feeding the invasion forces. Their ships were now providing direct support to the ground forces, and with the fleet's cruise missiles, they had destroyed the enemy airfields and any remaining aircraft they had. The Allies now had complete air superiority. It had been touch-and-go at first; the PLAAF had mounted a concerted attack against his fleet as they approached San Diego. However, although they had sustained damage, they had been able to beat back the attackers while inflicting significant losses.

As Captain Baker approached Admiral Stonebridge to bring him the latest images of the enemy fleet, he saw him signal one of the yeomen for a refill of his coffee. "Admiral, the satellites are showing the enemy fleet has put to sea and is heading towards us. What are your orders?" he asked. Baker was hoping that they would leave the coast and head to meet the enemy head on as soon as possible. He desperately wanted to finish off the enemy fleet and avenge his fallen comrades.

Admiral Stonebridge smiled at Captain Baker, and began to examine the images on his tablet. He zoomed in to see the fleet composition. It appeared the entire Japanese/Chinese fleet had set sail. "So, it looks like they want to have one final battle for supremacy of the Pacific," the Admiral remarked.

He didn't respond to the question right away; instead, he gazed out the window of the bridge, contemplating the situation. Off in the distance, he could see the sky filled with smoke from numerous fires; aircraft and Razorbacks darted back and forth, attacking ground targets in the city. LA had been a beautiful city prior to the invasion. They had been in the process of building numerous highspeed rail networks linking San Diego, San Francisco and Las Vegas together. It was truly disappointing to see the city now being systematically destroyed through the fighting. Thousands of civilians were being killed daily, caught between the two fighting armies with nowhere to go, cut off from food, water and electricity.

Stonebridge broke free of his thoughts and turned back to face Captain Baker, "Order the fleet to prepare to head towards Hawaii; we are going to finish this fight. Get the air wings ready and let's begin preparations."

During the past week while the fleet had been on station off the coast, they had received several new squadrons of F38A and F38B drones (now that air superiority had been achieved, they would not be needed in LA). The navy would need the additional aircraft for the upcoming battles. Fortunately, the Air Force, Navy and Marines operated the same type of drones, so transferring them from one service to the other was not as challenging as one might think.

Looking over the maps one more time, Admiral Stonebridge noted there was a lone *Seawolf* class submarine not far from Hawaii. He sent a quick order to the ship directing them to position themselves between the two fleets and then lie in wait for the enemy fleet to sail directly over them before engaging the enemy carriers. If they could damage the carriers or even sink one, that would definitely improve his own fleet's odds.

As the two fleets converged on each other, the tension between those who commanded these great naval armadas continued to grow.

Chapter 36
Heading Towards the Midnight Zone

12 January 2042
100 Miles East of Hawaii

Captain Thompson had taken over command of the *Seawolf* shortly after the war had started. The *Seawolf* and many Virginia class attack submarines had been slated for decommissioning as the Navy was moving towards a new more versatile attack submarine and underwater drones. However, when the war broke out, the decommissioning of all submarines was placed on hold, and emergency retrofitting and upgrading began in earnest. The US only had three *Seawolf* class submarines, and they had already served nearly fifty years. They were good submarines, but they had served their purposes. With the destruction of the Fifth and Seventh Fleets, even the older submarines were once again in great demand.

The *Seawolf* had spent the better part of a year being upgraded with new electronics and the Navy's new Hammerhead torpedoes. After a few false starts, the ship was finally ready for combat duty. Captain Thompson and the *Seawolf* had spent the better part of the past year patrolling the waters of the South Pacific and Indonesia. They had gotten lucky a couple of times and managed to sink several Chinese transports and two destroyers. When the Navy moved CSG12 into the Pacific to engage the joint Chinese and Japanese fleets, they had been ordered to head to Hawaii to standby for further orders.

They arrived on station just after CSG12 had won the first battle and had carefully monitored the enemy fleet as it returned to the Hawaiian waters. Captain Thompson wanted to get his ship into the action and attack the enemy ships, but he continued to hold his position until he received further orders. Now Admiral Stonebridge had finally given them a new directive, positioning themselves between Hawaii and the path of the approaching CSG12 to lie in wait for the approaching Japanese and Chinese ships. Once they converged on their location, they were to strike at will. Thompson was high on the rush of adrenaline. He couldn't wait until those carriers traveled over their position so that he could spring the trap on them.

Chapter 37
Difference of Opinion

12 January 2042
Tokyo, Japan

It had been a little over three weeks since the Chinese Japanese fleet had been nearly wiped out by the new American super weapons. Following the near annihilation of the combined fleet, the support ships and carriers that had survived escaped and returned to the safety of the Hawaiian Islands. In the subsequent days after their return, Admiral Tomohisa Kawano of the Japanese Navy and Admiral Hong Xi of the People's Liberation Army Navy had been ordered back to Japan to review a new battle plan being proposed by their superiors.

At first, Admiral Kawano was not sure if the new plan, which called for an enormous missile swarm attack, could work. Admiral Xi, on the other hand, whole-heartedly supported the scheme. He sternly insisted, "If enough aircraft and ships can fire the same number of anti-ship missiles as we used during the first naval battle, we can overwhelm the American missile defenses, especially considering the number of American support ships that we already destroyed."

Admiral Kawano, still not confident in the chance of success, proposed, "We should also consider the use of tactical nuclear weapons or nuclear-armed torpedoes."

PM Hata was aghast that a Japanese Naval Officer would even suggest the use of such a weapon, but the Chinese appeared to be willing to consider it. Hoping to get ahead of this before disaster struck Hata argued, "We cannot seriously be considering this idea. Any use of nuclear weapons would result in a swift and overwhelming response by President Stein. The American leader has already shown that he has no qualms about unleashing the United States' nuclear arsenal on anyone that uses these weapons against them. Are you all forgetting the holocaust of the Middle East and North Africa? I cannot believe that anyone's memory could be so short-sighted."

A rather nerdy-looking junior Japanese officer dared to address the group. "May I suggest that we incorporate the new micro-drones we have been secretly developing over the last several years?"

All eyes turned towards this unknown officer, and Admiral Kawano shot back, "Please elaborate."

"We have been creating micro-drones for use in our naval operations. Originally, they were intended to counter the PLAN, but now that we are allies, they could obviously be used against the Americans."

"Ok, but how do they work?" asked Kawano, irritated.

"One of our drone bombers would drop the micro-drone pod; once in freefall, it would open to release ten micro-drones. Those drones would then begin to race towards their pre-programmed targets, exploding once their proximity sensors indicated that they were close enough to their mark."

Everyone in the room sat there silently thinking for a moment before one of the PLAN officers inquired, "How many of these micro-drone pods does Japan have right now?"

The young officer replied, "We have 50 of them built right now, so that would give us 500 of these micro-drones. I should also note; the drones can be programmed to emit the same electronic signature as either an aircraft or just about any type of missile. We could set them to appear to be much larger anti-ship cruise missiles, which would trick the American defenses into thinking they pose a greater threat than they actually do. The Americans' targeting AI would automatically assign the micro-drones a higher priority for engagement, causing them to expend limited resources on a red herring instead of destroying the actual missiles."

Following this revelation, the group quickly agreed that the micro-drones would be used in the missile swarm attack. The JDF and PLAN also agreed to send as many additional aircraft to Hawaii as they could to aid in launching the anti-ship cruise missiles. They also began the process of moving as many cruise missiles as possible. They had no idea when the American fleet would move on Hawaii, so time was not on their side. If they did not move quickly, then they might lose control of the Pacific.

Chapter 38
Heavy Burden

14 January 2042
Near the coast of San Diego, California

Admiral Michael Stonebridge was being hailed an American hero for the near destruction of the joint Japanese and Chinese fleets, but what people had quickly forgotten was that nearly 1,100 American sailors had also died during the battle, making it one of the costliest naval engagements of the war. Stonebridge hadn't forgotten though, the weight of every sailor lost hung on him each day.

The Admiral tried to suppress thoughts of depression by burying himself in his work; the only way to get through each day was to put one foot in front of the other. While Stonebridge was drinking his coffee in the CIC, an intelligence officer walked up to him, handing him an intelligence intercept from the NSA. As he read the report, his eyes grew wide with alarm.

He looked up at the young officer and asked, "Do we have any of the specifics on this new micro-drone weapon?"

The young officer shook his head, "No, Sir, but I suspect their designs are probably based off our own micro-drone project. I have asked several of the weapons officers to research the issue so they can provide a brief on what these weapons may be like and how we can prepare to deal with them."

The Admiral thought to himself, *"Now this is a sharp officer; we need more forward thinkers like him in the Navy."*

Aloud, he replied, "Lieutenant, that is a great idea. Thank you for taking the initiative in getting this going. Please let the Captain and the other officers know, and we will have a briefing about this tomorrow during Commander's Call. Tell the weapons officers they have until then to finalize the brief." Then he dismissed the young officer so he could finish his coffee and draft a personal email to his wife.

He missed his wife severely; the past few years had been incredibly hard for him. Besides all of the sailors that he had just lost, he was still mourning the loss of all his old friends that he had gone through the Academy with in his youth. Beyond that, his eldest son had also been wounded while serving on occupation duty in Saudi Arabia last month.

His son, who had managed to become a captain and a company commander in the Marines, had been in the wrong place at the wrong time and had been traveling from one city to another when his vehicle had been hit by an Improvised Explosive Device, killing two of the four people with him. Fortunately, it looked like his son would fully recuperate from his wounds, but for the time being, he was on a long road to recovery. The Admiral was having a hard time not being able to see his son while he was in the hospital and then at a skilled nursing facility; the urgency of their deployment had prevented him from being able to see him.

Captain Mason could see that Admiral Stonebridge was deep in thought as he approached him. "Admiral, I am sorry to interrupt. General Gardner would like to know if we can stay on station for another two weeks while the rest of the Third Army continues to arrive in the area-- on the other side of things, Admiral Juliano and General Branson from DC want to know how soon we can begin to sail on Hawaii and finish off the enemy fleet there. How would you like to proceed?"

Admiral Stonebridge sighed before responding, "Thank you for breaking me from my thoughts...we do need to make this decision soon. How many aircraft is the fleet short of right now? Also, what are your thoughts on our ability to effectively defend against a missile swarm attack?" He wanted a better idea of their defensive capability before he made the decision.

The captain looked through some files on his tablet before responding, "Sir, we are short 48 manned aircraft and 143 drones. We can probably get replacements from the forces in California prior to our leaving. As to the drone swarms, that is a good question. With the loss of nine of our support ships, I am not sure we could effectively defend against another major missile swarm. I think we would take a lot of hits."

"That is a bit of a problem then. I'm sure you saw that NSA intercept. The enemy is planning a nice little welcoming party for us when we get closer to Hawaii. What are your thoughts on how we can overcome this?" asked Stonebridge, looking for ideas.

"Sir, we could request F41 support for this specific engagement. Also, the President has not changed our directive with regards to the use of nuclear torpedoes. We have a *Seawolf* class submarine off the coast of Hawaii, conducting surveillance. We could order them to use a nuclear torpedo against the enemy carriers once they have left the harbor and move to engage us. With more of the enemy carriers and support ships out of the picture, the number of anti-ship missiles they will be able to launch will be significantly reduced," Mason suggested.

Admiral Stonebridge shot Captain Mason a very icy look with his already blue eyes. "No!" he exclaimed. "We will *not* use nuclear weapons. Our situation is not that desperate that we need to use a nuclear torpedo or weapon to win. I want a message sent to Captain Thompson, the CG of the *Seawolf*, asking them to engage in a second attack using conventional torpedoes. Tell him that he is to do anything he can to damage the enemy carriers. I will make the case to the President that we need the F41s for this mission. We will rely on them and their laser weapons systems to help us defeat the enemy drone swarms. Unless directed by the President, I will not use nuclear weapons."

Stonebridge was visibly angry; you could see his blood pulsating through a vein on his forehead that was suddenly very noticeable. He had seen what those weapons could do up close and in person. His ship had survived a nuclear attack, but so many of his friends had died because of them. He would not be party to the use of such a brutal weapon.

"I did not mean to overstep," Captain Mason said, trying to calm the Admiral down.

Stonebridge took a deep breath. "No, it's OK. You are only looking for ways to protect our fleet. There are just some lines we should not cross. Nuclear weapons have been used enough in this war, I do not want to be the reason for why additional nukes are used." As he spoke, he realized he might have over-reacted a bit. The vein near his temple slowly became a bit less obvious. "I will make the call to the President now; have everyone ready for the Commander's Call tomorrow and we'll discuss our plan in detail."

"Yes, Sir," Captain Mason replied. With his orders issued, he turned to leave.
****

The following four days were busy for the fleet. Admiral Stonebridge did obtain permission to use the only remaining squadron of F41s for the attack. The F41s would fly off from the carriers, so they could be brought to bear immediately. They would loiter high above the fleet and be used for the sole purpose of engaging enemy missiles heading towards the fleet. Their added firepower would greatly increase the survivability of the fleet. Their effort, along with the additional attack from the *Seawolf*, should make enough of a difference to turn the tide in their favor.

As the fleet set sail for Hawaii, the apprehension among the sailors was high. A lot was riding on the ability of the *Seawolf* to damage or sink the remaining PLAN and JDF carriers and the F41s' ability to shoot down the inevitable missile and drone-swarm that was coming. Once the immediate threat had been neutralized, then the F38B attack drones and F35s could be sent in to attack the enemy fleet.

Chapter 39
Ultimatum

18 January 2042
Hawaiian Islands

In the dimly lit command center of the USS Seawolf, Commander Ramos approached Captain Thompson saying, "Sir, the enemy fleet is nearly on top of us right now. The carriers are approaching quickly."

Captain Thompson looked at the face of his XO and just nodded. Surveying the Command Center, the captain could see the nervous looks on the faces of the men and women around him. They all knew that this was the moment they trained for, but it was hard not to think that these might be their final moments on this earth.

Turning to his weapons officer, Thompson asked, "Do we have a firing solution on the carriers?"

The weapons officer looked up at the Captain and nodded. "Everything is ready, Sir," he replied.

The tension on the bridge was palpable; the crew were eager to attack the enemy capital ships but also scared and nervous that once they open fire, they may only have minutes left to live.

Looking at his XO, the Captain insisted, "Please go over our escape plan again." He wanted to make sure they had fully determined how they were going to slip away once they had unleashed their deadly cargo of torpedoes.

The XO activated the attack and evasion plan on the holographic display. It immediately began to show the preplanned scenario. "Once the torpedoes are in the water, we are going to launch our two decoys: one will dive while heading East at ten knots, the other will dive heading Northeast at eighteen knots. The smokescreen should distract the enemy long enough for us to silently slip away. While the decoys are going, we are going to dive to our maximum depth at five knots and then go silent." Commander Ramos spoke with confidence; he firmly believed that their plan was sound and would give them their best chance of success.

After running the scenario through in his mind, the captain nodded in acceptance. He paused for a moment, then looking to his weapons officer he ordered, "Fire all tubes! Chief of the Boat, launch the decoys and begin our dive!"

The crew had been prepared for the past twenty minutes to fire their torpedoes. Now that the order had been given, the tension in the room lifted; they knew their fate had been sealed and now it was up to them to outfox the enemy lurking all around them.

Within seconds, the entire sub began to shudder as all eight of their torpedoes left in quick succession. Then the two decoys left the sub and began their high-speed pursuit away from their current position. The Seawolf lurched downward, beginning its descent to its maximum depth, hoping to go unnoticed.

The torpedoes raced towards their targets quickly while the targeting AI determined where the weakest point in the target ships were and steered the torpedoes towards those points. As soon as the enemy fleet detected the incoming projectiles, they immediately sprang into action; multiple destroyers launched decoys, hoping to lure some of the torpedoes away from the carriers. Other ships began launching torpedoes of their own to go after the firing location of the American submarine. Several helicopters also dropped some of their own torpedoes on what they thought was the sub's location.

The water under the enemy fleet became a buzz of activity with nearly a dozen torpedoes racing after various targets. Within a few minutes, two of the American torpedoes hit one of the destroyer's decoys; the targeting AI had taken the bait. Seconds later, two other torpedoes hit one of the Chinese carriers, blowing an enormous hole along the keel of the ship. The remaining four torpedoes locked onto an individual carrier and exploded their ordinance directly under the ship, ripping a hole in the center of the hull and causing part of the ship to collapse into the newly created vacuum before the water rushed in to fill the gap.

The carriers shuddered from the impact of the explosion. It was not long before the lower decks of the capital ships started to fill quickly with water; the crew and damage control parties began to lock down the various compartments of the ship in order to try and save the undamaged parts. Hundreds of sailors were being sealed off below decks as they desperately tried to get beyond the quarantined decks. In minutes, the capital ships came to a complete halt as the damage control parties attempted to stabilize them.

In short order, the Chinese and Japanese torpedoes found and destroyed the Seawolf's two decoys. Following their destruction, the anti-submarine helicopters began dropping sonar buoys as they tried to determine if they had succeeded in chasing off any additional submarines.

Captain Thompson looked around the Command Center and felt a sense of relief sweep through the crew. They had carried out an incredibly dangerous mission and seriously damaged the enemy fleet, and it looked like they were going to live to tell about it.

Turning to the COB, the Captain ordered the ship to continue their slow and steady course away from the enemy fleet. A quick call from the sonar room determined that the enemy fleet was looking for them about forty miles east of their current location. They had also determined that there were two enemy submarines in the area, but could not pin down their location. The Captain directed the sonar room to continue to monitor the enemy subs and ensure they stayed clear of them. He wanted to get their ship away from the enemy fleet for the moment and reposition to attack again in another twelve hours.

****

The JDF/PLAN fleet had left the safety of Pearl Harbor ten hours ago, and had begun to sail towards the enemy. Admiral Kawano knew this was going to be the final naval battle of the war. They would either defeat the American navy once and for all, or they would have to accept that America could not be invaded, at least not from the West Coast.

As the fleet made their way towards the Americans, alarm bells began to ring. One of the action officers began to shout, "Warning! Incoming torpedoes!"

Admiral Kawano's carrier began evasive maneuvers, moving as quickly as a ship of their size could; they also deployed their drone decoys, in hopes that the enemy torpedoes might go for them. Several minutes went by, and then Kawano saw two explosions from one of the PLAN supercarriers. It appeared to have been hit by two separate torpedoes, one near the engine room in the rear of the ship, and the other under the keel.

Seconds later, Admiral Kawano felt the floor beneath him lift up…then his feet slammed down on the deck as gravity returned. He heard a deep rumbling through the ship and felt it quiver from what must have been the impact of a torpedo. The lights in the CIC flickered out and then came back on as the emergency generator kicked on.

"What in the blazes just happened?!" yelled one of the officers.

Admiral Kawano knew exactly what had happened; he figured that the torpedo had impacted along the keel, and if they were lucky, the ship might survive. "How bad is the damage?" He barked in a loud voice, trying to be heard over the murmuring of the others in the room.

One of the damage control engineers in the CIC was speaking quickly on a handheld radio to one of his men below deck. Another sailor was looking at the various systems readouts to try to determine what was still working and what was not.

The engineering officer turned to the Admiral saying, "Admiral, we sustained two torpedo hits. One hit our keel; it appears to have broken the hull in multiple locations. We are taking on a lot of water right now. The crews are trying to seal off the lower decks now in an attempt to keep us from sinking. The second torpedo missed the engineering room, but it hit near the propeller screws. It destroyed two of the three propeller drive shafts. We also have severe flooding happening in the rear of the ship."

The engineering officer received another message as he spoke and paused to read it. "Sir, one of the officers in the engine room just reported they need to do an emergency shutdown of the reactor. They think one of the hits may have caused a crack in the reactor and they need to take it offline while they investigate." The officer was not able to hide his concern; his voice trembled as he spoke.

If they had a crack in their reactor and they could not get it under control, then they might have a containment breach. The ship could quickly become irradiated, or worse, the reactor could meltdown. In either case, they would lose the ship.

"Do what you need to do, but we need to save the ship. Is that understood?!" Admiral Kawano yelled at everyone in the CIC. He got up and walked towards the bridge. He needed to see the situation around them with his own eyes and not on a computer screen.

When he got to the bridge and surveilled the fleet around him, he saw one of the PLAN carriers listing hard to one side; it looked like the ship was going to sink. Emergency rafts could be seen inflating all around the ship. Several of the escort ships were moving closer to help pick up the survivors. Looking to his left, he saw his sister ship starting to sit lower in the water as well. When he inquired about it, one of the officers on the bridge said it appeared they had been hit by one torpedo. He was not sure if the ship would sink, but it looked like it was taking on a lot of water by how much lower in the water it was.

Admiral Kawano knew the fleet was in trouble. They had just lost one of their four carriers and it looked like they may lose two more. The loss of the fighters from those carriers would seriously diminish their ability to launch enough cruise missiles to overwhelm the American fleet.

"Sir, Admiral Xi is on the radio for you," said one of the communications officers as he handed him a handset.

Admiral Kawano could hear a lot of commotion on the other end of the line as he placed the handset to his ear. "Sir, this is Admiral Kawano, what is your situation?"

"Admiral Kawano, we took two torpedo hits. The first one hit our keel; sixty seconds later, a second torpedo apparently hit the exact same spot and nearly ripped my carrier in half. We are going down. I'm transferring over to the carrier *Moa*. How bad is your ship hit?"

"We are in a similar situation. I believe we can get the flooding under control, but we have a larger problem. Two of our five drive propeller shafts have been destroyed, but worse, it appears we have a crack in our reactor. The engineering room is not sure if they can seal it just yet," the Admiral responded.

Admiral Xi didn't say anything for a moment "Admiral…if you are going to lose your ship, then we will need to turn the fleet around and head back to Hawaii."

Kawano knew that that was the best military decision to make; he also knew it would likely be the end of his military career. The new JDF/PLA command structure did not tolerate failure, no matter whose fault it was.

Two hours went by, and then it became clear that Admiral Kawano's supercarrier was not going to survive. The crack in the reactor was larger than they had initially suspected. They were able to shut it down, but it would take months of repair to fix. This was time that they obviously did not have. They were also dead in the water with no power.

With the fleet in the predicament they were in, it was determined that all of the mobile ships would have to pick up the survivors and head back to Hawaii. There they would have to prepare to meet the American fleet, hoping that the assistance of land-based aircraft would help their situation.

Chapter 40
Battle for the Skies

20 January 2042
Off the Coast of Hawaii

Admiral Stonebridge surveyed an interactive map display at the CIC. "Captain Mason, I want our aircraft (including the F41s) ready to engage the enemy aircraft and ships as soon as the battleships get in range of Pearl Harbor and the enemy fleet."

The surprise attack by the *Seawolf* two days earlier had thrown the entire enemy plan off. One Chinese carrier had been sunk, and a second Japanese carrier had been disabled. The remaining two carriers and their support ships where loitering around Pearl Harbor and would obviously rely on land-based air support. As the US aircraft began to assemble over the American fleet, the enemy air armada also began to gather, preparing to meet them. The Japanese/Chinese forces would be caught off guard once they realized that the F41s had been brought down from Alaska to participate in this fight.

As the American F35s and F38s began to engage the enemy aircraft, the F41s swooped in to attack the enemy from the rear. Then the two American battleships moved into range to use their railguns and pulse beam lasers, and they joined in the fight. The Battle of Hawaii lasted over two hours with thousands upon thousands of anti-ship missiles and drone-swarms being fired at both sides. The F41s immediately made their presence known and began to shoot down dozens and then hundreds of the enemy anti-ship missiles heading towards the American fleet.

The U.S. Air Force, which had also been developing micro-drone technology, was able to provide some useful advice on how to tell the difference between a micro-drone and an anti-ship missile. Within minutes of the battle starting, the radar operators were indeed able to tell the difference between the micro-drones and actual cruise missiles. This was quickly relayed to the AWACs above the fleet and the targeting computers of the American fleet defenses.

Nearly one-third of the contacts being tracked were micro-drones, which were essentially harmless if they impacted against one of the battleships or supercarriers. Had the radar operators not been able to tell the difference between them, then the likelihood of stopping the enemy missile swarm would have been greatly reduced. Hundreds of lives were going to be saved because of this critical intelligence victory.

By the evening of January 20th, the American Navy once again controlled the waters around the Hawaiian Islands. Now it was time to develop a plan on how to recapture the land on the islands; however, that would have to wait until the West Coast had been fully secured.

Chapter 41
Disrupting Traffic

05 February 2042
High Above the Arctic Circle

Major Lia Michaels was the squadron commander for the B5 drone squadron that was going to unleash a major cruise missile raid on the Central Asian rail and road network. Her squadron was tasked with launching their payload of X59 scramjet cruise missiles to go after the Chinese, Indian and Russian rail and bridge networks that connected the three countries in some of the most remote parts of Asia. Major Michaels' first target was the rail line that cut through the mountains along Lake Baikal in Russia. Her squadron was going to be hitting numerous rail bridges and tunnels that ran along the trans-Siberian rail line connecting China and East Russia in order to disrupt the primary route that the Indian reinforcements were going to travel.

After five hours of flying to her launch site, her missiles had locked onto their targets and in quick succession, she fired her bomber's four missiles. She turned to head back to the base, but then she heard over the radio that several of her bomber pilots were reporting enemy fighters in the area. Two of her pilots said they had been hit before they could launch their missiles. The other seven pilots reported a successful launch of their missiles, though two more of them were hunted down by enemy fighters and destroyed. The bombing mission was an overall success, but her squadron had lost four of their nine aircraft. Fortunately, they were drones, so none of the invaluable pilots had been lost during the mission.

The goal of the raid was to destroy as much of the transportation infrastructure linking Russia and China together as possible. This would greatly hinder the ability of the Axis powers from reinforcing each other and transporting needed manpower and material. It would also reduce the ability of the Indian army to get involved in any meaningful way in the war.

Chapter 42
No Hotel California

15 March 2042
Downtown Los Angeles, California

Captain Thornton and his company had been fighting Chinese, Japanese, Indonesian and Indian soldiers in the city of Los Angeles for nearly three months. In that timeframe, most of the suburbs that make up LA and the downtown had been torn to pieces by the block-to-block and house-to-house fighting. The enemy knew their situation was hopeless; they were effectively cut off from reinforcements and supplies, yet they would not give up. Many of the Japanese forces his company encountered were surrendering, but the others fought on with a fanatical zeal his Marines had not seen since the battles in Israel. The Chinese knew they had lost this battle, but they were intent on destroying as much of the city and its people as possible.

As the Chinese soldiers lost a block or key portion of a city, they would destroy the sewer system on their way out of the area. In doing this, the enemy was effectively destroying the critical infrastructure of the city. The sewer systems allowed the city to transport water, sewage, and run-off from the rains. This disruption was designed to create an enormous mess for the Americans once they recaptured the city and began the process of rebuilding.

Because of the density of the city, it was difficult to make use of tanks and armored vehicles; they could be used on the roads, but when it came to clearing buildings and houses, the option was to either level them or send soldiers in to clear the structures and then move on. Often homes and buildings were being rigged with booby traps and explosives, which required a lot of engineers to clear them. If a unit clearing a house or building was not cautious, they could end up setting off an explosive, killing or injuring everyone in the squad. It was a terrifying experience for the soldiers having to perform this task.

Captain Thornton was sitting at his Tactical Operations Center (TOC), which was one of his Wolverine armored vehicles that had been converted into a command center. He was watching some drone footage of one of his platoons circling around a small group of enemy soldiers. They had finally cornered this group of fighters after they had ambushed and destroyed one of the Army's tanks. As the platoon encircled the enemy, he radioed to the lieutenant in charge of the platoon, "LT, hold your men back, we are going to call in a couple of artillery rounds and flatten that building. Once the dust settles, send your men in and make sure they are dead," he directed.

"Roger that, Captain," replied the platoon leader.

Several minutes later, multiple artillery rounds flew in and hit the small apartment building, flattening it. The shell of the edifice was still there, although the roof and most of the walls had been blown out. Slowly, he could see his Marines moving forward, sifting through the rubble, making sure the enemy soldiers had been killed. After a few more days of cleaning out the enemy holdouts, the city was largely declared secured. There had been several engagements between the Marines and the enemy soldiers in the sewers, and though most of the enemy had been killed, it was suspected that some may survive and continue to fight sporadically. As far as Thornton was concerned, the city was effectively locked down. The few holdouts would be found and dealt with in time.

Chapter 43
Launch

17 March 2042
London, Kentucky

Despite the war raging on, plans for Operation Pegasus continued to progress and move forward. The minerals and resources of the Moon were greatly needed to create the necessary tools of destruction to win the war. Technology had so dramatically changed the way modern warfare was being fought; the need to stay one step ahead of an enemy was paramount to winning, especially when the odds were heavily stacked against you. The United States and her allies were facing a war against an enemy that had a population of 4.5 Billion people and a manufacturing capability of 63% of the global GDP; trying to win on sheer manpower alone would have been lunacy.

While Dr. Karl Bergstrom and Dr. Peter Gorka walked through the HULK on their final inspection, they could not help but be in awe of what they had helped to build. The HULK had been a secret DARPA project for many decades; it was not until the development of the EmDrive and the Angelic power source that the venture had suddenly become a reality. Working with numerous private entities, NASA, DARPA and the DOD collaborated to build the HULK and the two transport ships that would move between Earth and the mining colony on the Moon. After nearly fifteen months of construction, around the clock building and fabrication by hundreds of thousands of workers, 3D printers and robotics, the HULK had been completed and was ready to expand man's footprint in the universe.

As they walked through the hallways leading from one room to another, they saw dozens of engineers fastening bundles of wires to various sections of the inner wall, while others came behind them attaching the outer wall, sealing the wire bundles and the other guts of the ship together. It was a mad dash to the finish as the engineers and contractors completed the last details of the ship before the big test the following day.

Dr. Gorka could not contain his glee; the ship he had dreamed of building as a young child had finally come to fruition. In a couple of days, mankind was going to land on the Moon to establish the first of many off-world colonies. He attempted to contain his excitement as he began to examine the equipment that would be used for the mining operations.

That evening, the crew was going to be joined by several VIPs, including President Stein, for a celebratory dinner. In an unexpected move, the President asked to speak. "Some of you here in this room may not know, but when I was the governor of Florida, I took a flight into orbit with the CEO of SpaceX. From that moment on, I told myself that if I ever became President, I would do everything in my power to establish the first off-world colony and advance the exploration of space. You brave men and women that are here tonight are about to embark on a mission that will change the course of humanity. You will also be carrying with you the hope of the nation as we continue to fight for our survival. I have made a great gamble in dedicating so many resources on this project; please do everything in your power to make it pay off. I wish you all safe travels and Godspeed."

The following week, the crew boarded the ship to begin their final examinations and preparations. The crew had successfully tested the engines and systems a couple of days ago; now that the equipment had been fully loaded up and the known bugs worked out of the system, it was time to launch.

Captain Luke Rogers still could not believe that he was about to lead the first human effort to colonize the Moon. He had been selected to be a part of this mission four years ago, prior to the start of World War III. He had almost given up his position on the project so that he could join his fellow comrades as they fought in the skies across the world. Many of his lifelong pilot buddies had died during the battles over the Middle East, Europe and Alaska. It had been difficult for him to stay focused on the Pegasus project while his friends were fighting and dying for their country. He had to keep telling himself that his mission was important as well; the country desperately needed the Tritium4 they were going to mine from the Moon if America was going to be able to win.

Captain Rogers had started his career as a pilot in the US Navy nearly 26 years ago; at that time, he had been selected to be an F35C fighter pilot, and excelled at it. He rose through the ranks quickly, until a car accident injured him and killed his wife. He and his wife had never had any children; after her death, he chose not to pursue any other relationships, and instead recommitted his life to the Navy. Due to his injuries, it was determined that he could no longer fly the F35, so he was transferred to the drone program instead. After a month of flying drones, he realized the capabilities of drones was going to eclipse that of manned aircraft, and did whatever he could to stay on the cutting edge of this new field. He quickly transferred to the DARPA Drone X project, and before he knew it, he found himself working on the Pegasus project. As someone who was both a drone operator and ex-fighter pilot, he had the skills DARPA was looking for when they began to search for the flight crew to pilot the HULK.

As Captain Rogers fastened his harness, he looked out the windshield and could see the TV cameras set up, and hundreds of observers outside. It was so strange to him after being sworn to secrecy for so long, but once the HULK launched into space, there would be no way to hide the program's existence. President Stein hoped that by maintaining the silence for so long, their enemies would not be in a position to attack them or to make any sincere move to stop them. Their clandestine life had now served its purpose; now it was time for openness and celebration to play a role.

America had been through a lot these past two and a half years of war. Millions of Americans had been killed, and the end of the war still seemed years away from conclusion. The fate of Europe continued to hang in the balance and America was now beginning the process of assessing the damage in California and rebuilding the West Coast. President Stein wanted to give the American people and the Allies a sense of hope, of optimism, and a desire to see the war through to its successful conclusion no matter the cost. Captain Rogers and the crew of the Pegasus knew they were going to do exactly that.

The next thirty minutes were going to change the mood and hopes of America and the world. People had suspected that America was pursuing space-based weapons, but the secret of their project had been well kept. President Stein unclassified Operation Pegasus beginning on the day of the launch, and would allow the public to watch the launch as the HULK went into the sky. For security purposes, the video feed of the launch had a ten-minute delay and so did any news of what was happening. The launch of Operation Pegasus was also only announced thirty minutes before it happened, and only a select few were being told where the launch was taking place. This was done largely to minimize the possibility of the Axis powers trying a last-ditch effort to hinder the launch or try to intercept the HULK as it flew into space.

The greatest threat to the launch was from Russia and China, who might attempt to launch missile interceptors or aircraft to try and interdict the HULK as it clawed for altitude and the depths of space. To minimize the likelihood of this happening, the US had moved the battleship *USS Iowa* to Baffin Bay, between Canada and Greenland. The *USS Wisconsin* had been moved to Midway Island; both ships had missile interceptors and laser platforms to engage any Russian or Chinese missiles that may try to reach out and hit the HULK as it entered orbit. To counter the possibility of ground-based lasers from Russia or China, the HULK had been built with a modulated armor that would nullify the enemy's lasers as long as they knew the wavelength the enemy lasers were using. The wavelength information had been stolen, costing many lives to obtain, but they had finally captured the information, just prior to the launch.

Captain Rogers gave the order to the crew, "Prepare for lift off."

A few moments passed as everyone performed their final checks. Finally, the word came back, "Cross check complete, Captain."

Rogers looked down at the throttle lever and slowly began to move it forward, applying more and more power to the EmDrive. In seconds, the ship began to lift off the ground and slowly started to gain altitude. As he continued applying more power, the ship began to accelerate forward; then the captain pulled back on the flight controls, pointing the ship at a 75-degree angle towards the heavens above. In less than a minute, the ship had passed Mach 10 and was approaching the outer reaches of the atmosphere.

In less than seven minutes, the HULK had broken free of Earth's orbit and began to enter deep space in their journey to the lunar surface. They had not encountered any resistance or attempts by Russia or China to stop their journey. Now they had a 22-hour journey to the Moon, where they would make several circles in orbit as they conducted a few surveys and scans of the surface to ensure the pre-identified location was in fact the best location for them to establish their base of operation and begin mining.

As they approached the Moon and began their orbit, Captain Rogers marveled at the sight of the lunar surface; he still could not believe they were about to establish the first extraterrestrial colony. Karl

Bergstrom, the geology officer onboard interrupted his thoughts when he came over the radio, telling him, "Captain, during our second pass of the Moon, we found a new location that had a higher concentration of minerals. It has an adequate landing zone."

"And the surrounding surface?" asked Rogers.

"Sir, it's flat enough to establish the mining base camp."

"Well, we knew this was a possibility. Thank you, Karl. I'm going to contact ground command now."

"Control, this is Captain Rogers. Our geology officer has identified a new location that appears to be more advantageous. I plan on moving forward with changing the landing location of the ship unless we receive a negative response from you in the next four hours."

There was a moment of static before the reply came in, "HULK, this is Control. You are cleared to adjust your landing, and we want to commend you for finding a better location. Please send the new coordinates for our tracking purposes."

Once Captain Rogers completed the necessary communications with ground command, he began to address his own crew. "Attention everyone, we have received permission from mission control to proceed with our landing at the new location. Good catch Dr. Bergstrom. We are going to begin our descent now. Prepare for landing. As Rogers began the descent, the crew became both nervous and excited. This was one of the most dangerous parts of their mission.

Of course, everyone was also excited; this was mankind's first attempt at establishing a permanent base camp in space. As the HULK descended to the lunar surface, they encountered no significant problems. The ship slowly settled on to the surface of the Moon. Once the ship's engines had been powered down, it was safe for the crew to move about the ship; they began to get their individual stations set up and collected the various gear into the vehicles in the outer storage bay. There was a moment of realization as they stood there before the door opened; this was not just an adventure, this was going to be their new home.

When the HULK was built, it was designed with multiple storage bays and access points to both the lunar surface and the storage bays themselves. It was a modular design that allowed the crew to reconfigure the openings to be small or large, depending on the need.

The mining equipment consisted of a rock crusher, which would reduce the larger rubble and rocks down to smaller rocks, and a small conveyor belt that would move the debris into large containers that would later be moved to one of the loading bays on the HULK for further processing. There were several additional pieces of mining equipment that would allow the miners to scrape the surface of the Moon for the minerals they were in search of, and excavators to build a mining pit like the ones used on Earth, only they were adjusted to be able to accomplish this with very little gravity. There was also a boring device, which would be used to begin the process of digging out various caverns, tunnels and rooms inside one of the mountain ranges near the camp. The goal of this crew was to prepare a location that would later be developed into a permanent structure and command post.

Once the equipment had been transferred to the lunar surface, the miners and base builders would begin their separate operations. The miners were obviously focused on getting the Tritium4 collected and prepared for transport back to Earth. Once the smaller base product was collected into one of the bays, they would use electricity to smelt it down; this would drastically reduce the amount of space needed to store the unrefined Tritium4. The base builders would immediately begin construction of five temporary biodomes that would be responsible for growing the food that the colony would begin to consume. Several botanists were part of the crew, and their goal was to begin establishing the three garden biodomes that would grow about 60% of the colony's vegetables, fruits and nuts through hydroponics. Growing food in a low gravity environment was largely an experiment, but it was one that needed to be conducted to determine if a sustainable colony could be built. Another dome would be set up for the purposes of raising chickens; it was unknown whether or not they would be able to thrive and continue to lay eggs in a low gravity environment, but if they were successful in this experiment, it would provide a protein source for the colony's diet, and also produce a source of fertilizer to assist with farming.

People back on Earth were amazed when they could see live video updates of the what the astronauts were doing daily. They saw the construction of the biodomes, the movement of soil and the cultivation of the hydroponic gardens, chicken coops being built and then chickens being moved into them. They witnessed the beginning of the mining operation, though they were unaware of what specific material was being mined. Watching these awe-inspiring experiences unfold began to revitalize the Allies, and gave hope to a people who were becoming war-weary. It was also a sobering moment for the enemy, because it made the Axis powers realize that America no longer viewed itself as being on the verge of defeat. As big a boon as Operation Pegasus was for the Allies' industrial centers and people, it was an equally potent propaganda tool against the Axis leadership, people and their military forces.

******

A month after the colony had been established, SpaceX's transport ship successfully left Earth and made the sixteen-hour flight to the base camp. The transport craft SpaceX had developed was faster than the DARPA-designed HULK; it was also much smaller and sleeker-looking in nature. The ship was designed with the pure intent of transporting cargo and material from Earth to the Moon and back. Upon landing at the colony, the smelted-down Tritium4 was loaded up for the return trip back to Earth.

The very first load of unrefined Tritium4 would produce more pure material than scientists had synthesized up to that point in the war. This first load would enable the US to build 200 new F41 Archangels and several thousand Pershing battle tanks. The era of limited production of mission critical aircraft and tanks was over. Now the US manufacturing capability would be running at full speed, producing the most advanced weapons ever developed. The tide of the war would now shift in favor of the Allies.

Chapter 44
Back from Vacation

11 August 2042
Washington, DC
Presidential Emergency Operations Center (PEOC)

Michael Montgomery ("Monty," the Presidents Chief of Staff) had been busier than usual. After a lot of persuasion and insistence by the President's doctor, President Stein had agreed to take a short vacation. The President's health was starting to become a genuine concern as his migraines continued to get worse, often forcing him to have to take time to sleep them off or take some heavy medication while sitting in a dark room with no noise or distractions. The doctors insisted they were stress-induced and not something more severe; it was determined that the President needed to take some down time for the sake of his health. Henry decided to head to his home in Florida, where he could lounge around the pool in his backyard and leisurely read a book. It was hard for President Stein to take time off; the war was still going, and he felt guilty taking a break while the country needed him.

Monty and the Vice President had been handling the day-to-day affairs of the country; the President only inserted himself if something major came up. Fortunately, the week had passed quietly, and now Stein had returned to the capitol. As Monty got everything ready for the afternoon briefing with the President, he couldn't help but be excited. After years of war, the end was finally in sight.

Admiral Casey walked into the room and made a beeline towards the coffee, making sure to get his fill before the others got to it and drained its content. He was still not 100% sure why the President had invited him and some of the other military leaders to what appeared to be a standard weekly cabinet update. However, like a true man of the military, he thought to himself, *"Ours is not to reason why; ours is but to do or die."* He grabbed a seat along the back row of chairs and prepared to do his best to listen.

As Admiral Casey sat down in his chair, his mind wandered to the national security brief he would be giving following this meeting. There was a lot to discuss, particularly with the operations in the Northern Atlantic. Carrier Strike Group 13 (CSG13) had completed construction and a rushed sea trial, this newest American Carrier Strike group would soon be moving towards the North Atlantic. The Navy had also finished completion of 12 Submarine Unmanned Drones (SUDs). Eight of them had been unleashed in the Pacific, with the remaining four sent to operate in the Artic, hunting Russian submarines. The Chinese and Japanese navy had retreated to their coasts, abandoning those forces in Alaska that could not retreat. It was unfortunate that China and Russia had been able to execute a well-run evacuation of their forces from Alaska. The Allies had hoped to trap most of the enemy soldiers in the Kodiak and let them wither on the vine; now those fighters could be redeployed elsewhere.

Admiral Casey wanted to end the war quickly. To him, if winning meant plunging America's enemies into complete darkness through his teams of hackers, then so be it. However, the President continued to insist that the war needed to be maintained against the enemy government, not its people. As far as Casey was concerned, they were one and the same. Casey was also aware of the Secretary of State's ongoing efforts to bring the war to an end through a diplomatic process. Although the admiral acknowledged that an end to the fighting would be great news, he was not excited about any situation where the enemy could retain their ability to restart the fighting again in a few years. In his mind, the enemy needed to be defeated, not negotiated with.

Suddenly, the large double doors leading into the PEOC opened, and in walked President Stein with his Chief of Staff in toe. The President looked rested for a change, and he even had a slight tan from his vacation. He walked around the table, shaking a few hands as he worked his way to his seat. Once he sat down at the center of the table, the meeting began.

"Good morning, everyone. It's good to be back. I'm glad to be here so that we can all discuss the status of the country." Pausing for a minute, the President looked around at his cabinet members and zeroed in on DHS. "Secretary Perez, where do we stand with capturing the remaining Japanese and Chinese Special Forces units still running around the country right now?"

Perez straightened up in his chair as he responded, "Sir, I've had my department working feverously with the FBI and local law enforcement on tracking these individuals down. We believe we are down to just two teams left. One is the unit that landed in Charlotte,

North Carolina and the second is the group that originally landed in Phoenix, Arizona. We still do not know their current exact locations." He put his head down after he finished speaking, knowing that the President was not going to be happy with his response.

Stein was a little taken aback at the way Perez had responded; he decided to take a softer approach. "Why the uncertainty? Do you need additional resources?"

Jorge sighed. "We have the resources we need; they are just good at evading us. We have a wide net, and once they make a mistake, we will catch them. Until they move out of hiding again, there is not a lot of we can do other than to keep a vigilant eye out for them."

Director Smart, the head of the FBI, interjected to add, "Mr. President, we are close. My agents are tracking down each lead that comes in and it won't be long before we have them."

The FBI had been working with DHS on tracking down these groups since they arrived in the country eight months ago. Slowly and steadily, they were either apprehending them or killing them. The Chinese and Japanese Special Forces groups had stuck to military and critical infrastructure targets, refraining from attacking civilians when possible. For that, everyone was grateful.

The meeting continued for another 90 minutes as the various advisors brought the President and each other up to speed on their specific aspects of the government that they managed. The economy was running at full speed, and was as close to full employment as it was going to get. The stock market was still going strong, despite the periodic domestic attacks and the war.

Now that the enemy had been fully defeated in Alaska and California, hundreds of billions of dollars were being poured into the affected areas to rebuild the destroyed infrastructure and housing. Tens of millions of people across California had lost their homes and were living as refugees in their own country; the President had already visited many of the refugee camps, encouraging them and letting them know the government was going to ensure it did everything it could to help rebuild the cities and towns they had fled from during the invasion. The damage to California was extensive; nearly all of the major roads, overpasses and bridges in and around LA, San Diego and Oakland had been destroyed. It was going to take years to remove all the rubble and rebuild what had been lost. The only good thing to come from it was city planners now had the ability to completely redesign the transportation system of these cities and improve upon them with the latest in maglev trains and mass transit systems.

Following the meeting, the President dismissed his domestic and law enforcement advisors so that he could meet privately with the national security and military advisors. Before the second half of the meeting started, Stein had more beverages and some finger foods brought to the room; the President was sort of like a friendly grandma in that he never wanted anyone to work on an empty stomach.

Once everyone had a chance to grab some food, the President began the meeting again. He surveyed the room full of professional killers. "I know these past 90 minutes may have seemed like a waste of your time, and you may be thinking that you really did not need to sit through all these domestic reports and updates of what is going on in the country. I assure you it was not just an exercise in increasing your patience."

The President saw the looks on his military advisors' faces, and clearly, they were not impressed. "I wanted you all to be a part of that discussion so that you could remember that this is ultimately what we are fighting for. It is these people's lives, and a vision for the prosperity of our great country and the world—that is what this is all about. It is not enough that we win this war; we need to also win the peace. That is going to be harder than anything we have ever embarked upon, and I am going to need each and every one of you to push your people harder and farther than ever to not just bring this war to a close, but to push through and win the peace that will follow. We need to identify those who will oppose peace and wipe them out."

The President saw the faces of these hard men and women soften. Maybe they realized that the challenge he was laying out for them was not just the military one, but what to do after the war had been won. Maintaining the peace and rebuilding the world would be as challenging and fraught with danger as the war has been.

Admiral Casey was the first to break the silence and address the President's challenge. "Mr. President, the war is still some ways off from being won. While I appreciate the lesson on why we fight and who we are fighting for, the conflict is far from over. The intercepts that we have received from the enemy governments indicate that they plan to continue fighting, despite the battlefield losses."

This was becoming a source of contention among the military and intelligence leadership. The Chinese had been forced to return their armies back to Asia, and Russia had lost Poland and parts of the Ukraine during the summer offensive in Europe. Despite these defeats, none of these enemy powers were willing to discuss an end to the war. The Indians, on the other hand, had approached the American embassy about a separate peace. The cyber-attacks against their country had begun to so cripple their economy that the government was on the verge of collapse, and many of the provinces had fallen into complete anarchy. The implosion of their financial system and collapse of select portions of their transportation system had nearly ground the country to a halt. Starvation was starting to run rampant through their country as the logistical network needed to move resources from the farms to the city had ground to a halt.

Despite the initial success in the cyber-attacks against the Japanese, they had managed to restore most of their systems within a couple of weeks. The strikes had caused some serious economic damage to Japan, but nothing they could not recover from. What was plaguing Japan now was an internal resistance to the government's decision to continue to support China and the war against America, despite the devastating naval losses and invasion of California. The Japanese had lost nearly 283,000 soldiers in the first four months of the war; much of their navy was gone. They were now relegated to providing the Chinese manufacturing support for the war and allowing the PLAAF to use their land as forward operating bases to house their aircraft. Once the American SUDs had cleared the waters around Alaska of enemy ships, they had moved to the waters around Japan and were causing havoc on a nation that depended on imports to survive. They were slowly being economically choked out of the war, and the people of Japan had had enough. The reduced rations, consumer goods and continued presence of Chinese soldiers was becoming more than they were willing to tolerate.

The President knew that the Admiral had a point; he needed to bring them into the loop on Project Terminator. "Everyone, this next portion of the meeting is going to be highly classified. Everyone will need to be read onto the program before we continue."

Everyone's eyes opened wide in surprise. Admiral Casey's jaw dropped; there were very few secrets within the government that he did not know about. Clearly, the President still had a few aces up his sleeves.

Dr. Gorka and Professor Rickenbacker walked into the room, and everyone shook hands and welcomed them to the room; Casey was particularly excited that whatever the President had in mind involved these two secretive and brilliant men. After a few moments, the President signaled that it was time for them to get the meeting going. Monty opened a vault on the side of the wall in the PEOC and pulled out several folders. Before each person could read the contents inside, they had to sign paperwork swearing them to secrecy.

Once the formalities had been completed, the room was darkened as Dr. Gorka prepared the holograph brief he and Professor Rickenbacker had brought with them.

The President smiled and announced, "Gentlemen, I believe it is now time for everyone to learn about Project Terminator."

A few of the men in the room snickered at the reference, but everyone was still very eager to see what the President had up his sleeve.

"As you know, the Bodark project had its ups and downs in Alaska. It was our first attempt at using a humanoid drone for combat. It was also a test of a newer system that Professor Rickenbacker had been developing for some time. I will hand the meeting over to him," the President explained, signaling for the professor to take over.

The professor stood up and began his presentation, switching on the holographic display. As soon as the first image of the new humanoid machine came up, someone let out a whistle; they were all in awe. "Ladies and gentlemen, what we are looking at is the next evolution in modern warfare, the Enhanced Humanoid Drone or EHD. We have named this EHD the Reaper, which seemed appropriate because it will reap death and suffering upon our enemies. The wars fought during the last one hundred years relied heavily on humans waging them. This war, however, has changed that reality. Since the beginning of this conflict, we have used increasing numbers of drones; now we are nearly ready to shape the face of war with the next evolution."

The professor could see the raised eyebrows on the faces of his audience. They had so many questions written on their faces that they were practically raising their hands, but the professor wanted to press on with his presentation before he allowed the group to respond. "As you can see by the dimensions, the Reaper is about 6'6" and weighs about 340lbs. It is built out of the same enhanced armor our tanks and other armored vehicles are, so it's a tough beast."

On the screen, the drone began to run through a variety of scenarios, from loading and unloading the M5 AIR infantry rifle to throwing a grenade. It ran as if it were a human, dropping to a knee to fire a few shots with its rifle before diving behind cover. It moved as if it were a human clone and not some sort of machine.

"Before anyone asks, the machine is not an AI. We have not moved forward in that direction, at least not yet. The Reaper is a drone. It is still operated by an individual." Another screen was brought up that showed the soldier operating the drone. He was wearing a set of sensors, helmet and other equipment that tied him to the drone.

"Like our fighter aircraft drones, these are also controlled by a human operator, though they do have the option of being turned into a semi-autonomous platform. When the operator needs a break, the drone can be turned on semi-autonomous mode, which turns the drone into a sentry. It will stand guard at its present position and challenge any target that enters its field of engagement. This mode also allows a single soldier to operate several of these drones when used in sentry or guard duty operations. We do have an AI version, but we want to further refine it before we move forward with deploying it."

The presentation on the screen finished, and Professor Rickenbacker held his hand out to the group with a "bring it on" motion. "Now I will take some of your questions before we move on," he said.

General Branson, the Chairman of the Joint Chiefs, was the first to ask, "Why were we kept in the dark about this project? This will have a huge impact on the battlefield." His brows were furrowed and he was obviously somewhat annoyed at not being brought in on the project earlier.

"General, we experienced a lot of challenges and problems with the Reaper last year, and until we were able to iron them out, we did not want to get everyone's hopes up. We had initially hoped to release the Reaper at the same time as the Bodark; however, we could not establish a secure enough link between the drone operator and the drone itself. When we deployed the Bodarks, we were able to figure out how to fix a lot of the issues that we had been observing. We simply did not want to place the Reapers behind enemy lines before we were sure that we could maintain control of them; to do so would have allowed them to fall into enemy hands."

Rickenbacker signaled to the Marine Commandant next.

"When do you plan on introducing the drone, and how many do you have ready?" asked General Lynch. The Commandant immediately saw the impact this would have on the coming battles. If this could save more of her Marines from dying, she was all for it.

"Now that we have a steady supply of Tritium4, we have been able to ramp up production of the drone. It's kind of ironic really; we have EHDs making additional Reapers as we speak--"

One of the generals interrupted, "--Now that is a scary idea, kind of reminds me of a movie I saw as a kid." A few people snickered, realizing that he was obviously thinking of "The Terminator," like the project's name.

"The thought is not lost on us either," retorted the professor. "However, we have purposefully not gone the route of AI, so the drones will not be able to function beyond a limited protocol without an operator."

"Back to the question--we have 100 of them right now, 2000 are being built right now, and we will crank out another 2000 a month going forward. Soon, we will be able to produce about 10,000 a month. Presently, 50 of the new drones are slated for the Moon colony as their use in space is almost limitless; the rest are being slated for the war. What we need to do next is identify our potential drone operators and then get them pulled from the line and trained up. We would like to have the first battalion of Reapers ready to deploy within the next 45 days."

The President signaled for the professor to take a seat, "Gentlemen, the war is about to enter its final stage. By employing this new technology, we are going to bring the war to enemy with as few casualties as possible on our part. I am directing the Secretary of State to issue a final ultimatum to the enemy leaders; they will either surrender and allow the world to return to peace, or we will move the war to the next level and wage unrestricted warfare on their countries, economy and people. Nearly two Billion people have died across the world during the war, and it is time to bring the suffering and killing to an end."

Mike Rogers, the National Security Advisor, spoke up first, "Mr. President, if we can, I would like to recommend we deploy our first batch of these drones to Japan with some of our Special Forces. The majority of their population now believes it was a terrible mistake to have gone to war with the United States. The support for the government has nearly collapsed, and if we were to help give it a shove, we might be able to topple the government and force one of our enemies out of the war."

Director Rubio from the CIA cleared his throat and said, "I agree. The situation in Japan is becoming unstable. The people are incredibly suspicious of the government and angry at the loss of their soldiers in California and near Hawaii. Many people in Japan have family and friends in America. The war has placed an enormous strain on the country. My agents believe that if we can provide weapons, explosives and support, many of the disaffected groups would revolt against the government."

Several others in the room also spoke in favor of supporting a popular uprising against the government. The President also liked the idea of the people being the ones to lead this effort. He had detested the idea of being at war with Japan; the two nations had been close allies and friends for nearly 100 years. The present Japanese government had not only betrayed America, its ally, it had cost the lives of hundreds of thousands of its people. Moreover, the treachery had not achieved anything for their nation.

After a few moments of discussion, the President raised his hand for everyone to be quiet. "I agree that we should move forward with a plan to assist the people of Japan in taking their government back. I want our efforts to focus on helping a popular uprising in Japan succeed. We will need to identify new leaders who are credible with the population that can take over. We also need a plan in place to assist the new government, in case the Chinese decide they do not want to accept Japan's surrender and leave the Island."

Chapter 45
Misaligned Priorities

02 September 2042
Tokyo, Japan
Kantei (Prime Minister's Official Residence)

The situation in Japan had gone from bad to worse since the defeat of the navy off the coast of southern California and then Hawaii. The subsequent surrender of their ground forces in California several months later was a defeat that nearly brought down the government. As it stood, the people of Japan had been demonstrating on an almost daily basis, pleading for an end to the war. The populace was angry with their government for getting them involved in the World War, and they were infuriated by the alignment with China over their traditional ally, the United States.

Foreign Minister Hirohita had just finished a holographic meeting with his Chinese counterpart about the latest protests happening in Tokyo. The Chinese were getting nervous that the government might not be able to maintain law and order, and had offered to send additional troops to Japan, if needed.

Minister Hirohita felt nervous after the conversation. He thought to himself, "*I need to talk to the Prime Minister about this. He needs to put down these protesters before the Chinese decide to intervene. I better go find him.*"

Unaware and aloof, PM Hata was walking in the gardens behind his residence, enjoying the late summer morning before his day began. Out of the corner of his eye, he caught Minister Hirohita walking towards him. "Prime Minister, I have an urgent matter that I need to discuss with you," he said as he approached the PM, bowing.

"You are disturbing me before our morning meeting. What is so important that it could not wait for our scheduled meeting?" the PM asked, perturbed that he had been interrupted.

Hirohita did not care if he had broken protocol or if the PM was irritated. The country was starting to fall apart around them--this was not the time to focus on routine and personal comfort.

"Sir, I just spoke with the Chinese Foreign Minister, Fang Yung. The Chinese are not pleased at all with our handling of the protesters. They are concerned that we are losing control of things in the cities." Minister Hirohita spoke with a bit more sternness in his voice than he probably meant to show. He was growing frustrated with the PM's lack of concern for the situation.

"Hirohita, you are getting yourself too worked up over these protesters," replied Hata nonchalantly. "People are frustrated, but they were peaceful. There is no threat to the government. Please calm yourself...the people are just upset about the reduced rations. They are young, and they are venting their frustrations. Nothing more. Japan will continue to stay the course with our allies. Now, leave me, and we will continue our discussion during our scheduled meeting." With that, the PM turned around and continued his walk, leaving his foreign minister speechless.

Unbeknownst to the leaders of Japan, several high ranking military leaders and the Chief of Police for the city of Tokyo were quietly planning a coup to seize control of the government and sue for a separate peace with America. That Saturday evening, nearly two million protesters were gathered in various locations throughout Tokyo, while millions more gathered in other cities across the country, calling for an end to the war.
****

At the behest of the Chinese, PM Hata had ordered the military into the cities to disperse the protesters and work with the police to restore order. While the military was moving to secure the cities, units loyal to the coup leaders had also silently moved soldiers near the various Chinese forces in Japan, insisting that they were there to protect them from the protesters. The following day, at 0300 in the morning, forces loyal to the former general Tenaka (one of the generals that the PM had relieved of command when he refused to accept the Chinese alliance) were set to strike.

Five heavily armed soldiers walked down the hallway leading to the PM's residences and ordered the two security guards to stand down or be killed. Seeing that they were heavily outgunned and out-numbered, they placed their weapons on the ground and were quickly apprehended without incident. The soldiers continued to move down the hall and burst through the Prime Minister's bedroom door, awaking him from his sleep.

Hata instinctively sat up in bed, and demanded, "What is the meaning of this?"

One of the soldiers grabbed him by his pajama shirt and summarily threw him face-down on the floor, zip-tying his hands. His wife, who woke up when her husband was slammed to the floor, screamed in horror to find armed men had intruded their bedroom. Another soldier shouted at her, "Be quiet, or we will arrest you, too!"

"I demand to know what you are doing!" the PM shouted at the soldiers.

One of the men lifted the PM back to his feet and turned him around just as General Tenaka walked into the room. "Prime Minister Hata, they are acting on my orders. You are hereby under arrest and being charged with treason. I am assuming control of the government until a new election can be held," General Tenaka said forcefully. He then signaled for the soldiers to bring the PM with them. The group walked out of the bedroom and headed towards the armored vehicles that were waiting out front to take them to a more secured facility.

All throughout the country, soldiers loyal to General Tenaka began detaining Hata loyalists and those that supported the war against America. As Tenaka's men were making arrests across the country, the units that had been placed near the Chinese forces moved quickly to disarm and detain them peacefully. One Chinese Commander suspected that something fishy was going on when several of his units stopped responding to his calls, and he ordered his forces to full alert. A quick standoff ensued, and his forces eventually surrendered once several Japanese attack helicopters showed up. By the early hours of Sunday morning, most of the government officials who had supported PM Hata or been outspoken backers of the war had been arrested.

General Tenaka broadcasted a message to the people of Japan, informing them of the coup and letting them know that he had assumed control of Japan. He encouraged the people of Japan to rally around him and his forces and support an end to the war and the occupation of Chinese forces in Japan.

People took to the streets in joy and celebration that morning. Many of the military units who had not initially involved in the coup quickly lined up to support General Tenaka. The few military units who remained loyal to Prime Minister Hata stood down and were quickly arrested. Even though those men did not want to support the coup against the government, they were not willing to take up arms against their fellow Japanese citizens, and they went into custody peacefully.

General Tenaka announced to the world that Japan was withdrawing from its military alliance with China and Russia, and requested that all foreign troops leave Japan peacefully. He also asked for an end to hostilities between Japan and the United States while a more formal ceasefire deal could be worked out.

The response from China was swift and brutal. The PLAAF and PLA launched a series of cruise missile attacks against multiple Japanese air force bases in the south of Japan. These assaults quickly followed them up with an airborne assault of the Island of Okinawa. Chinese forces also began to move soldiers in to secure Kumamoto, to act as a buffer between the East China Sea and mainland China.

In reaction, General Tenaka immediately ordered the forces loyal to him to fight the Chinese invaders. Despite the recent Japanese betrayal of America, Tenaka also boldly asked for the United States to come to their aid.

Chapter 46
Geepers, Reapers

05 October 2042
North Atlantic Ocean
100 Miles Northeast of the Faroe Islands

Captain Elizabeth Mann had been the Commanding officer of the newest *Reagan* Class Supercarrier, *USS Donald J. Trump*, for the past year. Before that, she had spent a year as the executive officer on the *USS William Clinton* before she was promoted and given command of one of the new supercarriers. It had been a great honor; she had beaten out a lot of other officers for such an important command.

Captain Mann was nervous about this particular mission. Her carrier (along with her sister carrier, the *USS Barrack Obama*) were escorting the 32nd Infantry Division to invade the Kola Peninsula and the critical Russian naval base of Murmansk. The fleet was going to be sailing deep into Russian territory, and would be attacking what was perhaps their most important naval base in Russia. If the 32nd Infantry could secure the facility and the Peninsula, it might bring the war that much closer to being won. In addition to transporting the 32nd Infantry, she had been told they were also escorting 1,000 of these new humanoid Reaper combat drones. The senior captains were not given a lot of information about them during the pre-deployment brief, other than being told that they were going to change the way ground wars were going to be fought.

The fleet had three attack submarines running about 100 miles ahead of their position, and another two SUDs shadowing them in case any Russian subs managed to slip through their anti-submarine screen. Subs were her greatest concern. The *USS Seawolf* had managed to sink one of the enemy carrier ships in the decisive battle of Hawaii. She did not want to lose her ship or any other ship in the fleet to a sneak attack from below.

As the fleet continued to move further north into Russian waters, the weather remained cool and the water became choppier. Thus far, they had encountered little resistance from the Russians. The submarine screen had sunk two subs a couple of days earlier, and one of the fleet's destroyers had also sunk an enemy submarine.

Unfortunately, three coastal raider ships had managed to slip past one of the American destroyer's surface radars and fired off a volley of anti-ship missiles, sinking one of the destroyers and damaged another frigate. Some of the intelligence officers thought that the Russians had used some sort of new anti-ship radar technology that allowed the small ships to slip past them.

While the fleet continued to move closer to Murmansk, the ground forces that would be operating the new Reaper drones continued to train on them, trying to become as proficient with them as possible before their first big test.

****

Captain Paul Allen was still getting used to being on a ship. Of course, operating in a virtual reality simulator all day was not making it any easier. Once the Russian and Chinese began pulling the bulk of their forces out of Alaska, the 32nd Infantry Division had been pulled from the line and redeployed to the East Coast. Captain Allen's brigade had been selected as operators for the new enhanced humanoid drone program. Seeing the Bodarks for the first time at the start of the New Year had been scary; however, the reality of the Reaper drones was nothing short of terrifying. Their flat silver grayish exteriors, menacing looking faces and glowing red eyes were unnerving. These new killing machines were truly science fiction nightmares.

After being selected for the EHD program, his company had spent a week in a classroom learning about the Reaper drones' functions, how they worked, and what they could do. They spent another week learning basic maintenance of the drone, though the technicians assigned to each drone would handle the day-to-day maintenance. Following the familiarization of the drone, they were introduced to the equipment that would allow them to operate the machines.

The operation of the EHDs was similar in function to other virtual reality systems; there was a circular three-foot round platform that you stood on while wearing a special suit, shoes, gloves and headset. The shoes were frictionless, which essentially allowed the operators to walk or run in place on the platform. The users' gestures and movements would be matched by the Reaper the soldier was paired to. If the soldier walked, the Reaper walked, if it ran, then the drone ran. When the soldier raised his simulated rifle, the drone would raise its rifle and engage whatever the soldier had placed in his or her sights. The drone was essentially a surrogate, doing the bidding of the soldier without risking the life of the soldier.

Allen's soldiers had spent three weeks learning to operate in a virtual reality environment: conducting patrols, storming a beach, conducting house-to-house searches and any other combat scenarios that the trainers threw at them. They were given a week of leave to enjoy some downtime before their brigade boarded the *USS America* and head to Russia. The *USS America* was a massive amphibious assault ship that could transport 2,000 soldiers and their combat equipment anywhere in the world. Paul had never been on a naval ship before; as he approached the ship, he was amazed at how utterly enormous it was.

After boarding the ship, they were introduced to their new surroundings; the vessel would become their home for the next several months. Unlike the rest of the soldiers in their division, they would not be going ashore. They would be staying aboard the *America*, operating the suite of virtual reality stations that had been installed throughout the belly of the ship where the landing craft and vehicles used to be stored. Those areas had been converted into a space large enough to hold up to 600 virtual reality stations. The bays had been broken down by battalions and then companies. The aircraft bay was currently filled with the Reaper drones and the maintenance crews assigned to support them.

Because each of the drones were being operated by human beings with biological needs, the army created drone teams. Each team would consist of three drone pilots and three maintenance technicians. The plan was simple; one soldier would operate the drone in four hour intervals and then swap out with a team member. This would enable the drone to be operated twenty-four hours a day while in combat, and give the operators time to rest.

When the pods got dropped off out in the field, there was a whole system set up out there. Several Reaper drones would be activated in sentry mode to guard spare drones and drone parts. In that cluster of pods, there were also be a few that were designated maintenance pods, filled with spare parts and staffed with technicians to repair the Reapers as needed (these soldiers were not there to fight, but solely to support the EHDs in their mission). As drones became damaged or needed repair, a spare drone would be activated until the original was fully functional again. If the technicians were not able to fix one of the Reapers with the spare parts and tools on hand, then it would be flown back to the *USS America* for a more advanced maintenance crew to work on.

Between the rest of the division using the Raptor combat suits and the Reaper drones, the Russians would have no idea what hit them. It was hoped that the Army would be able to secure this northernmost Russian base and provide the Allies with a platform from which to launch further attacks deeper into the Russian mainland, pulling additional resources away from the frontlines in Eastern Europe.
****

After nearly two weeks at sea, the invasion force was nearing their launch position. As Captain Allen sat in the briefing room with the other battalion and company commanders, looking over their objectives, he couldn't help but wonder if they were finally nearing the end of this bloody war. After nearly three years of combat, he was ready to be done with fighting.

The plan for the invasion was simple; the Reapers would be flown in via the Razorbacks to assault the Severomorsk naval base along with regular troops who had been equipped with the Raptor exoskeleton suits. Once they landed, the first wave of EHD pods would be delivered and the Reapers would then begin to fan out and secure the facility. The same process would be replicated all throughout the peninsula as small units in Raptor suits secured various landing sites for the Reaper pods and then let the drones go do the dangerous and dirty work of securing the broader area. Once the port facilities were fully secured, the transport ships would move down the channel to offload the armored vehicles. The Air Force would work on getting the nearby airfields up and running while several squadrons of fighter drones and additional Razorbacks were flown into the area.

With a forward operating base situated deep behind enemy lines, the allies would be able to launch any number of raids against the Russians, and they would have virtually no defense against them. Paul thought the plan sounded simple, but maybe it was too simple. "*Typical higher ups,*" he thought, "*Always making these grandiose plans. I wonder if they realize that the Russians get a vote in the matter, too.*"

As Paul walked through the rows of virtual reality pods on his way to brief his company, he couldn't help but think to himself how detached war was becoming. When World War III had first started, he was a rifleman, a soldier with the first railgun to be used as an infantry rifle. Two years later, he was outfitted with an exoskeleton combat suit. Now he was commanding a company of soldiers who would operate the latest mechanical killing machine, the enhanced humanoid drone, a mechanical clone that would enable his soldiers to throw themselves at the enemy without fear of death. It was strange to think how fast the business of killing had advanced and what the next evolution would entail. While talking with one of the computer technicians, he had heard the military was developing an Artificial Intelligence version of the Reaper drone that would enable the military to drop the drones behind enemy lines and let them operate autonomously, on their own without human involvement. That was truly a scary idea to him and he wondered, *"What if the machine decides not to listen to its human masters? What if it becomes 'self-aware'?"*

"Room, Attention!" yelled the Company First Sergeant as Captain Allen walked in.

Paul was still not used to the formality and attention every time he entered a room. He had been an NCO most of his military career. As he surveyed the men and women of his command, he could see the apprehension written all over their faces. This was the first time they would be using the Reapers in combat, and they were carrying a heavy burden; the men and women of the division would be counting on them to successfully secure their objectives. If they did their jobs right, a lot of lives would be saved by not using live soldiers in Raptor suits.

"Listen up, everyone. I know there is a lot riding on our success, but I don't want you to concentrate on that. I want you to focus on the tasks assigned to each platoon and squad. You worry about doing your specific job, and let others worry about doing theirs. I want you to fixate every thought you have on operating your Reaper...don't get bogged down by the bigger picture. If you run into a problem, get your squad leader's attention quickly so we can address it. I spoke with our support company, and they have several computer technicians assigned to our company to help address any problems that may come up."

Pulling up a holographic map of the area, Captain Allen began to highlight the individual platoon and company objectives. "Things are going to move quickly once we are on the ground. Once our initial mission has been completed, there is a chance we will be given new orders and expected to capture more ground."

Showing some areas highlighted in red, Captain Allen pulled up more information showing the enemy unit composition. "As you can see, the Russians have moved a brigade of their own soldiers (who are equipped with exoskeleton suits) to the area as well. You can expect these guys to be ready for a fight. The Russians know that if we capture this peninsula, the war is that much closer to being won, so expect them to fight like cats backed into a corner."

"Remember, just because we are tied to virtual reality simulator equipment does not make what you are about to see, hear, and be a part of any less real. Keep your wits about you, and your head on a swivel. Do not take unnecessary risks, and do what you can to protect your EHD. Oh, and before we leave, I want you to remember one very important thing…we are going to crush them!" he roared to the delight of his men.

With that, he dismissed the troops to their individual commanders and they quickly exited the briefing room to head to their simulator pods. As the soldiers got themselves strapped in, Paul walked over to his own simulation pod and began the process of hooking himself up.

He changed into the skin-hugging jumpsuit that would mimic his every move and allow him to feel what the EHD felt. He put on his gloves and frictionless boots, then stepped onto the simulation platform and began to attach his helmet. Once the power had been activated, he immediately began a quick system check, just as they had been taught.

Shortly after completing his system check, a message was sent across the battalion net, letting them know the helicopters would be lifting off shortly to begin the assault. As Paul looked from left to right, his EHD mimicked his move, and he could see the others in his transport pod doing similar checks. It was strange looking at the other Reapers, each had a name and rank written on its right chest area just as it would have if it were a regular soldier or Raptor suit. What he never got used to seeing was the soft glowing red eyes of the EHD. The lights for the eyes could be dimmed or turned off all together, and typically were darkened when operating at night. However, the physiological warfare folks believed that the soldiers should leave them on all the time, even if it gave away their positions at night. Their reasoning was simple; the strange sight was a powerful cause of intimidation and fear.

A few minutes later, the transport pod began to lift off the deck of the *America*, carrying the Reapers towards their drop point. Paul couldn't see that much while the EHD was in the transport pod. Switching channels on his visual input, Allen was able to see what the pilot saw as the helicopter travelled quickly at treetop level. In the distance, Paul saw anti-aircraft fire emanating from the direction of the Russian base and city nearby. Several missiles streaked towards some of the helicopters. He saw a Razorback take a direct hit--it exploded violently.

A few minutes later, Paul saw the airfield his company had been assigned to secure. They were going to be landing towards the tail end of the runway, where the area was cleared of trees. There were no buildings nearby, which is why they had chosen this area to land the EHD pods. It would allow the helicopters enough time to drop the pods and then run back to the *America* to pick up the next load of EHDs.

In seconds, the transport pod was on the ground, and Paul and his soldiers began to detach the restraints holding their Reapers in place. They quickly began to exit the transport and began to move as squads towards their objectives. Paul was moving with the second squad from first platoon towards what had been identified as the command building for the airfield. The targeting system on the EHD quickly identified several enemy soldiers, who immediately opened fire on the Reapers with their machine guns.

Green tracers could be seen heading towards their position. Paul saw one of his fellow soldier's EHD get hit with several rounds and fall to the ground. As he ran past the drone, he saw it get back up and continue to fire its rifle; soon it was running towards the enemy position with the rest of his squad. While Allen was sprinting towards his objective, he raised his rifle and shot at a small cluster of soldiers he saw emerging from the building in front of him.

The targeting system on the EHD was amazing. Despite running across rough terrain, the Reaper could keep the rifle stable while tracking whatever target it had identified. Paul found himself awestruck at the integration of the virtual reality technology; the digital and physical world had blurred together in the EHD.

The Russians began to pour more and more soldiers out of the surrounding buildings to attack the Americans. The Russians were truly caught off guard; they had been expecting the Americans to attack them, but had anticipated soldiers in Raptor combat suits. They did not know how to respond to this new threat.

A Russian officer observing the attack from the window of one of the buildings a little farther away from the base headquarters would later write that in his memoirs of the war that when the Americans attacked with their new weapon, it looked like something out of a Sci-Fi novel. He saw a small cluster of soldiers' attack one of the EHDs and hit it with at least a dozen rounds, only to see the drone get back up and continue to attack. Another drone had been hit by a heavy machine gun, ripping one of its arms off. The drone continued to fight on with it's one good arm, until the heavy machine gunner hit it with a stream of rounds that eventually disabled the drone.

Within an hour, Paul's company had secured the airfield and their objectives. Of the 132 EHDs that participated in the attack, they had lost nineteen. Three of the soldiers from their maintenance platoon had been injured when a mortar round landed nearby their maintenance pod; however, aside from their injuries, his company had captured the enemy airfield with no casualties at all. This was a feat that would have cost his company dozens of dead or injured soldiers if they had carried out the attack with only the Raptor suits.

The success of Captain Allen's company was repeated throughout the peninsula as they continued to take control of each objective the EHDs had been given. By the end of the first day of the operation, they had secured half a dozen enemy airfields, and several small cities and port facilities. The 32nd Infantry Division immediately began to unload the rest of their armored vehicles and tanks as they began the task of turning the peninsula into a forward operating base and launch pad for further deep penetration operations into the Russian heartland. By the end of the first week, they had secured all their objectives with very few casualties. The division had 2,600 EHDs at the start of the operation and had lost 431 to enemy action and 214 to maintenance issues. The first combat test of the EHDs had proven successful and now their implementation across the rest of the army would begin in earnest.

Chapter 47
Honey Pot, Not so Sweet

12 October 2042
Moscow, Russia

It was cloudy and dreary outside. A light mist was starting to fall as Petr Gromley entered the Pivnoi Bar. The tavern was a small, out of the way place that afforded those government officials who did not want to be seen with unsavory characters the opportunity to conduct meetings unnoticed. Mr. Gromley was not comfortable meeting Sasha Petrosky in Moscow, even if this was a secluded backroom bar. There were too many curious eyes and ears in Moscow for Gromley's liking. He pulled his ball cap down a little lower as he moved to a small table against the wall, not far from the door. He took a seat with his back against the wall, waiting for Sasha to arrive.

Sasha is what people in the intelligence circles called "a honey pot." She had been specially trained by Russian intelligence to use her looks and sexuality as a weapon for the purpose of gathering intelligence, and to eliminate those her superiors directed her to kill. Sasha was still young at thirty-two years old, and highly intelligent. She had studied economics at the London School of Economics and obtained a Master's in finance at the Wharton School in Finance by the age of 24. Following a year of specialized training with the Russian SVR, the external intelligence and espionage arm of the FSB (Russian Secret Service), she had been recruited by Goldman Sachs to work as a financial analyst and consultant. This position afforded her favorable placement, and access to a wide range of influential people across the world. Her handler at Goldman Sachs ensured that Sasha had a loose consulting schedule and little oversight, which allowed her to work on a wide variety of opportunities.

Sasha had been on assignment in London, tasked with obtaining information about the American Moon-mining operation. She had befriended the Chief Financial Officer of a British space mining corporation, who had just signed a joint venture agreement with Deep Space Industries, the leading company managing the mining operations for the American base on the Moon. Her company had helped them acquire the funding needed for the joint venture and her "new boyfriend" was only too eager to tell her all about the minerals being mined on the Moon and how the Americans were incorporating the materials into their new armor and technology.

She was finally obtaining the valuable information she had been after, and now she had been called back to Moscow for a secret meeting. She risked blowing her cover; she had to travel through several different neutral countries without drawing suspicion. It was a risk, one she was not happy about having to take.

As she walked into the bar, a place she had frequented during her SVR training many years ago, she spotted Petr. It had been said that Petr was the man behind the rise of President Fradkov and many of the other leaders within the Russian Federation. When she had been told that she would be meeting with Mr. Gromley, she was a bit taken aback. Why would such a powerful man want to meet with her? Not that she had a choice--she arranged for them to meet, and chose this place because it was a hole-in-the-wall place where two people could talk and go relatively unnoticed.

Petr recognized Sasha as soon she walked through the door into the bar. His contacts had been right. She *was* a very attractive woman, though she was wearing a coat and headscarf that did a good job of hiding her beauty. As she walked up to his table, she greeted him with a soft kiss on both cheeks and then took her seat next to his, as if they were close friends.

Blushing slightly, Sasha said, "It is a pleasure to meet you...but I must say I am not sure why you have asked for me."

Sizing her up before responding, he told her, "I have recalled you because I have an important mission for you. I need someone of your skillset and trust to do what I am about to ask."

Her eyes darted about, searching his for any signs or clues of what he meant. Not sure what this cryptic response meant, she asked, "What tasks do you have for me? I cannot be away from my original assignment for very long without drawing suspicion."

Gromley slid a capsule across the table towards Sasha, who casually picked it up and quickly placed it in her Louis Vuitton handbag. "You are going to be brought to President Fradkov's Dasha tomorrow night along, with one other woman. Each Wednesday night, he has two whores brought to his Dasha for the evening. We are replacing one of his regulars with you for the evening. He may be suspicious, but you will need to dissuade him from turning you away. Once he has accepted you, you need to swap out one of his Viagra pills with the one I just gave you, without being noticed."

Sasha thought about the capsule that had just been given to her and what was most likely in it. She did not like the thought of killing the President and being one of two prostitutes in the room with him when the poison took hold.

Seeing her sour facial expression, Petr added, "The poison is time-delayed. It will take 48 hours for it to release in his body. Once it does, it will appear as if he has had a sudden heart attack. You will already be on your way back to London by the time the poison kicks in," he said, reading her mind.

Gromley handed her a cell phone and a piece of paper with additional instructions on it before leaving. As he got up, he said, "Do this assignment well, and you will go far in the SVR. Screw it up, and you'll be dead before you know what happened."

As Sasha watched Gromley walk out of the bar, she was glad she had asked him come to her stomping grounds. This was only the second time she had met Gromley. Few people met him more than once. There were the figure heads in the SVR, who everyone knew, and then there was Petr Gromley, the spy who ran the spies. Very few people could even identify Petr Gromley, but he was probably the most powerful man in the Russian Federation. In many circles, he was only known as "The Shadow," the unseen powerful force that pulled the puppet strings behind the curtain.

Petr walked down the alley way, ducking into another bar to check that he had not been followed. He exited the rear of the bar, and then slipped into another restaurant, repeating the process before he eventually arrived at the subway station. He boarded two different subways and passed through three different stations before he arrived back at his office, confident he had not been followed. He then resumed his work, transferring generals from one unit to another and dispatching orders for certain military units to be rotated to the capital while others were sent to the front. It was all a well-orchestrated charade to ensure that units loyal to him and his benefactors were in place when Fradkov had his heart attack.

Gromley had helped place Fradkov in power, along with his generals and cronies. Now he was removing them from command because of their incompetence. He had advised against attacking the Americans and Europeans, arguing that they should wait at least a year to let the IR and Chinese weaken America first. Fradkov and his generals would not listen. Now Fradkov wanted to join Premier Jinping's Pan Asian Alliance. Giving up Russian sovereignty in a vain attempt to save his war was one step too far for the oligarchy who really ran the Russian government to endure. Fradkov needed to be removed and replaced before the war was truly lost. There was still time to make an honorable peace, but not if they waited much longer. The sudden loss of their Artic bases in Murmansk was the final straw.

Chapter 48
The New Colonizer of Africa

12 October 2042
Pretoria, South Africa

Wang Ma was the Chinese Ambassador to the African Confederation; over time, he had become perhaps the most important man on the continent. For nearly four decades, China had been investing heavily into Africa and, in particular, South and East Africa. They had invested in developing industrial ports, heavy rail networks, international airports and other major infrastructure projects. During the 2020s, while the rest of the world was suffering a global depression and food shortages, the Chinese government had been working with their African partners to develop industrial-sized farms and an intricate water system that turned large swaths of previously unusable land into fertile farmlands for commercial farmers.

The Chinese began to cultivate leaders and political parties over the course of several decades, ensuring there were always political leaders and parties that were sympathetic and friendly to Chinese policies and initiatives. The Chinese also encouraged their own citizens to emigrate to the African nations and removed any limits on the number of children a Chinese family could have if they relocated to an African country. After several decades, this had led to a massive Chinese diaspora in multiple African nations; they began to exert immense political and economic sway over these countries.

When World War III broke out, many of these African nations chose to remain neutral. However, once it appeared that America was going to lose, many of these nations chose to join China in declaring war against America. Led by handpicked leaders in South Africa, Botswana, Namibia, Mozambique, Madagascar and Zimbabwe, the African Confederation had been born in March of 2041. With assistance from the PLA, the "African Confed" (as it was being called) began a conquest of their neighbors, with the intent of uniting Africa under one banner, one policy.

While Europe and America were fighting for their very survival against the Islamic Republic, the Russian Federation, and the People's Republic of China, the African Confed had been conquering one African nation after another. By the end of 2041, the nations of Zambia, Tanzania, Kenya, Uganda, Rwanda, Burundi and the Democratic Republic of the Congo had fallen. Angola had willingly joined the Confederation and provided the Chinese Navy with South Atlantic naval ports.

By the summer of 2042, when the war in Europe had started to turn against the Russians and the Chinese had lost control of the Pacific, the African Confederation had conquered all of Central Africa and half of Nigeria. The brunt of the fighting taking place on the continent now centered around parts of Cameroon and Nigeria as the Americans and the South American Multination Force began to provide military assistance to the fledgling governments, trying to do their best to fight against this new force.

Ambassador Wang Ma's purpose in Africa was simple--assist the African Confed in winning their war and in developing a sustainable long-term government and economy that could continue to support and sustain Chinese global dominance. Though Wang had been born in mainland China, he had spent most of his life in Africa. His father was a prominent businessman and had earned billions in mining and railroads; he had helped stitch Africa together through hundreds of thousands of miles of train tracks and brought enormous economic prosperity to the continent by linking their vital mineral resources with the very hungry Chinese manufacturers who would purchase those goods. The railroads he had helped to build also linked the countries together, growing the economies and bringing the people of the continent together. His legacy had helped to cement China as the nation who had brought Africa into the 21st century and beyond.

His son, Wang Ma, not only inherited his father's wealth, political connections and business, he was later appointed the Ambassador to South Africa and then the African Confederation. He was well liked and trusted by nearly every leader and businessman on the continent, and was considered to be an African, even if he was Chinese.

America, on the other hand, had paid little attention to Africa during the past thirty years, focusing instead on internal domestic problems and their continued antagonistic relationships with the Middle East, Russia and China. This had enabled the Chinese to cultivate a multi-decade long relationship with the current and future leaders of the continent.

Ma's directive from the People's Republic of China (PRC) ruling committee was simple--guide the African Confederation in their conquest, but prepare them to support China in the war against the Americans if needed. Shortly after the loss of the PLAN fleet near Southern California and Hawaii, it became apparent that Africa would need to play a larger role in the Chinese plans for global dominance. America was slowly taking back control of the Pacific; that much was apparent. What the PRC needed to do, was solidify their hold in Africa and southeast Asia and ensure that no matter what happened, they would be too big for the Americans to conquer.

Wang Ma had worked with the President of the African Confederation to sign a military pact with China, and began construction of a military industrial complex that could support and sustain a modern military. The military forces the Confederation had were merely adequate for the regional conquest they had been undertaking. They were used to fighting other poorly trained and equipped armies. The Allies, however, were anything but poorly trained and equipped.

Ambassador Ma worked with his African counterparts to identify young men and women who could be trained as drone pilots to form the backbone of a new Air Force. Drone aircraft were cheap and easy to manufacture in comparison to an advanced fifth generation stealth fighter. It was also easier to train someone how to operate a drone than a plane. Ma's counterpart, General Ming, had 100 drone pilot instructors brought to Africa, and they immediately began an aggressive program of training new drone pilots.

Four new military airbases were built, an intense ten-week drone pilot training school was constructed, and the new crop of drone pilots began to be trained. Multiple state-of-the-art 3D printing fabrication facilities were built across the confederation, and the construction of thousands of fighter/bomber drones had begun. The challenge Ma and General Ming faced was finding enough skilled workers who could man these advanced manufacturing plants and repair the machines to keep them operational. Most of 2041 and 2042 was spent training a workforce that could handle these tasks and develop a nucleus of skilled workers who could, in turn, train more people.

President Aliko Dangote had been the leader of the African Congressional Congress during the 2020s, and was the instrumental leader who advocated for the creation of the African Confederation. He had championed this cause for nearly twenty years, advocating for a stronger, unified Africa. He believed the 21st century was going to be the century of Africa, the rise of the continent from its past colonialization and resource pillaging from the West. With aid from the Chinese, Dangote built a grassroots network across many countries, garnering support from every political circle and walk of life he could. He was the young revolutionary leader the continent needed.

When the formation of the African Confederation began to take shape, he was nominated to become the leader of the movement, and later put forward as the nation's figurehead. He had worked closely with the leaders of China and Russia in developing the needed foundations of a successful government and country. They needed a functioning economy and the ability to feed their own people. Through a myriad of trade agreements, the African Confederation became a major global food producer. This provided the needed counterbalance to the American-led Grain Consortium, which had formed under President Stein.

President Dangote admired President Stein's rise to power and what he was doing in America. In many ways, Dangote wanted to emulate what he saw Stein doing in America, but he also had to be cautious. Dangote owed his rise to power and the formation of the African Confederation to the Chinese, not the Americans. It was China that had poured hundreds of billions of dollars into infrastructure and education across Africa, not the Americans. It was China who had provided them with the engineers they needed to bring stable and renewable power sources to Africa. Who had established a manufacturing base and increased food production using genetically modified crops and dozens of irrigation projects? China.

Dangote had done what he could to keep the Confederation's focus on Africa and not the global war being waged against the major superpowers. He was of the mind that Africa would work with whomever won, but that was not to be the case. His Chinese leaders had other plans in mind. While he wanted to focus on uniting Africa under one banner, his Chinese bosses wanted him to train a military force that would be used against the Americans. He had reluctantly agreed and authorized the creation of a new International Force that would serve with the Chinese wherever they deemed necessary.

The Chinese had nearly 260,000 soldiers stationed in the African countries, spread across numerous provinces. They had assisted

Dangote's forces in the capture of many countries and in the institution of law and order. Now, they were being used as military trainers and advisors to train the nearly 850,000-man army he had been told to draft. Most of the people being drafted into the army could barely read and write their name. The Chinese did not seem to care. They had established a dozen training bases, and began to filter the recruits through their training program. By the end of 2041, the PLA had trained 330,000 soldiers. As they completed training, they were quickly moved to the north of the country to fight with other PLA soldiers who were moving in to capture the Horn of Africa and some of the other provinces from the now-defeated Islamic Republic. Clashes with American and Israeli soldiers were becoming more common, but no direct military engagements between the armies had yet been fought. The PLA was more concerned with grabbing land and consolidating their gains.

What concerned Dangote was the treatment of the civilians in the former IR provinces. He knew the PLA could be brutal when they needed to be, but if the rumors were true, then he was horrified. The PLA had been eliminating nearly every civilian in Somalia and South Sudan. Rather than feed the people they were conquering, the Chinese began a process of systematically killing the population off. While China may have been allied with the Islamic Republic, they did not like or agree with the Islamic faith. The People's Republic of China had been brutal in their treatment of their own Muslims, and now that they were conquering former Muslim lands, they were doing whatever they could to eradicate the religion and the people who practiced it.

President Dangote had already brought the issue up to Ambassador Wa once, and he was quickly told not to concern himself with what the PLA was doing and to focus internally on winning the war with Cameroon and Nigeria. Dangote was not comfortable with how the Chinese were using his soldiers and was becoming less content with the PLA's ever-increasing control of his own military. His best officers were being transferred into the International Force that the PLA was training at an alarming rate. Secretly, he feared the Chinese would depose him and just assume control of Africa once he had done the hard task of unifying the continent.

Up until that point, the Americans had left the African Confederation alone. They had no real diplomatic ties with the country, and were solely focused on the wars in Europe and on their own soil.

However, once the PLAN lost the majority of their naval forces near California and Hawaii, Dangote began to wonder how long the Americans would stay away from Africa. Just when it seemed they had been defeated, they rose from the ashes and squashed their enemy. Would they repeat this history in Africa?

Chapter 49
Liberators

12 October 2042
Washington, DC
Presidential Emergency Operations Center

President Stein was sitting in his chair at the head of the table in the PEOC, listening to the military advisors around the table talk about the next steps in the war. America had been in conflict for three years now. Millions of people had died as war had been brought directly to Main Street, America. At least after a bloody summer campaign in Alaska, the Chinese and Russians had been defeated and had withdrawn the majority of their troops, leaving those that could not be rescued to surrender. Nearly 128,000 Chinese and 83,200 Russian soldiers had been captured once it was clear they were not going to be rescued.

The re-capture of the Hawaiian Islands and Midway Island a month ago meant the American navy was finally back in control of the Pacific. The US had completed construction of two additional Supercarriers and moved them to the Pacific to join the three operational carriers of CSG12. President Stein had appointed Admiral Michael Stonebridge to be the new Seventh Fleet Commander, and directed him to work with General Gardner on developing a plan to liberate Japan and the Pacific from the Chinese.

Admiral Juliano observed that Stein only appeared to be half listening. "Mr. President," he said, gently tapping the desk and hoping to gain his fully attention. "We have to be realistic in our expectations regarding taking back the Pacific from the Chinese. I know we have just scored two huge victories in recovering Alaska and in seeing a successful coup in Japan, but the liberation of the Pacific is going to take time."

The President understood the challenges; the Pacific was a big ocean. Despite the defeat of the Chinese fleet, they still possessed dozens of submarines and other surface ships. They had also established a network of military bases throughout the South China Sea that had been turned into missile bases. Penetrating the Chinese missile swarms to get close enough to their shores and industrial heartland was going to be difficult, but not impossible.

"What I want from everyone is a realistic plan of how we are going to bring this war to a close. We have popular uprisings that we are supporting in the Philippines, Vietnam and now Japan. The Chinese will squash these uprisings if we are not able to offer more assistance. What are your suggestions?"

Admiral Juliano jumped in saying, "Sir, I have redirected our SUDs to the South China Sea to start engaging Chinese shipping. We are also going to start placing a bigger emphasis on going after the shipping between the African Confederation and China as well. Not nearly enough has been done to try and sever the mineral and natural resource pipeline between Africa and China that is keeping their factories going. I also believe we should step up our insertion of Special Forces to these countries."

General Branson agreed. "We need to send more Special Forces to these countries to help. I also think we should increase the number and type of weapons we provide them. The Chinese are deploying their own version of the M5 AIR, so I do not believe we should hold out on providing them to the insurgent forces any longer. These weapons would greatly increase their ability to conduct hit and run attacks."

"I agree" echoed CIA Director Rubio. "We held these weapons back in the past because we needed them for our own forces. Now it's time to step up the scale and type of weapons we provide them."

"All right then," said the President. "General Branson, Director Rubio, move forward with the new plans, and let's see what more we can do to help sow some chaos. In the meantime, I want to know--what is our strategy and plan for liberating Japan and the rest of the Pacific? What forces do we need, and when will we have them?"

Admiral Juliano brought up a new image on the holographic monitor for them to look at. "Sir, what you are looking at is our initial plan for re-securing the Pacific. We have four of our new *Reagan* class Supercarriers and three of our older *Nimitz* class Supercarriers in the Pacific. We also have four of our *Webb* class Battleships." On-screen he also showed the list of cruisers, destroyers and frigates that were also assigned to the Seventh Fleet. It had taken several years, but the navy finally had the ships it needed to take the Pacific back.

"Our plan is to liberate Japan first, then move to assist Taiwan. To free Japan, we are going to need to secure a launch platform from which we can move in air support to help on the main Island. We have identified the island of Hokkaido as our best location to use for housing our aircraft." A map of the Island was brought up with several identified landing zones, airports and other strategic targets that would need to be secured.

"The assault against the Kola Peninsula in Russia with the EHDs was a resounding success. We are going to use that same strategy to capture Hokkaido. Four of our *American* class amphibious assault ships are currently being outfitted with EHD simulator pods just like the ship that we used in Russia. These four ships will be able to carry an assault force of 8,000 Reaper drone operators. Once the key objectives have been secured, we will begin to ferry in tens of thousands of Raptor-equipped soldiers to capture the rest of the Island. With the Island under our control, we'll begin to move in additional men and material and get ready to liberate the rest of the Japan."

The President looked over the information, and asked several clarifying questions, but in general, he agreed with the premise of the plan. Then he probed about a more pressing issue. "What I want to know is when this plan will be ready to execute?"

General Branson saw this as his opportunity. "Sir, it is going to take time to get everything ready and in position. We anticipate launching the invasion of Hokkaido in February, and then moving to the rest of Japan in May of 2043. At that point, we will have 12,000 EHDs available for the operation, and the necessary ships to support the mission."

After thinking about the information provided, the President responded, "I'd like to take the rest of the evening to think about it. Why don't we dismiss the meeting for now, and we can come back tomorrow?"

There were no arguments from the group, so the President returned to the Residence to mull things over.

Chapter 50
The Man No One Was Supposed to See

14 October 2042
Moscow, Russia

The loss of the Kola Peninsula was a heavy blow to Russian morale, and the darkness sat in the air. As President Mikhail Fradkov sat in his office, he was wondering why Petr Gromley had insisted they meet today. Today was not a good day for a surprise visit; he had a strategy meeting with his foreign minister and military leaders to discuss the Pan Asian Alliance. He wanted to see if there was a way for Russia to join the alliance and still maintain their sovereignty. Fradkov knew Gromley and the men he represented were against the deal, but he did not care. He was the President, and this alliance was Fradkov's way of ensuring he stayed in power despite what Gromley and his benefactors thought or said.

Mikhail had woken up that morning feeling a bit strange. He was more tired than usual, and his heart had been racing all morning. As the palpitations continued, his hands started to feel clammy, and he thought to himself, "*I had better check in with my doctor after my meeting with Gromley. Petr had better have a really good reason for insisting on meeting today. I have a busy schedule, and this meeting is an interruption.*"

As President Fradkov got up from his desk and began to walk towards the door in his office, the pain overwhelmed him. He grabbed his chest. It felt like an elephant was sitting on him. He could not breathe. He was frozen there for a moment before he realized that he must be having a heart attack; he gasped for air, but could find none. As his world turned black, he couldn't help but wonder if this was Gromley's doing.
****

Petr Gromley's smartphone vibrated slightly in his pocket. He pulled it out and saw the message; President Fradkov had had a heart attack and was confirmed dead. The President's doctor would confirm Fradkov had died of a massive coronary arrest, citing "natural causes" and leaving no suspicion that he had actually been assassinated. As Gromley approached the entrance to President's office (where the other leaders of the Russian government were expecting to meet with Fradkov), he reveled in what was about to take place.

The double doors were opened for him by the President's personal guard, who had been personally selected by Gromley and his associates. As he walked into the room, he saw General Gerasimov, the Head of Russian Military, LTG Igor Dmitrievich Sergun, Director of the GRU (Russian military intelligence), Sergei Puchkov, Minister of Defense, Nikolai Bortnikov, Director of the FSB, and several other members of the ruling council.

Nikolai Bortnikov was not able to hide his facial expressions when Gromley walked in the door; his eyebrows seemed to reach for the ceiling. He was also the first to speak. "Petr--what are you doing here? We are about to meet with President Fradkov."

As the rest of the men in the room noticed the half a dozen armed guards standing just outside the office, they all started to look as surprised as Bortnikov.

Gromley barely managed to hide a smile as he sat down at the table cavalierly and addressed the group, "President Fradkov has just suffered a heart attack and died."

As several of the men gasped in shock, Gromley pulled a pistol outfitted with a silencer out of his jacket, and shot director Bortnikov in the head. Before anyone else in the room could respond in any way, he fired off two more bullets, shooting General Gerasimov and General Sergun, killing them instantly. He motioned to the others, insisting that they stay calm and seated. The guards that had been standing outside the room stepped in and immediately began to move the bodies of the men Gromley had just shot.

Petr calmly walked over to the head of the table, placing the pistol down in front of him as he took a seat. He calmly announced, "A change of leadership has been called for, and I have stepped in to implement it. The rest of you sitting here have been determined to not have been a part of the corruption at the core of this government. You will be allowed to live so long as you do as you are told."

The others in the room let out a collective sigh of relief.

"It has been determined that I should assume control of the Russian Federation. I have the full backing of the men who matter, and you will either fall in line and support me and this government, or you may leave. If you stay, there is no turning back, and no questioning of my orders." Petr's statement made it sound like he was giving everyone a chance to leave...of course, no one left. To leave would have meant a bullet in the back of the head.

Seeing that he had their undivided attention, Gromley snapped his fingers, letting the guards know to send in the others. Eight other men in dark suits, some known and others unknown to the men at the table, walked in and sat down at the empty seats and opened their tablets, ready to begin work.

"Effective immediately, Russia is stopping our work on the Pan Asian Alliance. We are not going to join the Chinese and become a puppet to them. Russia will not surrender its sovereignty to a ruling committee."

Petr gestured towards a few of the others in the room as he began, "These three men are going to handle the negotiations with the Chinese, and will convey our decision to not continue with the alliance."

Those three men nodded, and then proceeded to get up and leave the room, heading out to implement their tasks.

"The loss of the Kola Peninsula has placed our country in a precarious position. The Americans have once again surprised the world with yet another breakthrough technology, their enhanced humanoid drone, the Reaper. We have no counter to this new superweapon. We also do not have the ability to create our own version of it, at least not right now with our current technology and available resources."

One of the newcomers to the room linked his tablet with the holographic display at the center of the table. He immediately brought up several clips of the EHD in action. The group watched as several of them advanced on a Russian machine gun position in the Kola Peninsula, and saw the EHD get hit several times but still continue to advance. In short order, the drone had killed the men operating the gun position and then moved on to the next target.

"Gentlemen, I do not need to explain to you what will happen when the Americans begin to deploy tens of thousands of these drones on our soil. Combing through the footage, we estimate it took our men nearly 50 soldiers to kill or disable one of those drones. These are odds we simply cannot sustain. The war is lost. The question now is--when will we accept that?"

"I am immediately promoting General Viktor Lodz to take over as commander of all Russian military forces. He will oversee the winding down of the war with NATO and bring us an honorable peace we can live with."

As Gromley was explaining this, one of the other generals at the table, a man who was clearly angry that he had just been passed over as the next in line to take over, asked, "And what if he cannot secure us an honorable peace? Will the war continue?"

Knowing this was also a possibility, Petr had a prepared response. "If General Lodz is not able to secure an honorable peace, then we will remind President Stein and the allies that Russia can and will still bring this war to their streets. We may not be able to use our nuclear weapons as a deterrent or threat like we had in the past, but we certainly can unleash biological weapons and cyber-attacks in perpetuity."

The general was clearly taken aback by the mention of biological weapons. No matter how bad the war had gotten, President Fradkov and President Stein had come to an understanding that neither side would use weapons that would destroy the people of either nation. This included the use of neutron and biological weapons. The devastation of the neutron weapon used against the IR was still being calculated, and had been responsible for the death of over a hundred million people up to that point.

Petr motioned that he was gearing to wrap up the meeting. "After we announce the death of President Fradkov and my taking over as the leader of the Russian Federation, I am going to call for an immediate 48-hour ceasefire and ask for an opportunity to talk with President Stein directly to determine if we can work out an honorable end to the war."

They looked solemn but also accepting of the fact that Russia could no longer win the war. The best that they could hope for now was obtaining a ceasefire that allowed Russia to maintain its dignity in defeat.

Chapter 51
Negotiator in Chief

16 October 2042
Washington, DC

The sudden death of President Fradkov and the change of leadership within the Russian Federation sent shock waves throughout the world. The Russian government requested a ceasefire and direct talks between the man who had emerged as the new leader of Russia, Petr Gromley, and President Stein. The key questions being asked in Washington were--who is Petr Gromley, and how did he become the President? No one seemed to know the answers, and this concerned President Stein and his senior staff. How did a seemingly unknown individual suddenly become the President of Russia?

President Stein did ultimately decide to agree to a 48-hour ceasefire and direct talks with President Gromley. As the intelligence community scrambled to learn as much as they could about Petr Gromley, an appointed time for a holographic telecom was set. Twenty-three hours after the ceasefire went into effect, the two leaders would have their first discussion.

As the President sat on one of the two couches in the Oval Office, he stared out the window for a second, collecting some of his thoughts. The President nervously asked Director Rubio, "Have we learned anything more about who Petr Gromley is? I'd like to know a bit more about the man I will be speaking with in a few hours."

Director Rubio gestured towards a middle-aged analyst he had brought with him to this meeting. "Mr. President, this is Dr. Jason Strom. He's from our Russian division, and had studied and worked for many years in Russia for us before returning to the US and official cover with the Agency. I will let Dr. Strom brief you on what he has been able to dig up."

Dr. Strom was clearly anxious about briefing the President. He stammered at first before clearing his throat to start over. "Mr. President, while I was in Russia, I came across the name Petr Gromley only once. I learned that he was a successful businessman, but also had deep ties with the SVR, part of the FSB foreign intelligence arm. There was relatively little information I could compile while in Russia and through my subsequent dive back into his history these past 23 hours; however, we were able to link him to several the major oligarchs that run the various industrial sectors in Russia. We also linked him to several senior military and intelligence officials who are also now in charge of the government. What we found interesting about his connections was how diverse they are. He is well-connected both with Russian power brokers and military leaders, and also with members of the financial sector, both domestic and abroad. For instance, his wife is an active member of the Rothschild family."

The President digested the information and sat silently thinking about what it meant before asking a follow up question. "So, what you are saying is, this guy is a very well-connected man both in Russia and outside of Russia. He has money, influence and contacts in critical areas within the government. Yet he also appears to have some sort of connection, a deep connection, with the SVR. What was his connection with Fradkov before he died?"

Glancing at his notes for just a second, "Gromley knew Fradkov; they had attended the same military school and college, and they worked in the FSB together for a short period. I have not had enough time with my sources still in Russia to really gain a full understanding of their relationship, but it is safe to say they knew each other for a very long time." Dr. Strom spoke with increasing confidence as he started to feel more comfortable with briefing the President.

President Stein took a sip of coffee; he was in the process of cutting out his steady diet of Red Bulls. His physician had said they were partly to blame for his headaches, so he had to find another source of caffeine. As the President placed his mug down on the table between his guests, he looked at Director Rubio and asked, "Do you believe there is a bit more to Gromley than we may think? Looking at what I've read and now heard from Dr. Strom, Gromley seems to be more of the spy master or chess master, moving players around the board. I find it strange that most of the individuals with whom we know he had strong connections prior to the death of Fradkov, suddenly find themselves in critical positions within the Army. Not to mention the very suspicious sudden deaths of nearly a dozen other figure heads within the government right around the time of Fradkov's death--it almost seems like his death was planned, but that's just me speculating."

Director Rubio nodded in agreement. "I believe you may be right, Mr. President. This could have been an internal well thought out plan. The question then, is if this is, then what is their end state?"

Dr. Strom knew he should probably not say anything since it was clear his section of the brief had concluded, but he could not help himself. "Mr. President, if I could, I believe Gromley's intensions will be to bring some sort of honorable end to the war. If he truly represents the oligarchs and elites within the country, then they know the war is no longer winnable, at least not without destroying Russia in the process. They have too much to lose in that scenario, and they must have believed that Fradkov would probably never pursue peace."

The President thought about this for a moment. "You may be right, though I think their decision probably had more to do with the likelihood that Fradkov was going to move forward with the Pan Asian Alliance. Joining the alliance was probably the only way to save his war. Our capture of Murmansk has shaken them to their core, and we are now positioned to strike deep behind their European lines."

CIA Director Rubio responded, "I think that is a safe assumption, Mr. President. From the intercepts we have from China, they were not going to provide Fradkov with reinforcements or additional military equipment unless he agreed to join the alliance. They had promised him one million PLA soldiers if he agreed to join, and it looks like he was probably going to get Russia to accept the agreement."

The President let out a soft sigh and looked out the window again, drifting away to a far-away world before returning. "Gentlemen, you both have given me a lot to think about. If you will excuse me, I am going to spend the next hour thinking about this meeting and formulating some questions and potential responses to them." With that, the President indicated that it was time for them to leave the Oval Office and allow him some time alone.

As President Stein sat at his desk, he began to pen several scenarios out, and wrote some goals he wanted to achieve during the meeting. He also put together a list of demands, if the Russians did want an end to the war.
****

Two hours later, President Stein walked down to the PEOC to have his virtual meeting with President Gromley. As the President walked into the communications room, he sat down at the center of the table. Just out of sight was General Branson, the Chairman of the Joint Chiefs, Jim Wise, the Secretary of State, Eric Clarke, the Secretary of Defense and Patrick Rubio, the Director of the CIA. Monty, the President's Chief of Staff and senior advisor was seated next to the President with a pad of paper and a pen. The President signaled that he was ready to receive the call. In seconds, a message was sent to the Russians to let them know President Stein was ready to start the meeting.

A minute later, the holographic screen came to life, and a life-size image of President Petr Gromley appeared opposite of President Stein at the table. President Gromley spoke perfect English, and initiated the discussion saying, "Mr. President, thank you for agreeing to meet with me and for the immediate ceasefire. As you know, President Fradkov suffered a massive heart attack. I was asked to step in as interim President until a new election can be held in two years. One of my goals as the new President is to work with you to find a way to bring this war between our nations to an end."

With the ball now in his court, President Stein now had to decide; did he want to pursue an end to the war then? Or did he want to fight on and end the war on their terms, as an unconditional surrender?

"Thank you for reaching out to me, President Gromley. Congratulations to you on becoming President. I am glad to hear that your government would like to pursue an end to this war. I must tell you; I am not sure Russia is willing to agree to our terms. We have been committed to nothing less than an unconditional surrender of Russia," Stein said, laying out his initial starting point for these talks. He wanted the new Russian leader to know that America was committed to continuing this war out to its conclusion; they did not need to agree to a peace just yet.

Gromley knew President Stein would want to set his terms. From everything he had read about Henry Stein, he knew he was a shrewd negotiator…tough, but fair. Russia had inflicted some serious wounds on America, and President Stein was going to want America's pound of Russian flesh in return.

"I am sure you understand, Mr. President; the Russian Federation cannot accept those terms as they are presently laid out. We have suffered some battlefield defeats, but we are far from defeated as a nation. My government's goal is to end this war and the bloodshed. As you are aware, the reinforcements from our Indian allies have arrived.

Their forces have not been committed yet, but their introduction to the European front will have an impact. I would like to negotiate an honorable end to the war and not have to commit them to the defeat of NATO."

The President shifted slightly in his chair before responding, "Thank you, President Gromley, for being open and more importantly direct. So, let me be direct with you as well, so we can save each other a lot of time and remove any confusion. The Russian Federation, in coordination with the Islamic Republic and the People's Republic of China, launched a massive surprise attack against the United States, Israel and our NATO allies. This was an unprovoked attack that has claimed the lives of tens of millions of people in the United States and our allied nations. I would like to find a way to end this war with your nation, but it will be on favorable terms to the United States and our allies, or we can continue this war until my forces have either captured or killed you and your government." Stein spoke forcefully but respectfully.

Gromley shifted uncomfortably in his chair. "Mr. President, what terms would you find acceptable?"

"For starters, Russia would need to withdraw all military forces from NATO member territories. Russia would also need to begin an immediate demobilization of your military force, allowing no more than 330,000 active duty soldiers. This number is consistent with your force structure from ten years ago, prior to your military buildup."

President Stein glanced at his notes very briefly before he continued, "Next, the Russian government would have to take responsibility for any war crimes your forces may have committed in the occupied territories, and pay reparations to the families. The exact amount would be determined by an international tribunal. Russia would also have to agree to an end of the ongoing cyber-attacks, cyber-espionage and cyber warfare being conducted against the United States and our allies. Finally, Russia would have to agree to a ten-year moratorium on any space exploration or space activities."

Gromley had figured that the President would most likely ask for everything he had just mentioned, with the exception of the space exploration moratorium. That was one area the oligarchs wanted to pursue since the advent of the EmDrive. Once the news had been made public about the American Pegasus project, space exploration and mining had become a top priority of the oligarchs. The mining and exploration possibilities were endless, and the war was the inhibiting factor in allowing Russia to pursue them.

"Mr. President, I can agree to most of these terms. What Russia will not give up is our possession of our former satellite nations, including the Caucus region and the 'Stan' countries. We can agree to withdraw our forces from the Scandinavian countries, Eastern Europe and Turkey. Would this return of territory be acceptable?"

Looking to his advisors for guidance, the President saw General Branson, Secretary Wise, and Director Rubio nod their heads. Stein summoned a bit of acting to make himself appear very reluctant as he replied, "We can agree to those terms; Russia can keep the Caucus region and the Stans."

Gromley continued, "I am not sure I can agree to the force reduction to 330,000 soldiers. We have more than four million men and women in uniform right now. I cannot simply release that many millions of soldiers without experiencing severe unemployment and civil unrest. We can work towards that number over a multiple year period, but I cannot cut that many soldiers overnight." Petr said as he offered his first bit of resistance to the American President.

President Stein's advisors just shrugged their shoulders and nodded. "Thank you for that clarification and justification. Let's agree to a force reduction down to two million soldiers over the next six months, one million soldiers in eighteen months and five hundred thousand soldiers in two years and we leave it at that level," Stein said, trying to offer a concession.

Gromley and Stein continued to negotiate for an hour about other details of the peace agreement, hammering out the major sticking points leaving the smaller points to their advisors and assistants who would pick it back up later.

Finally, things seemed more or less settled, until Gromley interjected, "Mr. President-- about the space moratorium--the Russian Federation cannot agree to a ten-year moratorium on space exploration and activities. Our government has done many years of research on the EmDrive technology Just as America is now establishing space mining operations, with the war concluded, Russia would like to pursue this opportunity as well. It would be a boon to our economy, and help aid Russia in recovering from this devastating conflict. It would also create a lot of employment opportunities for our citizens in the domestic economy as opposed to in the defense industry," Gromley explained.

Stein felt caught off guard. "Humph," he grunted. "My concern with allowing Russia unfettered access into this new frontier is that Russia would use these new-found resources and capabilities to rearm, and once again threaten the free world." Stein had felt optimistic up to this point, but he was concerned that this might by the sticking point that would kill the whole negotiation.

Gromley assumed President Stein would fight him on this area; he also knew that he needed to assure President Stein that Gromley's government was not interested in fighting America again. His benefactors wanted to return to making money, and they ultimately just looked forward to not having to constantly watch their backs because of the risk that they might possibly get killed by an American airstrike or Special Forces unit.

"This is a point I cannot negotiate away, Mr. President. I understand your concern and your unwillingness to trust or take my word that Russia will not look to find a way to restart the war. To give you a more steadfast assurance, what if we offered to have American or NATO observers work within our civilian space program? We are not asking for a joint venture, but allowing NATO to observe our civilian program would ensure that we are not militarizing our space industry. We can agree to a ten-year observation regimen. Would that be an acceptable outcome?" Gromley was truly hoping that they could come to an agreement on this area; if Russia was going to turn away from its military economy, then it was going to need to have a new sector of the economy to turn to and the space industry represented that opportunity.

President Stein hated the idea of letting Russia benefit from establishing a civilian space economy and industry. Russia had cost the lives of millions of people, and now they wanted to be rewarded with this new lucrative industry. However, Henry also understood that if an equitable peace was not achieved, it would only lead to further animosity and conflict. The US *could* continue the war until they had thoroughly defeated the Russians. The challenge was, if they did persist in the conflict, it would probably drag on for another year; hundreds of thousands of soldiers would be killed, and eventually, America and NATO would have to occupy Russia, which would bring its own unique challenges.

President Stein contemplated his options until he made a firm decision; he realized that not everyone would agree with his choice, but he hoped to be able to bring them around after logical explanations. Resolute, he responded, "President Gromley, this is going to be a tough sell. I need to consult with my fellow allied leaders before I give a definitive answer. If we do agree, we would want to have an observation group for at least fifteen years, not ten."

Knowing that this was probably the best deal he was going to get while still accomplishing his benefactor's goals, Gromley nodded in acceptance of President Stein's terms. "If the other allied leaders will agree to these terms, then the Russian Federation will accept them. I understand a lot of other details need to be worked out, and you need to discuss things with the other allied leaders. I would like to request that we extend the ceasefire for the duration of these talks. The fighting can resume if the talks break down, but I would like to put a stop to the killing while there is hope that the war may finally be over." Gromley hoped to gain his forces a bit of a reprieve. His forces could use the time to shift units around and prepare to restart operations, should the negotiations not progress.

"I am not willing to extend the ceasefire indefinitely. We will prolong the ceasefire for another five more days while I consult with our allies. If we are able to come to a consensus in that time, then we can move to formally end the war at that point. If all parties cannot come to acceptable terms over the next five days, then hostilities will continue," Stein said forcefully. The two leaders agreed, and the meeting was terminated.

Everyone in the room let out a collective sigh, and then the excitement emerged. The thought of ending the war with Russia in less than five days was something that none of them had thought possible just two days ago. America had been planning for at least another year of conflict with Russia. American factories were now using a nearly unlimited supply of Tritium4; this allowed them to produce nearly 1,000 Pershing tanks a month, and close to 200 of the F41 Archangel fighters. As new fighters were completed, they were quickly being formed into new squadrons and deployed to Europe. With the Chinese defeated in Alaska and California, and Japan having surrendered and now fighting China, the US had moved the bulk of their forces to Europe; not having

to fight Russia would allow America to consolidate their forces against the Pan Asian Alliance, and possibly end this war once and for all.
****

The next five days were a flurry of negotiations between the allied leaders and military advisors as they collectively discussed the terms of ending the war. Most of the leaders agreed that an end of the war should be pursued. Most of Europe had suffered horrendous damage to their infrastructure and economy. Refugees had also become a serious problem as countries scrambled to find enough suitable places to house them; there was also a significant economic strain as many of the refugees required at least some government assistance. As the fighting continued and intensified in Eastern Germany, Poland and southern Europe, more and more people had been displaced from their homes. The idea of stopping this mass humanitarian crisis was very appealing.

The one aspect of the peace terms that the allied leaders were having a hard time agreeing to was allowing Russia to pursue a space program. The EU and UK were reluctant to allow the Russians into the space industry, partially because they also wanted to participate in space exploration and mining, and they did not want the additional competition in the market. President Stein lobbied hard for the proposed international monitoring force that could keep tabs on the Russian program. He also reminded the British and the Europeans that this was a necessary evil if they were to end the war. Stein also reminded everyone of the lessons of World War I; implementing punitive policies against the vanquished foe did not end well then, and no one was eager for a new world conflict.

After three days of intense negotiations, the allied leaders agreed to the terms after adding several provisions to the stipulation about the NATO monitoring group of the Russian space program. With the final details hashed out, President Stein met one last time with President Gromley and laid out the minutiae of the agreement. After many hours of reviewing the document, which surprisingly was only 24 pages in length, President Gromley approved the terms and signed the document. They had effectively just ended the war.

The following day, a news conference was held, announcing to the world that the war between NATO and Russia had officially concluded. While not all the terms of the surrender were revealed, enough of the details were showcased to demonstrate that America and NATO had the upper hand in the negotiations.

The news, of course, was met with harsh rhetoric by the Chinese and the member states of the Pan Asian Alliance, who vowed to fight on despite the Russian treachery. China immediately cut off any ties they had with the Russians, and began to shift large numbers of troops to their northern border with Russia. As the intelligence community continued to monitor the troop movements, it was becoming clear that the Chinese were considering options to attack the Russian eastern territories since the Russian military had little in the way of forces in the area to defend against a possible Chinese invasion. The Allies had also devastated the Trans-Siberian Railway and road network that connected western Russia with their eastern provinces; this would make countering a Chinese move nearly impossible.

The Russians had anticipated something like this happening, and had begun to airlift thousands of soldiers to their military bases in the east. They also had several of their armored divisions withdraw from Poland and the Ukraine, moving these fighters towards their eastern provinces via the road network. As they would encounter a destroyed portion of the railroad, they would repair as they went. The Allies began to be grateful that they had agreed to delaying the drawdown of the Russian military by six months; hopefully, this would allow them time to resolve the situation with China.

The US also began to shift forces back from Europe to the West Coast of America, and all of the EHD Reaper drones were also brought back to domestic territory. New plans for occupying Japan (and assisting them in removing the Chinese) began in earnest. The US would need to use Japan as a base of operations if they were going to consider a ground invasion of China. Secretary of State, Jim Wise, also began secretive talks with Korea. The Koreans had stayed neutral throughout the war, per their agreement with China. Secretary Wise hoped to change that decision once they saw that China was going to be invaded. His hope was to gain approval from the Koreans to allow the US to use their land as another invasion point into northern China.

As hostilities in Europe concluded, Israel, the EU, and the UK began to move soldiers and aircraft to the West Coast of America. They would also participate in the occupation of Japan and the eventual invasion of China. It had been decided nearly a year ago, at the Saint Mary Islands Conference, that China would need to be broken up. No permanent end to the war could be achieved unless China became a less powerful entity.

Chapter 52
Mr. Speaker

22 November 2042
Washington, DC
Capital Building, Office of the Speaker of the House

The Speaker of the House and deputy chair of the Freedom Party, George Fultz, was a close friend of President Henry Stein and his Chief of Staff, Michael Montgomery. The three of these men had fashioned the blueprint for the Freedom Party, and through their business savviness, self-funding, and brute determination, had formed a fierce political machine in Florida that saw them capture the Governor's office and then the state assembly and senate. Two years after taking the Governor's office, Speaker Fultz ran for Congress in 2030, and then began the grassroots work with Monty to establish hundreds of field offices across the country. They began to identify congressional districts that they felt they could capture and candidates that shared their same views for the country.

By 2042, the Freedom party had gained control of four-fifths of the governors' offices and State legislatures. The party had pushed through a lot of changes in federal laws and the Constitution. They limited the role of the Supreme Court back to the original intent of the Founding Fathers, removing their ability to legislate from the bench. No longer would judicial supremacy be allowed. They also changed the tenure of the chief justices. No longer were they life time appointments; they were now limited in their appointments to fifteen years. Following their service on the Supreme Court, they were ineligible to hold any future public office. The decision to move in this direction was met with a lot of resistance from both parties; even some in the Freedom Party disagreed with it. However, the average tenure of a Supreme Court judge is 19.6 years, so establishing a 15-year tenure seemed fair. It also helped to ensure judges would not serve on the bench until they literally died in their seat.

On this Tuesday before Thanksgiving, Speaker Fultz was meeting with Monty to discuss a very important topic. He wanted to restructure the number of years in each Congressional, Senate, and Presidential term, and implement term limits. The Freedom Party wanted to get these changes passed while they still had the votes to do it. They needed to ensure the ideals and principles of the Constitution remained intact long after the supremacy of the Freedom Party.

Monty walked into the Speaker's Office and saw George standing near the window with a glass of cognac in his hand. As he walked towards George's desk, he saw a second glass waiting there for him and took it.

"I take it you have something important you want to talk about? That, or we are celebrating something," Monty said raising the glass of cognac.

George smiled wryly as he responded, "I want to propose some legislation, and I want to know if President Stein will support it or be against it."

"OK, what legislation are you thinking about?" asked Monty, hoping it wasn't anything too extreme.

Walking towards the two leather chairs in his office near the fireplace, George took a seat, and signaled for Monty to join him. "I want to redo the legislative terms and term limits of our elected officials." Monty raised an eyebrow, but didn't bring forward any objections.

"...I also want to redo the Presidential terms," added George.

Chuckling softly, Monty downed the rest of his drink and looked for a refill. "For a second there George, I thought you were going to talk about something really ambitious...you really want to move forward with this?" asked Monty.

"I do. The Freedom Party has done a lot for this country. We have given the USA new life and a new start at greatness. However, we may not always be in power. We need to use our influence now while we have it, in order to set our nation on a better path. If we don't do this, you can bet the government and our elected officials will return back to their old ways. They always do. We need to be the ones that break the cycle." George said with conviction. He believed Monty and the President wanted this as well. At least he hoped they did. Power can have a strange way of corrupting people.

"George, this has always been a goal for the President and for me as well, you know that. What do you have in mind?" asked Monty, leaning forward.

George tried to read Monty's response for a second before replying, "First, I'd like to address the Congress. The two-year election cycle can be convenient when you want to get rid of a Congressional member you dislike, but it also presents a real problem. They are always having to campaign and raise money. They spend most of their time fundraising, and not nearly enough hours doing their jobs. This needs to change. I am proposing we change congressional terms from two years to four years. We will also set term limits of no more than five terms. That way a person can only serve a maximum of twenty years; no more of these Washington dinosaurs that hold on to power until they die. As to the Senate, their six year terms will remain, but they will be limited to no more than three terms in the Senate. For the President, I am proposing a more radical change. One seven-year term as President. Typically, most of the President's first term is spent preparing to run for his or her second term; that mentality needs to end. I know President Stein was never like that, but we need to make sure future presidents are not stuck in that same cycle." George was excited to have an old friend to share this idea with, especially now that they were in a position of power to make it happen.

Monty sat back in his chair, polished off his second glass of cognac, and poured himself a third. "I like the idea. I know Henry will as well. But I sense you have something else you want to propose? Am I wrong?" Monty had a quizzical look that said he knew Fultz had another trick up his sleeve.

George snickered before answering, "Am I really that easy to read? Yes, I do have one more thing I want to propose. I want to overturn the 22nd Amendment, which as you know, limits the President to two terms. Of course, this will become a moot point after we enact the new legislative terms, but for the time being we need to change it (I think we can get enough governors to vote for the change, as long as they know that this new legislation will make it impossible for future presidents to run for endless amounts of terms). I want to know if you can convince Henry to run for a third term? We have a national election in 2044, which is sooner than one might think, and one of the things I would like to do is propose that we place the new proposed term limits on the ballot and give the people a chance to vote on them at that time. This will add further legitimacy to the change and ensure the term limits are not challenged in the future. Following the election, President Stein would then serve a seven-year term and then be done. But this way, we ensure we have Henry at the helm for seven more years to see our country through the post-war years and our adventure in space."

"Hmm…that *is* going to be a big ask. Henry will certainly go along with the ballot initiative, but I am not sure he will want to run for a third term, especially a seven-year term," Monty said, his voice dripping with regret.

George was a bit taken aback; the President was going to turn sixty in April, he was still more than capable of serving. "Really? You don't think Henry would want another term? His vision is not complete yet--doesn't he want to finish the work he has started?"

"It's not that he doesn't want to serve any longer. I think he is physically and mentally beat. The war has really taken a toll on him, and I do not know if he can handle another seven more years. I think it might be too much for him," explained Monty, who was a bit disappointed as well.

Fultz absorbed the information, and though for a moment. "Perhaps he just needs to take another vacation for a little while and rest, plan out what else he wants to do and then make that determination. Can you please convey my message and idea to him? I have a lot of things to get finalized before the end of the year if we are going to get these initiatives on the 2044 ballot."

Monty nodded, and George indicated that their meeting was done. As Monty got up to leave, he assured Speaker Fultz that he would convey the message to the President and do his best to get him onboard with it.

Chapter 53
Space Exports

15 December 2042
Lunar Base Stargate

Dr. Karl Bergstrom was still in awe of what they had accomplished on the Moon's surface these last eight months. The SpaceX transports were making a delivery of supplies every six days, bringing back tons of partially refined Tritium4 and Helium3 Isotopes. The mining operation had increased dramatically as well. With each trip from Earth, the transports would bring additional building materials and personnel. It had taken several months to construct the initial buildings on the lunar surface, but now they were complete. The first two structures were the farms; These buildings were 300 meters in length, 260 meters in width, and 75 meters in height; each one provided nearly 75,000 square meters of warehouse space to grow food for the burgeoning colony. The third building was the same size but divided up into different sections to house the livestock (since the experiment in raising chickens had been going well, they were going to try raising goats as well to provide a source of milk and cheese). The key to establishing a permanent colony on the Moon, was establishing a means of producing a sustainable food sources.

Another building was nearly completed; it would be six stories tall, with two subbasement levels. This one was meant to house the colonist workers, and would include a medical facility, cafeteria, communications room and a recreation room. Once completed, it would have room for up to 300 people. Each building was connected by a series of tunnels that enabled the workers to move between buildings and airlocks without having to suit up and leave the facility to enter another one. Though the structure of these edifices had been completed and sealed, it would still be months before the electrical wiring, heating, cooling, water and recycling systems were completed. Each building also had multiple airlocks, which were used for moving materials in and out of storage areas of the facility.

The various engineers estimated that it would be close to two more months until the remaining housing facilities were completed and the additional personnel could start arriving from Earth. Dr. Bergstrom was enjoying his work on the Moon immensely, but his heart ached to see his family. He had hoped that once the new housing structure was completed, he might be able to arrange for his family to move here to be with him. Unfortunately, the answer he was given was "no." They simply did not have enough room yet to allow people to bring their families with them. Right now, people assigned to the Pegasus Project were expected to serve a one-year term with a 30-day R&R at the six-month mark.

Dr. Bergstrom had been conducting intensive surveys and soil sampling of the Moon, identifying in detail what minerals and resources were located at different points across the lunar surface. Others in his research group were working on designing several heavy factories that would, in time, refine the materials being mined and fabricate additional building materials needed to expand the colony and build additional spacecraft. The construction crew was already hard at work assembling the foundation for multiple new buildings and an adjoining tram system that would link all of the buildings together. It was a massive undertaking, and would take years to complete. Several of the new housing structures were going to be 40 stories in height. The colony would then be able to house around 12,000 people, and would only grow from there.

Heavy deposits of iron, tungsten, copper, magnesium, aluminum and most importantly, water were found in abundance just below the Moon's surface. There was also Tritium4 and Helium3 isotopes in heavy concentrations. Most of the minerals were relatively close to the growing colony. The long-term goal was to get the various mining operations up and running and build out the factories, refineries, and fabrication facilities needed to make the colony self-sufficient. Eventually, they would be in a position to start constructing equipment for larger space exploration and colonization ships.

Karl enjoyed his work immensely; he was now the world's leading geologist and the man leading humanity into the stars in search of new minerals and opportunities for humanity to spread beyond Earth. His position had grown beyond just geological work; he was now among the leadership of the colony and a member of the space exploration committee, which was headed by Dr. Peter Gorka, the President's Chief Scientist. His ideas and suggestions for how America should explore space and what needed to be done to accomplish those goals were being heeded and implemented.

While he felt like he was making a difference for humanity, he felt his family life was starting to suffer immensely. He had been sequestered to work on the Pegasus Project for nearly six years now, only seeing his family for short bursts on weekends, holidays and their yearly vacation. In that time, he had poured his heart and soul into space exploration and mining. While his wife understood his passion and what he was doing for humanity, his children did not. All they knew was that their daddy worked 80 hours a week and was gone for weeks and sometimes months on end. His living on the Colony for a year was really stretching his relationship with his children. His son was seventeen and a senior in high school. He was a smart kid, and all of his classes were now AP classes that he was completing through a dual enrollment homeschooling program with Liberty University. His daughter was sixteen, and like her brother, was also a bit of a prodigy. Both of his kids were well on their way to attending some of the best universities in the world. His son wanted to go into physics, his daughter wanted to be a doctor. He wanted so much to be there for them while they were going through this pivotal time in their lives, but long-distance fatherhood of teenagers was proving to be quite challenging.

Karl was due to head back to Earth in four months, just in time for his son's eighteenth birthday and graduation from high school. What his son and wife did not know, is that Karl had been working behind the scenes to get his son an internship with Dr. Gorka's research assistant, Dr. Nikki Travosky. She was scheduled to take his place at the Colony when his one year assignment was completed. Nikki was a leading physicist and was working on developing the next generation in EmDrive propulsion that would allow humanity to explore well beyond the solar system. He was pulling some connections and leveraging his position on the President's science team to get his son into the MIT Physics program. Because his son had completed so many college credits through his dual enrollment program, he would go to MIT as a sophomore. His internship with Dr. Travosky would give his son an edge over all other students in the same program. He wanted to surprise his son with all of this when he arrived back home in four months. Of course, his wife would kill him once she found out their son's internship would place him on the lunar surface at the colony, but what an experience it would give his son. He hoped this would do something to bridge the divide that grown between him and his son.

Chapter 54
Whose Side are We on?

20 December 2042
Pretoria, South Africa
African Confederation Headquarters

President Aliko Dangote was starting to grow a bit concerned about his Chinese allies. The recent change in leadership within the Russian Federation had given him pause, and was causing him and some of his military leaders and advisors to question the longer-term feasibility of their relationship with China. With the Allies now focused completely on China, it was only a matter of time until the Chinese economy collapsed and their military was destroyed. The Americans had been attacking dozens of key bridges and dams across the Chinese interior, which was starting to wreak havoc on their ability to govern and maintain control of their population of more than two billion people.

Then there was the war in Africa. The Americans and Europe had not taken an active interest in it just yet, and Dangote wanted to make sure they did not. The Chinese insisted that Dangote continue the war in the Horn of Africa, Central Africa and the Gold Coast. What Dangote himself wanted most was to work on integrating the half of the continent that he currently controlled. The Chinese had been using his soldiers to carry out a genocide of the Horn of Africa; from the reports that he had been receiving from his generals, they were killing nearly everyone that lived in Somalia and Sudan. He tried to concentrate on the bright spots. The war in Cameroon was finally winding down, and his forces had finished off what was left of the government forces there. The war in Nigeria was turning into a stalemate.

President Dangote had been a good soldier. However, he was going to go against his Chinese puppet masters soon. He was going to start working on a peace with the Nigerians after the New Year. His goal was to bring an end to the fighting by February. His forces and the Chinese had two and a half months left to accomplish their tasks before he would unilaterally call an end to the war. He was President of the largest country in the world, but his hold on the country was tenuous at best. On paper, he controlled more than half of the continent; in actuality, he really only controlled the major cities, ports, and mining and oil fields.

He needed to produce a functioning government and law and order if he was going to maintain power, and that was not going to happen if his people continued to stay at war.

As Aliko Dangote sat at his mahogany desk in the massive Presidential office, he knew he was going to have to reach out to the Americans soon. He hit the buzzer near his desk for his secretary to respond. A second later a voice came over the speaker, "Can I help you with something, Sir?"

"Please arrange a meeting with my Foreign Secretary."

"Yes, Sir."

The meeting had more than one purpose. He planned to make his Foreign Secretary the new American Ambassador. Their current Ambassador was going to be coming home shortly; he had done a good job of keeping the African Confederation low profile and out of the spotlight, but now it was time to begin serious talks with the Americans. Dangote wanted to prevent them from waging their war on his continent. A war he knew he could not win was one that he wanted to avoid at all costs.

Chapter 55
Thompson's Last Mission

03 January 2043
1,200 feet under the East China Sea

Captain Thompson was on his last combat patrol as the Commander of the *Seawolf*. He had just received word that he was being promoted to Rear Admiral and would be taking over command of the navy's submarine training squadron. It was a non-combat role, but one that would give him two years of shore duty and time with his family. It would also position him for his second star, so from that perspective, he thought it was going to be a great assignment.

His ship had survived multiple enemy engagements this year, and as a crew, had the most tonnage sunk of any US submarine. They sunk one of the Chinese Supercarriers (and one of the Japanese carriers) and damaged the others enough that it proved to be a turning point in the battle for Hawaii. Everyone on his ship had been awarded the Bronze Star with V device for Valor. He was given the opportunity to award ten members of the ship the Silver Star and had also presented two Navy Crosses. Captain Thompson himself had been awarded the Navy Cross as the commander of the sub. For their last patrol with him as commander, they had been ordered into the East China Sea, about eighty miles northeast of Shanghai, just off the coast of Qingdao, one of the largest shipping ports in the country.

With Japan neutralized and now functioning as a launch pad for the coming invasion, the Allies were now moving more and more subs and ships into the East and South China Seas, to begin locking down their ports. The Navy had finally cut the Chinese shipping lanes off from the rest of the world and their other captured territories. The Allies had been working hard to cut China off from Africa and the island nations of Indonesia, Malaysia and the Philippines. They did not plan on liberating the Philippines or invading Indonesia. Instead, their plan was to isolate them and conduct surgical air strikes against their forces to degrade them over time.

The *Seawolf* was given the mission of launching a series of cruise missiles at the port and then slipping away to return to their base of operations in Japan. As his sub came to launch depth, he looked at his

XO and said, "Ready the missiles, I want to launch them as quickly as possible so we can get out of here."

"Yes, Sir," the XO responded.

Captain Thompson continued, "COB, once the missiles have launched, I want us to dive to 900 feet and begin to move away from here at eight knots."

"Ay, Ay, Sir," replied the COB.

Turning to his weapons officer, the Captain simply nodded, indicating it was time.

Then he announced, "Fire all missiles."

It only took seconds, but then the ship shuddered slightly as the blast doors began to blow and a series of cruise missiles began to be ejected from the missile bays. Every three seconds, another blast door opened as a cruise missile was launched, until all sixteen had been fired.

Immediately following the launch of the missiles, the sub began a steep dive, picking up speed until it reached eight knots. "Conn, Sonar--do we have any contacts?" asked the Captain, hoping they were going to make a clean get-away.

There was a pause as they waited for the update. Petty Officer Wilks was listening intensely to his headset and watching the computer screen in front of him. They had not heard any Chinese subs in the last two days, but that did not mean they were not out there. A few minutes later the Captain called asking for an update. "Sonar, Conn--we are not showing enemy submarines in the area," Wilks said to the Captain.

They all breathed a sigh of relief. Launching their cruise missiles was probably one of the most vulnerable positions a sub could be in.

****

Twenty minutes after firing their cruise missiles, the Captain was fairly certain they had not been detected, so he ordered the ship to increase speed to 12 knots and deploy the towed sonar array. If an enemy submarine was out there, then chances are the towed array would be able to find them. It looked like his final combat mission of the war was a success.

Chapter 56
Maps and Schemes

09 February 2043
Yokota Air Base, Japan
General Gardner's Headquarters

Following the coup in Japan, the US Military quickly backed the coup leaders and helped the military seize control of the government and the country. The Chinese, of course, had their own response to the situation. The PLA had 35,000 soldiers in Japan, and those soldiers did their best to attack the government forces and try to hold on to the few military bases they operated on. The PLAAF also sent additional aircraft into the mix. After nearly three months of fighting, the US and the remaining JDF that supported the coup were able to push the PLA off the island. The US Navy put a lot of effort into preventing the PLAN from bringing in more reinforcements; the US lost a lot of ships attacking the remains of the PLAN, but after months of naval engagements, the US had defeated what was left of the Chinese navy and reasserted their dominance of the Pacific.

After the Chinese and Axis powers had been defeated in California and Alaska, General Gardner had been promoted again and given his fifth star. He had now been given overall command of all Allied forces in the Pacific. The last four months had been busy; the US had ferried over a million soldiers and supporting equipment to Japan. With the steady supply of Tritium4, the US had been cranking out F41s as fast as they could. The Air Force now had one 187 of them operating in Japan. They had quickly established air control over Japan and the East China Sea.

General Gardner's forces in Japan had now reached 1,400,000 soldiers, and were still growing. There was still some resistance domestically from holdouts of the previous government, but they were being hunted down and dealt with. What Gardner wanted to focus on now was how best to invade China and bring a swift end to the war. He was concerned with the casualty numbers, and the last thing he wanted to do was lose hundreds of thousands of soldiers. Of the soldiers that he had in Japan, nearly 230,000 of them were equipped with the Raptor exoskeleton combat suits. He also had 12,000 of the new enhanced humanoid drones and 4,000 trained operators ready to use them.

Intelligence and surveillance of the major cities and probably landing zones of mainland China showed a massive increase in activity. The Chinese were building up their shoreline, and appeared to be turning their cities into fortresses. This was the exact fight General Gardner wanted to avoid. He grumbled to himself, "*No one wants to fight in a city; it favors the defenders and it is a lot harder to root out the enemy. Unless I were willing to flatten all the buildings and kill the civilians in them, fighting in a city is going to cost us a lot of lives... I have to find a way to cut China up into manageable chunks.*"

He opened a map on his tablet and began strategizing. Shanghai was the first region of concern that he identified; there were nearly eighteen million people living in that metropolis and surrounding area. Intelligence showed the PLA had moved nearly 600,000 soldiers into the area to defend it as well. His second goal was the port city of Qingdao and the rest of the peninsula. Next, he planned to liberate Taiwan. This would allow him to position aircraft, troops and supplies a lot closer to southern China. He also wanted to capture Tianjin, which would put his forces in striking distance of Beijing. The real question was--where should he attack first? Fighting was going to be heavy in all four areas; he needed to figure out where to use the Raptor soldiers and EHDs versus regular infantry wearing standard body armor.

It was still dicey providing air support to the infantry. The F41s could operate at a higher altitude and because of their speed and stealth, the enemy laser and Surface to Air Missile (SAM) batteries were useless against them. The F41s were attacking every laser battery they could find, but they were never going to get them all...the PLA had tens of thousands of SAMs, not to mention shoulder-fired missiles, which were also able to pack a punch. In either case, the invasion was going to be costly.
******

General Tyler Black walked into the operations center and went straight for the coffee stand. He had been awake for nearly twenty hours after visiting several of the battalions of newly-arrived soldiers. He had made it a point to spend at least three days a week touring the various battalions, talking to the soldiers, sergeants and junior officers to get a feel for the mood of the soldiers and their morale. He tried to offer words of encouragement and give them hope that the war was finally ending. He told them the President and General Gardner were in negotiations with the Chinese government, but if they did not surrender, he expected them to do their duty and bring this war to an end.

The war in Alaska had taken a lot from General Black. He had lost so many soldiers, and ultimately, they still lost. If it had not been for the Navy, they might *still* be fighting the Chinese there. He wanted payback for the invasion of America. He wanted payback for the Chinese providing all the weapons to the IR and starting this war. Too many young men and women had died. Too many more were still going to die if President Stein ordered them to invade.

As he stood there for a minute holding his coffee, he lifted it up to his nose and took a big sniff, letting the aroma fill his lungs before he took a long sip. In seconds, he felt the warmth of the liquid move down into his body; within minutes, he could already start to feel the caffeine slowly starting to kick in. Once he had his fix, he looked around to see if he could find General Gardner.

General Black spotted him talking to one of the Air Force generals and began to walk towards him. He had just finished up his conversation when he saw him approaching. Gardner then extended his hand, "General Black, it's good to see you. We have lots to discuss," he said.

They walked down the hallway towards General Gardner's office, which sat just off of the operations center. Gardner liked to be near the heart of the war, which these days meant being near the operations center, which was filled with TV monitors of drone feeds, headcams and an endless feed of data from all sorts of sensors and maps.

As they sat down to talk, General Black was the first to speak. "The troops are in high spirits. They are eager to get this fight going, if that is what it's going to come down to."

General Gardner smiled for a second as he replied, "That's good to hear, Tyler." His face then reverted into a stone-cold, serious expression. "I just got done talking with the President and the National Security Council about twenty minutes ago. We've been given the order. We are to begin preparations to invade."

He paused for a minute to let his long-time friend collect his thoughts before he continued, "The President has given me some leeway in when we can begin the operation, but he wants it to begin within the month. We can pick the date, time and location, but he wants us to move forward with the four-pronged approach we briefed him on." General Gardner was somber. This was a big decision. They were about to commit millions of soldiers to one last major campaign of the war.

The two generals had known each other on and off again for the last fifteen years, but had really become close over these past five months. When General Gardner was given his fifth star, he immediately requested General Black to be his field commander. General Gardner knew that he was not going to be able to be at the front leading his soldiers as much as he wanted to, and he needed someone he could trust to be in that position for him. He had seen how Black had fought tooth and nail against the Chinese, and he admired that. He had finally found someone as aggressive as he was.

General Black took a deep breath in and then puffed it out as if he were blowing out an imaginary candle. "This is going to be a tough one, Gary. Have you already determined which front we will hit first and what troops we are going to use?"

"Yes. We are going to go after Shanghai. Using the Raptor troops, I want them to hit Nantong first, then cross the Yangtze River and capture Changzhou. I want that area completely sealed off. Then I want to use our airborne and heliborne troops to hit Shaoxing and drive towards Hangzhou on foot with the Wolverines. They need to move fast and secure the docks and the airports. Once the docks are secured, you need to get reinforcements into those guys quick and firm up their position. We are not going to attack Shanghai right away. I want to get the area completely surrounded and cut off from further supply," Gary explained as he showed Tyler the plan on his tablet map. He went over the numbers of troops, timeline for reinforcements, number of aircraft assigned for ground support as well as helicopters and Razorbacks available. He also went over the direct fire support the Navy would be providing with their battleships.

General Black leaned back in his chair. "That is going to be a tall order, Gary.". He knew there were a lot of concerns. They still did not have nearly as many Raptor suit troopers as they wanted, and wouldn't for nearly a year. The private sector was cranking them out as fast as they could, but they could only produce so many a month. Presently, they were manufacturing 150,000 a month.

Gardner nodded, aware of the difficulties. "I'm going to have the Air Force start hitting the rail and road systems in the area tonight. They are also going to start going after the pre-identified targets we went over last week. We will let the Air Force and the Navy pound them for the next three days, then they will shift to our second objective, Taiwan. After the third day of them hammering Taiwan, they will shift their focus back to Shanghai and we will invade. This will hopefully throw them off a bit."

"When do we hit the other objectives?" asked Black, knowing those attacks would come sooner rather than later. The goal was to overwhelm the PLA by hitting them at multiple points, forcing them to have to pick which front was going to be the priority.

"This is the tough part--hitting the next objectives is going to place an enormous strain on the Navy and our sealift capability. We will hit Taiwan within the next four months, using regular infantry. All of the Raptor troops are going to be needed in Shanghai. They are already going to be heavily outnumbered. As to the other objectives…I am not sure just yet. I want to hit Tianjin with the EHDs. We are going to be seriously outnumbered in that invasion, and I think the drones are going to be our best bet. We will follow them up with regular infantry once they have established a beachhead."

Standing up and stretching his back, General Black looked his friend in the eye and said, "I know that you've done everything you could to prepare for this moment. Now it's time to put the plan into motion and let the rest of us execute it. We will see it through to victory and bring this terrible war to an end."

He left General Gardner's office and began to marshal several the operations officers and senior NCOs around him to get things started. From that moment on, the operations center was beehive of activity as the greatest military invasion in history began.

Chapter 57
Controlled Chaos

12 February 2043
0400 Hours
Rudong, China

As Captain Thornton sat strapped into the seat of the Razorback that would fly him into the port city of Rudong, he just wanted to make it out of this situation alive. He had fought in Mexico, the Middle East, California and now China. He just hoped his luck would not run out on this mission. As he sat there with his helmet on, he could see the men around him looking anxious; some had a blank look, others were ready for a fight. As he sat there looking out the door at the water moving quickly below them, he couldn't feel that the air was chilling or smell the saltwater below; his exoskeleton combat suit was a fully-enclosed system.

What he was certain of was that they were flying very fast. He could tell by the looks on the door gunner's face and from the pilot when he first got on that they were nervous. Thornton's company, along with the rest of his battalion, was going to be flown in from the troop ships offshore and be deposited right in the center of Rudong County, which controlled dozens of smaller docks and ports that were going to be critical to secure if the invasion was going to work. Hundreds of Pershing battle tanks were waiting to be offloaded at those docks, along with thousands of Wolverine infantry fighting vehicles.

His Razorback was flying low and swiftly. He had ridden in the Razorbacks dozens of times, but was not sure he had ever ridden in one that was flying this hastily. In the distance, he saw waves of Razorbacks. Just behind them, and a little higher in altitude, he saw dozens of additional gunships. The sky was full of helicopters. After nearly fifteen minutes in the air, he could start to see land off in the horizon. It was the pre-twilight hours of the morning, so the land still looked dark and ominous, but he could see shards of light starting to penetrate the night. He knew they were getting close, and things were about to get crazy. He had no idea if he was going to live another five minutes, five hours, or five days. What he did know is life was never going to be the same for everyone on board this helicopter.

Joe did not have to wait long for the silence to be broken. Within a minute of first seeing land, enemy tracer fire began to rise from the ground headed straight for them. The dimly lit green lights grew in size and intensity as they approached his helicopter. Explosions began to shake their craft as they few through the air, Thornton's heart began to race and his chest tighten up. He knew there was nothing he could do, but that did not relieve the anxiety he was feeling. Their pilot began to deftly evade the enemy fire, moving their Razorback seconds before a missile would have hit them. Joe thought to himself, "*This pilot is good.*"

As their craft flew over land, the volume of enemy fire began to pick up even more. Joe did not think that it was possible, but the number of enemy tracers flying all around them was so thick that he could not believe he had not already been ripped apart by them. He felt his craft shake multiple times as they began to take some hits. Then an explosion nearby threw the Razorback to one side and then the other; their pilot tried desperately to duck and dodge while also going with the flow.

Joe saw the door gunner, who was sitting about ten feet from him, begin to use his gun. He began shooting at unknown targets at the ground. Joe wished he could shoot at something, anything. He hated being helpless like this, strapped to a seat hoping and praying that he was not killed by some unseen hand before he was able to get on the ground.

They were approaching what he thought was the center of town. The pilot banked hard to one side and let loose a volley of anti-personnel rockets. Seconds later, they jerked to the other side and fired several anti-tank missiles at an unseen target. There was a loud explosion and their Razorback lurched swiftly towards the opposite side. Smoke, began to fill the cabin, alarms began to blare, and he heard several of his men let loose a number of swear words; some shouted out a few prayers. As their craft began to slide out of control, Paul thought for a minute, "*Is this it? Am I about to die?*"

Then their Razorback slammed into the side of a building and bounced off of it. They thudded hard and crashed into a parking lot next to several mid-sized office buildings. Once the Razorback stopped moving, Joe realized that they were still alive. He could still see smoke, and felt some heat, which meant the Razorback was on fire, but at least for the moment, they were alive. He immediately yelled to everyone in the craft, "Grab your gear and get out!"

In seconds, ten of the men in his squad were off the Razorback and moving to the side of one of the office buildings for cover. Two of his soldiers had been killed in the crash and one of the door gunners had also been killed. The two pilots survived, though they both had some injuries and broken bones. Three of his soldiers ran back to help the wounded and retrieve the dead bodies of his soldiers that died. Thornton began to issue orders, "I want you six to set up a perimeter around our current position."

"Yes Sir," they responded.

He turned to his communications sergeant and continued, "We need to let the rest of the company know our location. I want to get a situation report from all of my platoon leaders ASAP."

"Yes, Captain."

Thornton loaded a map and found the GPS plot of their location. He saw that they were only a few hundred meters away from their original landing zone. He also discovered one of the Razorbacks carrying his soldiers had been completely destroyed, with no survivors. Two more had been shot down and had casualties but those Marines were on the ground and moving to their objectives. The other two platoons had landed successfully and were moving to secure their targets. Seeing that he was not far from his original objective and looking at his surroundings, Joe opted to move his headquarters to the first floor of the office building they were now using as cover. He ordered second platoon to move to his position and sent his remaining squad members into the office building to secure it and set up spotter positions on the roof. Once the other platoon arrived, they would be relieved.

He needed to get his base of operations established; his objective was to secure a perimeter so they could begin to bring in more soldiers and get some light armored vehicles and mobile anti-aircraft vehicles set up. He had 45 minutes to secure his area before the next wave of reinforcements would begin to arrive, and two hours before eight Wolverine infantry fighting vehicles would be airlifted in.

As he surveyed the area around him, he realized the office buildings were located on the edge of a densely populated residential area. His position was also relatively close to several anti-aircraft heavy guns, which were still shooting away at the Razorbacks and gunships moving around the area. He called the platoon leader for third platoon, gave them the location of the enemy gun position, and directed them to take it out. It appeared to be in the center of several large apartment buildings. It was likely placed there to discourage the Air Force from dropping a bomb on it, killing a bunch of civilians. It was a smart play on the PLA's part, but his grunts would take it out.

While two soldiers from his headquarters squad began to set up the communications antennas and run the cables back into the reception area of the office building, a dozen PLA soldiers appeared about fifty yards from his position at the corner of the intersection nearby. They immediately began to shoot at him and the soldiers pulling sentry duty.

One of Thornton's men fired his M203 grenade launcher in their direction, while another soldier moved behind a small brick wall and began to fire controlled bursts from his M5. Joe took cover behind a parked vehicle in the parking lot and took aim at one of the Chinese soldiers. He saw the fighter move to the corner of a building and begin to fire at his men. As he took aim at the soldier, he sighted in on his head and fired a single shot. The man's head jerked back, and he collapsed where he was standing. Joe immediately began to move on to the next soldier, repeating the process several times. The PLA seemed to be so focused on shooting at the other soldiers behind the building that they had taken over that they did not seem to notice him off to the side, behind a parked car.

Thornton had picked off seven PLA soldiers before anyone began to fire at his position. Seconds later, a Marine gunship flew nearby and fired off several anti-personnel rockets in the direction of the PLA soldiers, blowing them up. Joe saw one enemy soldier get thrown in the air, landing maybe ten feet from where he had just been standing. He saw the man desperately grab for his left arm, which had just been ripped off by the explosion. Joe took aim and shot him in the head, ending his misery.

The attack helicopter that had randomly appeared near them quickly darted off to find another target to attack. Now that the enemy had been neutralized, Thornton and his men continued to clear the area for the follow-on forces that would arrive soon. They needed to push several vehicles in the parking lot to the outer edge and create a clearing for additional helicopters to land. Once they finished, the parking lot would have enough room for two Razorbacks to land at a time.

When Joe walked into the reception area of the office building, he saw his two coms Marines had their laptops up and running and had pulled up the portable digital map board. As he began to study the map board, he learned the current positions of the Marines in his battalion and company. A couple of drone feeds were also being piped in. The drones were identifying pockets of enemy soldiers and overlaying them on the map in relationship to the Marines' positions. Several red flashing symbols represented the battalions' primary objectives and targets that had not yet been neutralized, while others were now listed as blue, indicating that they had been destroyed.

Studying the map for a second, he could see that the third platoon had successfully taken out those enemy anti-aircraft guns and were now en-route to his position. First platoon appeared to be bogged down, still trying to accomplish their primary objective. It looked like most of second platoon had been killed after two of the three Razorbacks carrying them had been shot down. The remaining squad of soldiers was still pressing on with their mission, securing a nearby road junction. He was going to need to detail off a squad from third platoon to assist them once they arrived. As he located his fourth platoon, he was able to determine that their first and second squad had secured one of the key bridges near the S324 highway.

An hour after their crash landing, a steady stream of Razorbacks and heavy helicopter transporters began to arrive at Thornton's position. Nearly four hundred additional Marines arrived, along with eight Wolverines. Captain Thornton's Company had cleared one of five initial landing zones, to assist the incoming battalions of Marines in securing the rest of the city. The rest of his battalion had secured three ports, which were now being used to offload the more heavily armored Pershing tanks and other armored vehicles that would begin to make their way to Nantong and the Yangtze River.
****

General Li Zuocheng had been promoted to Eastern Theater Commander two months ago. He knew this was an important promotion because he would most likely be defending against an American invasion, one that could take place anytime. He was not without resources. He had 1,300,000 soldiers to defend nearly 500 miles of shoreline, along with some of the most important industrial cities and sectors in the country. His force was broken down into 82 divisions; 14 of them were heavily armored divisions, while the rest were a mix of mechanized and light infantry division. To augment his force, he had 22

PLA militia divisions, which were lightly equipped and poorly trained infantry.

He knew the Americans were going to launch an invasion of mainland China, the question his officers and planners were trying to decipher was when and where. They knew that Nantong had the majority of the deep water heavy ports in Jiangsu Province, a key foothold to Shanghai; this made it a prime target. The capture of Shanghai and the industrial centers around it would be a big blow to China. General Zuocheng knew the American President wanted to break China up because they had grown too powerful; he could not let that happen.

At 0300 in the morning, one of his aides knocked on his door and woke him up. Li was upset. He had been getting one of the best night's sleep he had had in the past week. The Americans had been attacking the various airfields in his military district with high altitude bombings and cruise missiles. Most of the cruise missiles were shot down, but the F41s had been modified to now carry two 500 lb. Joint Direct Attack Munitions, an old-fashioned dumb bomb with a specialized GPS and laser-guided nose, and guidable tail fins. It was fortunate that the Americans only had a few hundred of these aircraft, or they could single-handedly dismantle his armored forces. Once it became clear what the Americans were doing, he had ordered his forces to disperse into the cities.

There had been a lull in the bombing the past couple of days as the Americans shifted their bombing attacks to Taiwan. It was during this lull that Li had ordered 34 divisions to the Shanghai area. His gut was telling him the Americans were about to attack. When his aide had knocked on his door, he just knew that the Americans must have launched their assault. After he hurriedly got dressed, he followed his aide down the hallway, to the stairs that would lead to where his operations center was set up.

Several guards at the entrance to the operations center snapped to attention and saluted General Zuocheng as he arrived. He returned their salutes and continued into the nerve center of his command. What he saw when he entered was controlled chaos with officers on the phone obtaining status reports from various sectors, and others analyzing the dozens of live drone feeds being piped in from Rudong and the nearby ports and harbors. He stood there for a second looking at the drone feeds of the Rudong. He saw the sky was lit up with tracers, flying in nearly every direction. He also saw what appeared to be hundreds upon hundreds of helicopters arriving from the direction of the sea, landing in dozens of areas across the city.

One of his generals walked up to him asking, "General Zuocheng, I would like your permission to order the 14th Army to Rudong and Nantong to throw the Americans back into the sea."

General Zuocheng just nodded his approval, leaving his subordinate to make it happen while he moved over to the PLAAF liaison. "General Feng, I need your forces to start attacking those American helicopters," he said as he pointed to the drone feeds and radar screens showing hundreds of helicopters and aircraft over the city.

The Air Force liaison replied, "Yes sir. We are scrambling aircraft and drones from across the military district to head towards the Americans now." The invasion was still in the first hours, so Li knew things were fluid and likely to change quickly. What he did not want to do was make the same mistakes the Germans did during the Normandy invasion. They had not rushed all of their forces to the beach, and by the time they had realized that this was the main Allied attack, the Allies had landed too many soldiers and tanks to be pushed back into the channel.

Zuocheng turned to one of his other generals. "I want the militia divisions rushed forward as well. Have them try and break through to the ports and interrupt the enemy operations."

Before the general issued the order, he asked, "Sir, the militia units will probably be cut to pieces without armor support. Should we have them wait until the 14th Army is in position to support their advance?"

"No. They are quick and mobile, and we need to get them there now. I know they will be ravaged, but they will buy the 14th time to get into position and hit the Americans with our heavier armored and mechanized forces," General Zuocheng replied. He had a huge pit growing in his stomach, knowing that tens of thousands of militia soldiers would probably be killed within the next hour.

Chapter 58
Hold the Line

12 February 2043
Rudong, China

"Captain Thornton, Colonel Lee was looking for you," said one of the sergeants as he walked into the operations room.

Thornton nodded and began to walk towards the door leading to the parking lot helipad. It had been three and a half hours since they landed in Rudong, and things were still very chaotic. His company had secured a suitable landing zone and expanded the perimeter enough to allow follow-on forces to continue to arrive. Helicopters were landing as fast as they could and offloading dozens of soldiers, munitions, water, food and other supplies that they would need. So far, two full battalions of Marines had landed at his landing zone (LZ), and were pushing further into the city. The eight Wolverines that arrived thirty minutes ago were already heavily engaged just a few blocks away.

As Thornton approached Colonel Lee, he could see that he was apprehensive about something. "Captain, there you are. I have some disturbing news...." he started.

Joe sighed. Then, sitting next to the colonel along the brick wall some of his soldiers had used for cover a few hours ago, he asked, "What's coming our way?"

"Intelligence intercepted a message from the PLA district commander, directing the Chinese 14th Army to head to Rudong and Nantong. They also intercepted some additional orders to the local PLA militia units. I'm not sure why we were not warned earlier; apparently, they intercepted these orders three hours ago. The brigade recon team sent a FLASH message saying they had spotted a massive troop movement heading towards us. Here's the video image they sent," he explained, passing a tablet to Thornton.

Looking at the screen, he saw multiple side streets and alleyways crawling with militia. There had to be thousands of them. Thornton handed the tablet back and asked, "How far away are they?"

"They are approaching the brigade perimeter right now. We have several airstrikes inbound right now that will hopefully thin them out. I've asked for several additional Wolverines to be dropped. We are going to need a lot more firepower to beat back that mob. Their sheer numbers could overwhelm us if we are not careful," Colonel Lee stated.

Thornton nodded. After a pause, he asked, "What do you want me to do, Sir?"

"I'd like you to have several heavy machineguns moved up to the roof of the surrounding buildings overlooking the LZ. See if you can't get a few more barricades built near the perimeter and have them start placing a lot of claymore mines out there. I'm confident they won't break through our main lines, but we need to be ready to hold the landing zones and ports. I'm going to move to Delta Company's position next and make sure they are doing the same. You and Bravo Company have the two closest LZs to the frontlines right now."

Before the colonel could leave, Thornton asked, "When are we getting some heavy armor from the ports?"

"Soon. They should be arriving with the next wave of transports, along with nearly 100 Wolverines. I would expect them to start showing up in a couple of hours, but until then, it's going to get a bit dicey around here--so be ready," Colonel Lee said as he got up and walked over to one of the armored trucks, hopping in.

Thornton quickly walked into his command center and began to look over the digital map as it was being updated with the data from the various drone feeds and intelligence reports. The colonel was right; it was not looking very good at the outer perimeter. He immediately called his platoon leaders and sergeants, gave them an update on what was coming their way, and issued new instructions to get their perimeter ready to repel the enemy should they break through the lines. It was imperative that they keep the air bridge into Rudong open.

Chapter 59
They Are All Bad Choices

12 February 2043
Yokota Air Base, Japan
General Gardner's Headquarters

As the reports continued to flood in from the Rudong and Nantong, it was becoming clearer that the invasion was not going according to plan. They had anticipated stiff resistance by the PLA, but what they were encountering was nothing short of madness. The PLA had started to throw multiple militia divisions at the invasion force while they positioned the 14th Army to join the fray. The battle for Rudong was turning into a complete slaughter--not of the US Marines who were spearheading the invasion--but of the militia forces that were attacking them.

The drone feeds from the battle and some of the videos they had been reviewing from the battle helmets of the Marines was brutal. The number of bodies piling up in the streets and parks was horrific. The Chinese kept throwing more and more militia soldiers at the Marines, despite the endless slaughter. At the same time, the wave-after-wave assaults were starting to inflict a terrible casualty rate among the Marines. What was worse, the PLA was not allowing the civilians to flee the city. They had blocked the roads, clogging the streets up and creating an even worse humanitarian crisis. The General was not going to be pleased with what was happening. The US had been working hard to avoid civilian casualties, but it appeared that the PLA was going to use the people of Rudong, Nantong and Shanghai as human shields.

Major General (MG) Peter Williams walked over to where General Gardner was standing and waited for him to finish speaking with General Black. MG Williams had been with General Gardner since the start of the war in the Middle East over two years ago, and he had continued to remain his executive officer as he transferred from one Command to the next. He had a relatively good understanding of how the general thought, what he wanted to have done and how he wanted things to run.

A minute later, General Gardner turned to MG Williams and said, "I assume you've gotten caught up on the reports flooding in?"

MG Williams just nodded and waited to see what his friend would say next. Gardner began, "We are taking significant casualties, even though we are slaughtering their militia forces. It also appears the PLA is using the civilian population as human shields preventing them from fleeing the city," he said, disgusted.

"I think we should revise our invasion plans and send the EHDs into Rudong," Williams proposed, hoping Gardner would agree.

"I had wanted to save them for our summer invasion, but I think you may be right. This is a fight that is more suitable for the EHDs. What I'm not sure of is what to do with the civilians. If the PLA is not going to let them flee the area, they are going to get caught up in the fighting. I do not want to limit our ability to provide air or artillery support for fear of hitting civilians," he stated.

"What are you going to do?" asked Peter, also very concerned about the situation.

"I have a call with the President and General Branson shortly. I am not going to do anything until I have clarity and support from the President." Gardner checked his watch again; his telecom was going to start in five minutes.

****

President Stein had been monitoring the progress of the invasion since it started, sifting through miles of information and data feeds in the bowels of the PEOC. Like the others in the room, he was appalled by what appeared to be the senseless slaughter of the PLA militia forces. Now they had to contend with the PLA's blockading of the civilians from fleeing the cities.

Stein had tried to call President Jinping to implore them not to use civilians as human shields. Unfortunately, Jinping would not take his call. Instead, one of his functionaries told him, "China does not use human shields. We expect the Allies to not intentionally target civilians who are trying to flee the city."

When General Gardner came on the call, he breathed a sigh of relief. "General, I want you to do whatever is necessary to support our forces on the ground. Obviously, Jinping has no value for human life, using his people as speed bumps and bait. Enough is enough."

"What do you want me to *do* about the civilians, Sir?"

Stein responded, "This war has been dragged out long enough. I am not going to lose more soldiers because the PLA refuses to protect their civilians. If you have to kill every civilian in the area to defeat the PLA, then so be it. This war is going to end."

Chapter 60
Morally Reprehensible

12 February 2043
Rudong, China

Twelve hours into the invasion, several thousand PLA militia solders (supported by the PLA's 14th Army group) had broken through the American's outer perimeter and were quickly squeezing close to the U.S. foothold.

After his meeting with the President, General Gardner ordered the 32nd infantry division and their enhanced humanoid drones to move into Rudong to support the Marines. In addition to ordering the drones in, he also told the infantry division commander to have the drones' combat AI turned on and programmed to kill every person who did not emit a friendly Individual Identification Frequency (IIF).

Typically, the EHDs were operated by a human, just like the drone tanks and aircraft. A human was always required in the loop because there was a concern about having the drones operate on their own and somehow going rogue. However, the American soldiers operating in the Shanghai area were being slaughtered by the sheer numbers of enemy soldiers that the PLA was throwing at them. The President had determined that something more extreme needed to be done.

The Marines conducting the fighting retreat from the outer perimeter were reporting that the PLA was forcing thousands of civilians to advance in front of their soldiers to act as human shields. The Marines were doing their best to not kill the civilians and focus on the enemy soldiers. However, it was becoming increasingly difficult to do. Then brigade had sent a FLASH message ordering them to engage and kill the civilians. Thornton read the FLASH message a second time, to make sure he fully understood what he was being asked to do. He felt a lump in his throat. He did not like this order one bit.

The orders also told them that the 32nd infantry division and their EHDs were being deployed shortly. Once deployed, they would take over the operation of clearing the city. A loop of endless thought ran through Thornton's mind. *"This is terrible; now they want us to kill any civilians being used as human shields? This is wrong on so many levels...but can we even survive if we don't do something? Those PLA soldiers are a miserable excuse for humanity. How can they lead their own people to slaughter?"*

Captain Thornton cleared his throat, and motioned for quiet. "Everyone, listen up. We just received a new set of orders from brigade. The PLA is not only deterring the civilians from leaving the area for safety; they are now actively pushing them out in front of their advance as human shields. The outer perimeter has already collapsed, and our forces are retreating. They will arrive our perimeter shortly. Brigade has just sent a FLASH message directly from General Gardner on orders from the President. We are to engage and kill any civilians being used as human shields." There was an audible gasp in the room. "I know most of you may not like this idea; however, if we do not stop the PLA advance, we are *all* going to die. We need to hold our landing zone until reinforcements arrive."

Pausing for a second to take a breath, he then continued, "I was just told the 32nd infantry division is being deployed to our position, which means they will be delivering thousands of those new enhanced humanoid drones. Once they arrive, we are to let them advance and deal with the PLA and the civilians being used as human shields. They should start to reach us shortly, and will continue to come in until the entire division is here. Our LZ will be one of the primary locations they will be landing at. I know this mess about killing the civilians is beyond horrific, but we have a duty to do, and I need everyone to remember that our lives and those of every other American involved in this invasion is depending on us doing our jobs."

With his new orders issued and his officers and NCOs acknowledging that they understood, Thornton went back up to the roof of the building he had been using as a headquarters since they first landed. As he arrived at the rooftop, he moved quickly to one of the corners, where several of his men had a heavy machinegun set up.

One of the soldiers looked at Captain Thornton and asked, "Sir, are we really supposed to mow down any civilians we see rushing towards our perimeter?" he probed, clearly distraught with the thought of killing unarmed innocents

Sighing for a second, Thornton sat down next to the Marines and looked each of them in the eye before responding, "These orders are the vilest thing I have ever been tasked with--shoot, the orders are illegal, and against the Laws of War and every rule of engagement we have ever been given or told. If I had my druthers, I'd refuse the order, just as I am sure many of you are thinking of doing. But here's the deal…the PLA is doing this *intentionally*. They know our rules of engagement and are trying to use them against us. They are trying to make us second guess ourselves and then overwhelm us with their sheer numbers. We can't let that happen. If we do, then everyone is going to die and this invasion will fail. We cannot let that happen," he said, trying to justify what would traditionally be an illegal order.

The Marines thought about it for a few minutes before a young black Marine spoke up for the group, "None of us like these orders, but like you said, Sir, if we do not do it, we are all going to die and this invasion is going to fail. We'll do it. We will follow your orders, Sir, and we'll make sure the PLA does not overwhelm our position." He spoke with such confidence and conviction that all of the other Marines nearby nodded their heads in agreement. This was the only course of action if they were to survive.

Captain Thornton got up slowly and left the machinegun crew to go talk with the other Marines in his Company. He wanted to make sure his soldiers understood the gravity of their situation. It took him close to thirty minutes to visit the majority of his men before the sounds of machinegun fire in the city began to creep closer and louder. Then, small clusters of Marines, first squads and then platoon size groups, began to fall back to their defensive line, shoring up Thornton's position.

Less than ten minutes after the outer perimeter force fell back to Thornton's location, the enemy soldiers started to show up. Looking down the street, Thornton's stomach just sank as he saw throngs of people being forced forward by Chinese tanks, armored personnel vehicles and soldiers with bayonets on the ends of their rifles. It was disgusting to see how callous the PLA was in the treatment of their own people.

Thornton knew what needed to be done and knew he needed to lead by example if he wanted his men to follow such tough orders. While crouched down behind a barrier that his Marines were using, he raised his rifle, took aim and began to fire countless rounds on burst into the crowd of civilians being pushed towards his perimeter. He saw one, then two, then dozens of civilians drop to the ground, dead from his rounds.

In seconds of firing his shots, the rest of his company and the Marines from the retreating group began to open fire as well.

A couple of his Marines on the roof tops began firing their anti-tank missiles at the PLA tanks rumbling towards them, taking several of them out. Thornton got on the radio and began calling in for naval gun support. Several Zumwalt destroyers off the coast began to rain down 155mm high explosive rounds across the streets where the PLA continued to lead their own people to slaughter. It was gruesome; thousands of civilians were being slain by the naval gun support and the machinegun fire of his Marines. In less than five minutes, most of the human shields were either dead or wounded, laying on the ground. The PLA infantry then began to advance, using their traditional human wave tactics. It did not take long before the Chinese soldiers were within grenade range, then both sides began to throw dozens of grenades at each other. As company-sized elements of PLA soldiers would rush forward after throwing a volley of grenades at the American lines, one of the Marines would detonate a series of claymore mines, obliterating most of the charging soldiers.

Just as Thornton thought their position was about to be overrun, he looked back to see two Razorbacks arrive on station. They quickly unleashed a torrent of anti-personnel rockets at the charging PLA soldiers, and then proceeded to land. They swiftly unloaded their payload of 16 EHDs each. The EHDs immediately ran towards the perimeter of the Marine positions and began to engage the Chinese soldiers. It was an overwhelming sight to take in--more than two dozen mechanical killing machines were running at full speed while delivering high-speed, accurate fire at the enemy. Once the Reapers reached the perimeter, they quickly advanced past it, with complete disregard for their own safety. The EHDs were after all, drones.

Many of them were being shot multiple times. Some would eventually have a leg or an arm shot off or those that were hit by larger caliber rifles might ultimately lose their head; However, the rest of them just moved forward at a quick pace, methodically killing everything that moved that did not have a friendly IIF. By the time the first group of EHDs had moved twenty meters in front of Thornton's position, a second wave of drones landed and began to speedily reinforce the first group. Thornton's men continued to provide fire support for the Reapers, but they were quite frankly in awe of how fast the enhanced humanoid drones were methodically killing and advancing forward.

Ten minutes after the first wave of EHDs had landed and began to make their presence known, the third wave of drones arrived. Thornton received word that a total of twelve waves of Reapers would be flown into his LZ before the end of the day. The rest would be landing at three of the five ports the Marines still had under their control (in the last 90 minutes, the Marines holding on to two of the ports had been overrun and wiped out).

By the end of the first day of the invasion, the Marines and EHDs had regained control of their original perimeter, recovered the two ports they had lost, and secured three more ports. The Reapers had also pushed the PLA back across the Yangtze River and secured most of Nantong. Of the 3,000 EHDs that had been deployed, some 823 had been destroyed, but according to their kill counters, they had collectively killed over 33,000 enemy soldiers and nearly 113,000 civilians who had been intentionally placed in the line of fire.

Unfortunately, the Marine force that had landed in Yancheng had been wiped out before any EHDs from the 32nd infantry division could be rushed forward to assist them. The Marines at Ningbo were nearly wiped out, but 500 Reapers arrived at the last minute. They had helped to create a big enough perimeter for additional forces to land. By the end of the day, some two thousand enhanced humanoid drones had landed at Ningbo and began to push further inland, leaving the Marines to clear the city and surrounding villages.

Sometime around 0230, Colonel Lee pulled up to Thornton's position in one of the armored jeeps that had been brought ashore several hours earlier. His vehicle had been followed by seven Pershing battle tanks and thirteen Wolverines, which did not stop, but instead pushed beyond them, heading towards Nantong to support the EHDs before they moved across the river. Colonel Lee spotted Thornton walking out of his headquarters and approached him.

"Captain Thornton, we need to talk," Colonel Lee declared.

"I see you brought some additional armor with you, Sir," Captain Thornton replied as he observed the armored column moving past his post towards the enemy lines.

Colonel Lee looked at the armored column briefly, then his eyes settled on the enormous amount of dead bodies surrounding Captain

Thornton's position. He could tell they had been hit hard earlier and somehow managed to hold out long enough for the EHDs to land and help them regain control of the area.

Looking Thornton in the eyes, Colonel Lee said, "Captain Thornton, your Company did an amazing job today. You not only held your perimeter against multiple enemy assaults throughout the last 24 hours. You beat back their advances and held on to perhaps the most important LZ in the Shanghai area. I wanted you to know I'm putting you in for a medal again, for you and your men." Lee heaped some much-deserved praise on his best company commander.

"Thank you for the words of encouragement, but my men and I were just doing our jobs," he replied feeling almost embarrassed by the adulation and, more importantly, guilty about what they had done to ensure they held their position. "We held, Sir, but I lost a lot of good Marines today. We also killed a lot of civilians, something my men and I were not at all comfortable with."

"I know. It was a terrible order they issued, but you executed it flawlessly and because of that, you probably saved the entire invasion force in Nantong. If your position had fallen, we would have lost the last three ports and most likely the other LZ," the colonel asserted, reaffirming the gallant effort of Thornton's men.

Colonel Lee sighed. "Look, I'm here for more than just a social call and to tell you how good you and your men did today. As you know, we took a tremendous number of casualties. Two of my three battalions were completely wiped out, one at the north port and the other at LZ Liberty. I've also lost all three of my battalion commanders. Shoot--the division Commander was killed, and I'm now the most senior officer in the division. On my way over here, I was informed by General Black, the invasion force CG, that I'm being promoted to Brigadier General (BG), effective immediately; they want me to take over command of Third Marines."

There was a brief pause as Lee allowed Thornton a second to digest before continuing. "As I said earlier, most of the senior officers have been killed; of the three brigades that we have in the division, I'm the only O6 still able to fight. I only have two of thirteen Lieutenant Colonels who are not wounded and able to fight. I'm promoting both of them to full Colonel to take over their brigades. Right now, your brigade has no commander, and your XO was just killed thirty minutes ago.

Therefore, I'm promoting you effective immediately to Lieutenant Colonel (LTC) to take over command of your battalion. I'll send out the official orders to everyone in your battalion shortly." As he finished his speech, he handed Captain Thornton his new silver oakleaf rank insignias.

Thornton just stood there dumbfounded for a second; then, snapping out of his stupor, he reached out his hand and took the silver oakleaves from BG Lee. They both took a moment to put their new ranks on before Thornton spoke. "Sir, I do not know what to say. I had never thought I would rise above Captain, having been just promoted less than a year ago. What are my orders?"

BG Lee looked at Thornton for a second, then responded, "Look, Joe, I know you are still new to being an officer, and there is a lot you do not understand about being a Lieutenant Colonel, or what is expected of you at your rank and position. You are a fighter. Right now, that is all I need you to be. As we get more reinforcements, I'll get you a good XO who has experience and that can help you with the administrative parts of being a battalion commander. Right now, I want you to get your battalion organized. Find out how many soldiers you have left that are able to fight, see what equipment you have, where everyone is located, and then send your request for replacements to my staff. I will do my best to get you fully staffed."

Still in a bit of shock, LTC Thornton responded the only way he knew how to. "Yes, Sir." Then, wanting to get on with the business at hand, he inquired, "Where do you want me to deploy?"

BG Lee smiled. "That's the man I need...we have reinforcements coming in constantly; I'm going to start syphoning some of them off and will send them your way to get you back up to strength. Have your unit camp out in your headquarters building and give them some rest. As new units arrive, they will be sent here. Unless something drastic changes, I'll contact you in six hours with your new order. In the meantime, I need to find out what shape the rest of the division is in."

"Yes, Sir," responded LTC Thornton.

BG Lee shook Thornton's hand one last time, then turned around and walked back towards his armored vehicle and drove off to the next unit.

Thornton stood there for a second, trying to comprehend everything that had just happened. The division must really have been hit hard for them to have promoted Lee to BG and him to LTC. Finally, he shrugged, then turned around and began to walk back into his headquarters building. As soon as he got back to his operations center, he brought everyone else up to speed on his conversation with BG Lee. He also promoted several of his lieutenants to captains and the one other captain to major. He also informed his First Sergeant that he was now the battalion Sergeant Major, until another one showed up.

Over the next hour, Thornton got the rest of his battalion relocated to his position and bedded down for some sleep. As new reinforcements continued to arrive, about a third of them were being syphoned off and sent to his position as replacements, just as BG Lee had suggested. When Lee got back in touch with him later in the day, his battalion had received enough replacements to bring them back up to 85% strength. The Marines had been told to stand fast in their current positions while the rest of the 32nd infantry division's EHDs continued to advance across the Yangtze River.

The Air Force was bombing the enemy positions into oblivion. Between the Air Force and the Naval guns off-shore, the enemy was under continuous bombardment. By the end of the third day of the invasion, the Allies had secured a solid foothold around the Shanghai area and had begun to offload thousands of tanks and other armored vehicles. Hundreds of artillery units began to arrive, and started to add their own muscle to the offensive against the enemy positions. By day five, the Allies had the entire city and the surrounding area of Shanghai completely cut off. Tens of thousands of Allied ground forces were arriving every hour through the ports, beaches, landing zones and at the one airport they had managed to secure.

The Allies had also lost a tremendous number of soldiers. Nearly 68,000 soldiers had been killed, and nearly four times that number wounded. Not all the wounded needed to be evacuated; many could continue to fight on. The Allies had also lost several thousand EHDs, a loss that was going to affect the next several invasions. Because of the daily Allied losses, General Gardner postponed the Taiwan invasion for at least two months. Until the situation in the Shanghai area could be further stabilized, he needed to hold those forces in reserve. The PLA was throwing everything they had at his invasion force in Shanghai, trying to both break the siege and destroy the Allied landing force.

However, their forces in Shanghai were trapped and were daily being pounded from the air, sea and ground artillery.

Chapter 61
Taiwan's Role

29 June 2043
China

It had been four months since the Allies had invaded mainland China. The invasion of Shanghai had eventually ended in success, but not before it claimed the lives of nearly 136,000 Allied soldiers. The PLA had suffered a debilitating defeat, grinding four separate army groups into the dirt trying to crush the Allied invasion force. The Allied introduction of the enhanced humanoid drones and the large number of soldiers equipped with the Raptor combat suits had proven too much for the PLA to overcome, even with their superior numbers.

However, after the surrender of Shanghai, the PLA had fought the Allies to a standstill. The Allies had a 46-mile bubble around Shanghai that they controlled, but after several attempts to break out, a halt had been called to any further attempts. Once a pause to any further offensive operations had been ordered in the Shanghai region, General Gardner ordered the invasion of Taiwan. The PLA fought ferociously for the first eight days of the invasion, but then their forces collapsed. They began to run low on munitions, supplies, and more importantly, the morale needed to keep fighting. The US employed another 6,000 EHDs in the invasion, and the mechanical killing machines were having their desired effect on the PLA, forcing many of them to just simply give up and surrender.

As the PLA forces in Taiwan began to collapse, the Chinese high command knew they needed to end the war soon or they might have further desertions or surrenders. President Jinping reached out to President Stein, asking for a 72-hour ceasefire to discuss terms of an armistice. After months of horrific combat and casualties on both sides, President Stein agreed to peace talks, selecting Sydney, Australia, as the neutral meeting location. Jinping was reluctant to meet in Sydney, but knew if he did not agree, Stein was the type of man who would continue to fight on, despite how many soldiers he might lose.

Chapter 62
A New World

01 July 2043
Sydney, Australia
QT Sydney Hotel

The Australian government quickly accepted President Stein's request to secure several downtown hotels and the zone surrounding them for the peace talks with the Chinese. The world was on the cusp of ending the bloodiest war in history, and if the Australian government had to kick out a bunch of tourists from some swanky hotels and ask people in the local area to endure some stricter security for a few days, it was worth it.

The American delegation would be staying at the QT Sydney, a ritzy hotel with cozy meeting rooms that would host the peace talks. The hotel was one of the few locations that could be fully secured to the US Secret Service's standards as the President had previously stayed at this hotel, just prior to the start of the war. The Chinese delegation would be staying at another luxury hotel just across the street. Both nations' security advance teams had arrived within 24 hours of the location having been agreed upon. The security teams and the Australian government had less than a day to secure the two facilities before both President Stein and President Jinping would arrive to begin the talks. A lot of work needed to be done with very little time.
****

As President Stein sat in his office on Air Force One, he was going over several of the main points of the tentative terms of the peace deal the Chinese had sent ahead of time. The President was not surprised by the demands, though he was not about to let the Chinese get everything they were asking for. The question he had to ask was what negotiating points could be given away, and what were the points he absolutely would not bend on.

He looked down at his paper again at the highlighted portion, which discussed the return of Shanghai and the removal of all Allied Forces from mainland China. The Chinese also wanted the Allied forces to leave Taiwan and for China to retain all territorial gains they had made up to this point. This included Southeast Asia, the Philippines, Malaysia and large swaths of east Africa. They also requested that the Allies not attack or intervene with their ally, the African Confederation. The outline of the entreated peace deal also included India, which was part of the Pan Asian Alliance.

It was a nice starting point, but nothing President Stein was going to agree to. With the endless supply of Tritium4 arriving from the lunar base, the US was producing nearly 5,000 EHDs a month. In a few more months, they would have 20,000 of them they could unleash on China. Stein knew he was negotiating from a position of strength; he was willing to let the Chinese keep some of their territorial gains, but he was not about to let them walk all over the US.

As soon as he landed in Australia, the President's motorcade took him directly to the hotel. Once he arrived, the President immediately went to bed; he had worked throughout most of the flight, and he was now exhausted. He wanted to get a solid eight hours of sleep before his morning meeting began with the Allied leaders to discuss what they would be willing to accept from the Chinese and what their red lines would be. In the afternoon, the two warring parties would meet for the first time and begin the initial discussions. The following day was dedicated to further negotiations. The third day was left open, to allow the parties time to think about the terms that had been offered and handle any last-minute changes. If no deal could be agreed upon by the end of the third day, the warring parties would return to their countries and the fighting would resume.
****

The following afternoon, President Stein and President Jinping walked into the same room to meet for the first time in nearly five years. The meeting was very private; it was just the two leaders, their personal translators and one advisor per leader; this arrangement was designed to be more intimate and direct, a chance for the two leaders to talk directly and hammer out some of the major points of the peace deal.

As President Jinping walked into the room, he saw President Stein and his two representatives were already seated. They rose when he walked in, and extended their hands as a courtesy. Jinping thought to himself, *"President Stein looks tired, like he's aged an entire decade since our last meeting. He also has a burning rage in his eyes; he is going to be hard to negotiate with."*

243

As Jinping shook Stein's hand and then took his seat, he opened the conversation. "Mr. President, thank you for agreeing to a temporary ceasefire while our two nations work out an end to this war."

President Stein was also reading his opponent; he saw a man who was determined to fight to the death if he was not able to save face and end the war as close to his terms as possible. He thought, "*Well, that's too bad for him. I will wipe China and its people from the face of the Earth if I must.*" Aloud, he politely responded, "Likewise, Mr. President, thank you for agreeing to meet to discuss how we can end this terrible war. Shall we begin?" As he finished speaking, he opened the folder in front of him.

The two men talked for nearly thirty minutes about the fate of Taiwan, the Philippines and Southeast Asia. President Stein said he would withdraw his forces from mainland China but the PLA would have to withdraw from Thailand, Malaysia, Indonesia, Taiwan and the Philippines. The US would cede Vietnam, Cambodia, Laos and Myanmar. President Jinping immediately objected to the terms, insisting that they wanted Taiwan returned to China as well as control of Thailand and Malaysia.

President Stein ceded, "We would agree to giving up control of Taiwan if the Chinese agreed to withdraw from Cambodia and divided Vietnam into north and south, with the US retaining control of south Vietnam, and China keeping the north."

After nearly two hours of horse trading back and forth, President Jinping agreed to the terms President Stein put forth. President Stein then placed one more demand on the table—complete restriction of future space exploration and the militarization of space for a period of time to be determined through negotiations. Jinping knew President Stein might do this; he had heard from sources in Russia that this had been a major sticking point with the Americans. However, unlike the Russians, China was not willing to have a restriction on their opportunity to explore the stars now that the technology for continuous thrust engines had been made.

President Jinping insisted, "China will not give up its ambitions on space, or the ability to mine and establish our own settlements on the lunar surface or elsewhere."

Stein knew he ultimately could not get the Chinese to walk away from the new frontier now that it had been opened wide up to exploration: mining, settlements, and EmDrive and advanced Ion engine technology was too strong of a draw. His goal was to slow them down, just long enough for America to become a dominant force in space before it had any serious competition from either Russia or China.

Stein proposed, "The Chinese could accept an observation force of your space activities for the next 15 years, or you would have to agree to a full 15-year moratorium on all space activities outside of reestablishing satellite activities."

Unlike the Russians, China had no intentions of allowing monitors into their space program. The Chinese were much further along in their own developments of the Ion engines and spacecraft design; Although, until the war ended, they could not get their program off the ground.

After nearly four more hours of arguing and going around and around the issue, President Jinping capitulated, and agreed to a fifteen-year moratorium on space activities. He justified that decision by telling himself that he would use that time to rebuild his empire.

President Stein made it clear, "I am more than willing to continue the war. We can always employ space-based weapons to systematically destroy China if you decide not to agree to our terms." After nearly seven hours of direct talks, the two leaders had agreed to terms that would bring the bloodiest war in world history to an end. The following day, the two leaders and their aides worked out the formal details of the new borders of the countries, reparations to be paid and the process to implement the peace agreement.
****

Once Air Force One had reached its cruising altitude, the President got up from his seat and began to walk towards the conference room. The rest of his senior staff quickly followed him into the room and took their respective seats. An aide brought in some fresh coffee and snacks for everyone and then quietly left the room and shut the door.

Secretary of State Jim Wise was the first to speak, "Mr. President, I believe some congratulations are in order. The peace talks were a success…this war is finally coming to an end," he said with a broad smile on his face.

The others in the room smiled and congratulated each other. President Stein just smiled and nodded, lost in thought. "*Could it really be over? After nearly five years, and over a billion-people killed, is the end really here?"*

Clearing his throat to get everyone's attention, the President stood up while signaling everyone else to stay seated.

The President began, "Gentlemen, I cannot thank you enough for your steadfast strength and perseverance in guiding me and our great nation through this war. America has lost so much, nearly twelve million people killed and nearly the twice that number injured. Our brave men and women of the Armed Forces, and our civilians as well, have suffered so much in the defense of this great nation and the free world."

"We are now about to embark upon the next great challenge, winning the peace. We have won the war, no one will dispute that, but we must truly work to achieve peace. We are on the cusp of a new world order, a world that I am determined must be led by America. Over the next several months, Chinese forces will be withdrawing from most of Southeast Asia while our forces begin the withdrawal from mainland China and Taiwan. Not everyone is going to be happy with our ceding Taiwan to the Chinese, especially after having fought so hard to secure it. I hate to use the term bargaining chip, but that is ultimately what Taiwan became. In ceding Taiwan, we liberated the Philippines, Thailand, Malaysia, Cambodia and what will now become South Vietnam."

"As Chinese forces leave these countries, our forces will move in. We will provide security and stability to them while we rebuild a new civilian government and security force. I want the Pentagon to begin identifying where we should establish permanent military bases in these countries. We are not going withdraw from these countries and leave an empty void like what was done in the Middle East in the 2010s. We must continue to win the peace if we are to avoid another war in the future."

The President had been pacing as he was speaking; now he stopped and turned back to his staff, who had been paying rapt attention. "One of the problems we have faced in the past after a war, is that our nation has historically begun a massive demobilization and moved immediately back to civilian life. While this has ultimately been the goal of our forces in the past, it is not going to be my goal. America, and the world, need to have a shared vision for the future."

One of the advisors in the room asked what everyone was thinking, "What do you have in mind Mr. President?"

Stein believed in his gut that America would eventually win, so he had spent many hours in the quiet thinking about what to do after a victory was achieved. Just as President Truman had established the Marshal Plan at the end of World War II, President Stein needed to establish his own post-world war plan to bring the people of the world back together, this time for a greater cause than nationalism.

He explained, "We are going to lead the world in the colonization of space. It is time for man to begin his next great adventure and expand our presence beyond our own solar system. We have the tools and technologies to make this happen. Now we need to make it a priority. Over the next several weeks, I am going to work with Dr. Gorka, Professor Rickenbacker, and Dr. Bergstrom to develop plans to construct a space elevator, orbital space station and spacecraft construction yard. We will also look for ways to expand our presence on the Moon and plan to start a new colony on Mars, as well as on Europa and other moons in our solar system. It is time mankind moves beyond the earthly squabbles that have led to countless wars across human history. Our future is in the stars, not here on Earth. That is the vision I want to project to the world as we usher in a time of peace, and hopefully, tranquility."

The room erupted in spontaneous clapping. A global project and vision would not only give the survivors of this great war a chance to move on, it would inspire people to dream big again.

They all broke out into chatter, discussing various aspects of the President's vision, Eventually, everyone started to leave the briefing room, until it was just Monty and the President sitting there. Monty looked at his long-time friend and smiled. "That was one world-class speech you gave. You really think we can make it happen?" he asked, raising one eyebrow slightly.

The President smiled, then replied, "I think so. We need to at least try. We need to find a way to heal not just our country, but the rest of the world if we are to sow the seeds of long-term peace and not animosity." Stein was confident for the first time in the future of humanity.

From the Authors

Miranda and I hope you've enjoyed this book. We always have more books in production; we are currently working on another riveting military thriller series, The Monroe Doctrine. If you'd like to order Volume One of this action-packed page-turner, please visit Amazon.

If you would like to stay up to date on new releases and receive emails about any special pricing deals we may make available, please sign up for our email distribution list. Simply go to https://www.frontlinepublishinginc.com/ and sign up.

If you enjoy audiobooks, we have a great selection that has been created for your listening pleasure. Our entire Red Storm series and our Falling Empire series have been recorded, and several books in our Rise of the Republic series and our Monroe Doctrine series are now available. Please see below for a complete listing.

As independent authors, reviews are very important to us and make a huge difference to other prospective readers. If you enjoyed this book, we humbly ask you to write up a positive review on Amazon and Goodreads. We sincerely appreciate each person that takes the time to write one.

We have really valued connecting with our readers via social media, especially on our Facebook page https://www.facebook.com/RosoneandWatson/. Sometimes we ask for help from our readers as we write future books—we love to draw upon all your different areas of expertise. We also have a group of beta readers who get to look at the books before they are officially published and help us fine-tune last-minute adjustments. If you would like to be a part of this team, please go to our author website, and send us a message through the "Contact" tab.

You may also enjoy some of our other works. A full list can be found below:

Nonfiction:
Iraq Memoir 2006–2007 Troop Surge
Interview with a Terrorist (audiobook available)

Fiction:

The Monroe Doctrine Series
Volume One (audiobook available)
Volume Two (audiobook available)
Volume Three (audiobook available)
Volume Four (audiobook still in production)
Volume Five (available for preorder)

Rise of the Republic Series
Into the Stars (audiobook available)
Into the Battle (audiobook available)
Into the War (audiobook available)
Into the Chaos (audiobook available)
Into the Fire (audiobook still in production)
Into the Calm (available for preorder)

Apollo's Arrows Series (co-authored with T.C. Manning)
Cherubim's Call (available for preorder)

Crisis in the Desert Series (co-authored with Matt Jackson)
Project 19 (audiobook available)
Desert Shield
Desert Storm

Falling Empires Series
Rigged (audiobook available)
Peacekeepers (audiobook available)
Invasion (audiobook available)
Vengeance (audiobook available)
Retribution (audiobook available)

Red Storm Series
Battlefield Ukraine (audiobook available)
Battlefield Korea (audiobook available)
Battlefield Taiwan (audiobook available)
Battlefield Pacific (audiobook available)
Battlefield Russia (audiobook available)
Battlefield China (audiobook available)

Michael Stone Series
Traitors Within (audiobook available)

World War III Series
Prelude to World War III: The Rise of the Islamic Republic and the Rebirth of America (audiobook available)
Operation Red Dragon and the Unthinkable (audiobook available)
Operation Red Dawn and the Siege of Europe (audiobook available)
Cyber Warfare and the New World Order (audiobook available)

Children's Books:
My Daddy has PTSD
My Mommy has PTSD

Abbreviation Key

AFC	America First Corporation
AI	Artificial Intelligence
AWAC	Airborne Warning and Control
BG	Brigadier General
CAG	Carrier Air Group Commander
CG	Commanding General
CIC	Combat Information Center
COB	Chief of the Boat
CSG12	Carrier Strike Group 12
CSG13	Carrier Strike Group 13
COMSUBPAC	Commander of Submarine Forces, Pacific
EAM	Emergency Action Message
EHD	Enhanced Humanoid Drone
FSB	Federalnaya Sluzhba Bezopasnosti (Russian Federal Security Service; FSK successor since 1995)
GRU	Glavnoye Razvedyvatelnoye Upravleniye (Russian Military Intelligence)
ICS	Industrial Control Systems
IIF	Individual Identification Frequency
IFV	Infantry Fighting Vehicles
IoT	Internet of Things (anything that is connected to a network, from cars to printers)
IR	Islamic Republic
JDF	Japanese Defense Force
LNO	Liaison Officer
LT	Lieutenant
LTC	Lieutenant Colonel
LTG	Lieutenant General
LZ	Landing Zone
MBT	Main Battle Tank
MG	Major General
MNF	Multi-National Force
NSA	National Security Agency
PA	Public Announcement
PEOC	Presidential Emergency Operations Center
PLA	People's Liberation Army (Chinese Army)

PLAN	People's Liberation Army Navy (Chinese Navy)
PRC	People's Republic of China
QRF	Quick Reaction Forces
SACEUR	Supreme Allied Commander Europe
SAM	Surface to Air Missile
SCADA	Supervisory Control and Data Acquisition (system controlling electric power transfers along the grid)
SFGp	Japanese Special Forces Group
SUD	Swordfish Underwater Drone
SVR	Sluzhba Vneshnei Razvedki (Russian Foreign Intelligence Service; post-Cold War intelligence service)
SWAT	Special Weapons and Tactics
TOC	Tactical Operations Center
UHF	Ultra-High Frequency
VIP	Very Important Person
XO	Commanding Officer

Made in United States
North Haven, CT
18 April 2022

18358517R00139